ANNA J. EVANS
DECEMBER QUINN

DEMON'S *Triad*

ELLORA'S CAVE
ROMANTICA PUBLISHING

An Ellora's Cave Romantica Publication

www.ellorascave.com

Demon's Triad

ISBN 9781419959035

Edited by Briana St. James.
Photography and cover art by Les Byerley.

This book printed in the U.S.A. by Jasmine-Jade Enterprises, LLC.

Electronic book Publication January 2008
Trade paperback Publication February 2009

DEMON'S TRIAD

Trademarks Acknowledgement

The author acknowledges the trademarked status and trademark owners of the following wordmarks mentioned in this work of fiction:

ChapStick: Wyeth Corporation

Charger: Chrysler LLC

Cosmopolitan Magazine: Hearst Communications, Inc.

Keds: SR Holdings, Inc.

NFL: National Football League Unincorporated

Rolodex: Berol Corporation

Salvation Army: Salvation Army, the Corporation

Chapter One

✌

"How bad you want to know?" Keller's voice was deep, radio DJ sexy and hoarse from too many late nights bouncing at The Bitch's Brew. In spite of being one scary looking motherfucker, he had a killer smile, complete with dimple, and a pair of baby blue eyes that had lured many a drunk college co-ed back to his double-wide trailer for fun of the horizontal variety.

Too bad his breath smelled worse than the monkey cage at the zoo, or Aleeza might actually have enjoyed interrogating him.

"How bad? Real bad," she all but purred, tossing her long, black hair over her shoulder. She placed a hand on the bricks behind Keller and leaned close enough for her breasts to brush against his arm. It was October in the Pacific Northwest and she wore only a black satin corset and a pair of skintight jeans, so those breasts were possessed of rock-hard nipples she was sure the bouncer could feel even through his leather jacket.

"Real bad, huh?" he murmured, eyes glazed as he reached toward her chest.

"Yeah…real bad." Aleeza tried not to roll her eyes, and faked an excited little moan when Keller cupped her breast and flicked his thumb over her puckered flesh.

She was Gunera coven and Keller knew it, had known it since she started working the greater Savior City metropolitan area as a kid fresh out of high school. Gunera didn't put out, couldn't even if they wanted to. This entire seduction scene wasn't going to amount to anything more than a major case of blue balls, but hope still glimmered in Keller's eyes. He was just like every other man she'd ever worked for information with a little slap and tickle. They all thought they were going to be different, that they would be the man with a cock big and bad enough to break a centuries-old chastity spell.

Men. They could be a pain in the ass, but you had to admire their sanguinity.

"Keller, I don't know about you, but I'm really ready to cut the crap and get the action started." Aleeza arched into the hand working her breast, things low in her body tightening and a rush of cream dampening her thong despite the rot-gut stench of Keller's breath hot on her face. For the millionth time she wondered if it was possible to die from pure sexual frustration. She didn't want to die at twenty-five.

"Baby, I'm ready for action anytime you are." He reached down to flip the top button on his jeans, preparing to release what looked to be quite an impressive package. Keller was handsome *and* hung. If he'd break down and put up the cash for a halitosis spell, he'd be practically irresistible.

"You're amazing, honey, but I need that number before this goes any further," Aleeza said, caressing his thickened cock through his jeans. Even if it were possible and she did plan to fuck him, she certainly wouldn't get busy in The Bitch's Brew's back alley. The bar was one of the hottest entertainment venues in the city and tonight was an all-ages show. Getting caught *in flagrante delicto* by some fifteen-year-old kid was not the slightest bit of a turn-on, and the last thing her coven needed was another lawsuit.

"Business before pleasure, huh?"

"Always." Aleeza increased the pressure of her hand until Keller groaned.

"He's staying in unit number twenty-six. My old man rented to him last week."

"Is he still there?"

"Should be, he paid a month's rent in cash."

"What's he driving?"

"I don't know," he said, reaching for her breast again.

"What's he driving, Keller? Don't fuck with me." Aleeza slapped his hand away and gave him her best glare. She was only five foot three, but growing up with two older brothers had taught her how to play tough and fight tougher. Of course, being Gunera didn't hurt things either. People who got on the bad side of their coven had a way of disappearing...forever. Not such a good reputation to have when it came to dealing with human police but great for encouraging a helpful attitude in most everyone else.

"A green Charger, spell-fueled 'cause there's no gas cap." Keller's hand slipped inside the top of her corset, his roughened fingers coming into direct contact with her tight nipple.

This time her moan was real. A bolt of electricity zipped down between her legs. Immediately her clit began to vibrate and the eager flesh of her pussy to swell. She was slick, aching and ready in seconds, her breath coming faster, bright blue light flooding the alley as her magic gathered into a tight knot of power at her very core. She wanted, she burned, she lusted with all the pent-up frustration of years of denied satisfaction, and before she knew what she was doing her fingernails were clawing into Keller's strong shoulders as he spread her legs and hitched her up around his waist.

Aleeza's back hit the brick wall hard enough to bruise, but she hardly felt the impact. She was too busy grinding up and down the long, thick cock that Keller pressed against her pussy. Even through their clothing she could feel the heat radiating from his arousal, and was consumed with the need to get that heat inside her, pumping between her legs, shoving into her and filling up every empty, aching inch.

"God, baby, you're so hot." Keller's lips were on her neck, his teeth dragging over her skin. Aleeza shuddered.

"Keller, stop. We have to stop," Aleeza said, her voice a sexy whisper that did absolutely nothing to keep Keller from pulling at her corset until her breasts sprang free.

The cold night air hit her bare flesh, but it was Keller suckling her nipple into the wet heat of his mouth that made her gasp. The sensation was unlike anything she'd ever known. A shockwave of desire stole her breath, making her womb hum and the force of her magic grow so thick and heavy that she knew she would need to cast soon or choke on the unreleased power. It was hard enough keeping everything in check the night of the full moon, without the painful urgency of her body making matters worse.

"I've wanted to do this since the first time you walked into the bar," Keller said, his hand busy at the button of her jeans.

"Wait, no, you don't—"

Keller let out a sound halfway between a moan and a scream as his knees buckled. Aleeza, legs still wrapped around his waist, went to the ground with him, hissing in pain as the bricks scratched her bare shoulders and did irreparable damage to the satin of her corset.

"Shit!" She cursed as her tailbone hit the pavement and a very heavy, very unconscious Keller slumped over her legs.

"Better than a chastity belt." Her cousin's voice drifted toward her from the shadows near the end of the alley, and Aleeza barely bit back a scream.

"Have you been there the whole time?" she asked, tugging up her corset while she glared in the general direction of Raven's voice. Her cousin was only nineteen years old, but she had already mastered shadow-walking to the point that not even Gavyn, the head of their coven, could point her out in the darkness if she didn't want to be found.

"Not the whole time but for all the good parts." Raven laughed and emerged from the shadows, a naughty grin on her very wholesome-looking face. With pale blonde hair and light blue eyes, Raven's looks were certainly not the reason her mother had chosen her name, but who knew what her mother had been thinking? Aleeza couldn't remember much about Bridget.

Raven's mother had been Amiantos coven, and like most marriages between Gunera and Amiantos, her relationship with Raven's father hadn't lasted long. She'd abandoned her daughter when she was only three years old, heading back into the foothills of the Cascade mountain range, the brutal wilderness the "undefiled" coven called home.

Undefiled. Odd that such "holier than thou" witches would so regularly abandon their own children if they showed signs that their magic would develop Gunera rather than Amiantos. Even odder that the most powerful Gunera of the past two thousand years had cursed their entire coven with a chastity spell, which could only be broken after marriage to an Amiantos. That ancient witch had probably thought she was doing good for her coven, but that didn't keep Aleeza from hating her.

"I think he gave you a hickey," Raven said with a snort. "Maybe two."

"Charming," Aleeza said, turning her attention to rolling Keller off her lap, anything to keep from looking Raven in the eye as a blush heated her cheeks.

She was six years older and had been working in the family bounty-hunting business since her cousin was nothing more than a snot-nosed fifth grader with braces. She shouldn't let Raven get to her, but she did. Something about the girl had always given her the creeps, and finding out she was perverted enough to watch her getting felt up in an alley did nothing to ease the skin-crawling sensation Raven inspired.

"Do you need help?"

"No thanks," Aleeza said, wiggling out from under Keller with a grunt.

"I meant with your shoulders. Those cuts look pretty nasty."

Aleeza closed her eyes and willed the knot of power within her into a healing spell, casting the energy out like a net that settled over her skin. The stinging scrapes on her back immediately vanished, as did the bruises on her tailbone. By the time she was finished she didn't have so much as a hangnail. Even her chapped lips felt smooth.

"Show off." Raven laughed as she ran a hand over the newly healed skin on Aleeza's back, sending her skin-crawling meter off the charts. Had the girl never heard of personal space?

"We all have our gifts," Aleeza said, stepping back until a good two or three feet separated her and Ms. Touchy-Feely. "Did you find out anything inside?"

"Not much. He hasn't been in here tonight or last night, but he left one of the cocktail waitresses a nice fat tip on Wednesday."

"What time on Wednesday?"

"I don't know," Raven said with a disinterested shrug.

"Did you try to find out?" Aleeza tried to keep the censure out of her voice but failed.

What use was Raven ever going to be if she didn't even try to learn from her mistakes? This was the third time this week she'd failed to ask the right questions. If Aleeza didn't know better, she'd think her cousin didn't give a shit if they scored this bounty. But the girl liked to eat as much as any Gunera, and there just weren't any other jobs out there for members of their coven.

You either worked the family business or you became one of the many homeless witches who haunted the seedier streets of Savior City. Gunera usually looked human enough to pass in society, but sooner or later the telltale blue glow of a Gunera in power would start to shine at the wrong time. As soon as it did, that witch was out of a job, or an apartment or a college class.

Aleeza had finally given up trying to get her degree in criminology. The hassle of being kicked out of class after class as soon as the teacher realized that she was "one of them" wasn't worth the piece of paper. She'd learned everything she needed to know on the job, shadowing older coven members for the first few years as an apprentice. Speaking of apprentices…

"Maybe you should follow Pierce around next week. I think he might be a better fit for you."

"I don't want to follow Pierce. He's an asshole."

"He's an asshole who knows how to get information. *All* the information," Aleeza said, tossing her waist-length hair over her shoulder where she hoped it would hide the damaged portion of her corset.

"Sorry." Raven didn't sound sorry at all, and Aleeza's teeth started to grind together.

"No big deal, I found out where the target's renting. I'll call the office and get a team out there to see if they can pick him up."

"Why don't we just head over there and do it ourselves? I'm sure we can handle this guy. He's into identity theft, not murder, right?" Raven asked.

"I have plans."

"Oh, hot date?" Raven laughed and it wasn't a pretty sound despite the fact that her twin dimples made her look like the poster child for wholesome, all-American good times.

"Keller's old man's trailer park is over near the office. A team will be able to get there faster," Aleeza said, turning to walk down the alley toward where she'd parked her car a few hours before. Hopefully it was still there. Even parking an old clunker like her Vesta in this part of the city was dangerous after dark. Automobile theft was at an all-time high despite the new mayor's promises to clean up the streets.

"Hey, 'Leez," Raven called after her in a voice that was almost plaintive.

"What?"

"Didn't mean to piss you off."

"You didn't," Aleeza threw back over her shoulder, not bothering to turn around.

"I know how it feels you know…to *want* so bad."

Aleeza broke into a jog, her high-heeled boots clicking on the pavement, not even bothering to validate her cousin's words with a response. Give her six more years of "wanting" and maybe a month or two of the dreams that had made Aleeza dread sleep for the past year—then, *maybe*, they would talk.

* * * * *

Aleeza took the steps at her mother's house two at a time. The Craftsman bungalow looked charming at night, but the creak of the wood beneath her feet hinted at the decades of neglect obvious in the daylight hours. Mona needed a new roof and a few dozen other repairs in a major way, but ever since Aleeza's dad had run off when she was six and her older brothers nine and twelve, money had been tight in the Perkins house. The Gunera coven had money set aside for members in need, but the money was never enough to pay for a new roof or for clothes that didn't come from the Salvation Army.

It wasn't until her brother Blake had reached seventeen and been able to work full time for Gunera Bounty that they'd seen anything but ground beef or government cheese on the their table. Any fresh vegetables, they'd had to grow themselves in the tiny backyard where there was never any room to play between the tomato stakes and the rows of zucchini and cabbage.

"Mona? Are you home?" Aleeza stuck her head in the door and called a little louder. "Mona! Are you in there?"

Only the bright, impersonal glow of the overhead bulbs answered her. Her mom had either gone out and left the lights on or passed out on the couch after a few too many glasses of cheap wine. Mona wasn't an alcoholic, but she and the bottle had been friends for years. She wasn't the only Gunera who drank a little more than they should. Some said it helped take the edge off the endless sexual frustration that was reality for at least half of their coven. Whether you had already married and lost your Amiantos husband or wife back to the mountains and woods, or were too young to have given in and rolled the marital dice with a member of the undefiled coven, over half the Gunera population was in a constant state of unfulfilled lust.

Lust. Shadow hands reaching through the night, touching her in all those secret places where she longed to be touched. Thick fingers pressing into her aroused flesh, teasing in and out of her wet folds, making her ache, burn, building the horrible, beautiful need inside her until she was sure she would perish from pleasure denied.

"Mona?" Aleeza's voice broke. She squeezed her eyes shut and struggled to take a deep breath. She wouldn't allow the dreams to haunt her while she was awake, couldn't or she would lose her mind. Hell, if the spell she planned to cast tonight didn't work, she might lose it anyway, but she was never one to go down without a fight.

"In here! Close the door, you're letting in a draft."

"Well, answer sooner next time." Aleeza let the door slam behind her as she made her way into the kitchen. There Mona sat at the scarred wooden table, with a cigarette dangling from her mouth, attention focused on the tiny doll in her hands. "You got more orders?"

"Five more. Even had a couple fly in from New York. Said their fertility doctor referred them, that I was the best in the business if they were going to go with a spell instead of 'conventional medical wisdom'." Mona let out a deep chuckle that turned into a hacking cough.

"And they went ahead and ordered, even after meeting you in person?"

"Ha, ha. You're a little bitch—you know that?" Mona lifted her dark, nearly black eyes and winked at her.

"I learned from the best." Aleeza pulled up a seat, taking a cigarette from her mother's pack.

"Since when do you smoke?"

"Since tonight. I'm thinking of picking it up." Aleeza lifted the cigarette to her nose and inhaled the smell of tobacco.

"Put that down, you have enough vices," Mona said, smacking the cigarette out of her hand. "What are you doing here, anyway? It's not Sunday last time I checked."

"I missed you so much I couldn't wait two more days." Aleeza picked up the cigarette and stuck it in her mouth.

"You're so full of shit. What do you want, money?"

"When is the last time I asked you for money, Mom?" It came out as a hurt little whine and Aleeza winced.

No matter how their relationship had evolved, no matter how "friendly" they became, it still hurt that Mona never seemed to understand her, had never been able to see through to the heart of her the way she did her sons. But maybe that was her fault. Aleeza didn't let anyone see through her. She was too afraid of what they might find.

"Then what do you want? I'm busy, booger. I have to get this doll finished by tomorrow morning. The client is going to be ovulating in the next two days, so I can't put it off, no matter how much I'd like to hang out and have girl talk." Mona patted her hand and slid her lighter across the table before flipping her hair over her shoulder in a motion Aleeza recognized all too well. Sometimes it was downright eerie how much she resembled her mother. It was as if she had sprung from Mona's forehead fully formed, and those hazy memories of a tall man with light brown hair and a warm smile for his daughter were nothing more than a dream.

"I was looking for some Queen Elizabeth root. Thought you might have some in stock," Aleeza said casually, flicking the lighter on but not bringing it to the cigarette still dangling from her mouth. She didn't like smoking, never had. She just liked the sensation of holding the cigarette in her mouth. It steadied her nerves and placed another barrier, no matter how insignificant, between her mother and herself.

"Why? Are you going to set up shop as my competition?"

"No, I have a friend who's having trouble getting in the mood with her fiancé. She's thinking about calling off the wedding."

"She should. If she doesn't want to fuck him before the wedding, she's certainly not going to want to fuck him after."

"Her dad died a few weeks ago and she's depressed, Mom. She swears she used to love banging Ted. I'm going to give her the root and let her try it out for a few months." Aleeza shrugged, focusing on the lighter, refusing to look her mother in the eye. She was a fantastic liar, but Mona had always been able to smell a lie. Even from Aleeza.

"All right, go get some from the cellar, but make sure you give her strict instructions on how much to use."

"Thanks, Mona," Aleeza said, jumping up with a smile. She was getting smoother, or someone was losing her touch. Either way, she hadn't anticipated scoring the root so easily and figured it was best to grab it and go before her mother changed her mind. Mona didn't share potion elements lightly, and she certainly never parted with anything she used in her fertility dolls.

"Get her to sign a liability release. Don't think just because she's a friend that she won't sue," Mona said, lifting her face to catch Aleeza's peck on the cheek.

"Gotcha." Aleeza was nearly to the backdoor by the time her mother spoke again.

"And be careful, booger. Whatever you're really going to use it for, make sure you don't bite off more than you can chew."

Aleeza turned back to her mom with a smile on her face. "I don't know what you mean, Mom. I'm just trying to help a friend." Then she was out the door and making tracks toward the cellar entrance at the side of the house, trying to ignore the unease that prickled at the back of her neck.

She was going to be careful, and she wasn't going to risk anyone's wellbeing except her own. If she failed, only she would pay the price. If she succeeded…well, if she succeeded, anything would be worth it, wouldn't it?

Chapter Two

ꙮ

Dorand shivered, both from the chill in the evening air and the anticipation coursing through his veins. This would work. It had to. If he and Ferrin, the two most powerful deathspeakers in the Amiantos clan, couldn't make this work, even without their third…it couldn't be done.

And that was not an option.

"Dorand…you have to relax." Ferrin's hands, hard and cool, stroked Dorand's bare shoulders. Even if Dorand didn't remember what those hands were capable of, the massage should have felt good. Too bad he was too fucking on edge to enjoy himself. He took a deep breath.

"I'm working on it, give me a minute."

"We don't have a minute. Time is of the —"

"Don't preach to me about time!" Dorand regretted the harsh words as soon as they were out of his mouth. He'd always been the member of their triad with the worst temper, but now wasn't the time to indulge it. "I'm sorry. I'm just…"

"I know." Ferrin's voice was soft, almost as soft as the kiss he planted at the nape of Dorand's neck. The intimacy was simultaneously comforting and completely alien. How many times had they kissed? Probably a thousand or more, but not without her, never without her. "You miss her. So do I, brother."

Dorand turned to look into the shorter man's dark eyes. They called each other "brother", because that's what they felt like. It was how they were raised. But the bond connecting them was stronger than blood. It was love, their love for each other and the passion they'd shared with Carantha. He wasn't afraid to admit his love for a man, especially his clan-mate, but desire was an entirely different animal. "I don't know if I can," he said. "Forgive me for being an asshole, but I just don't know."

Ferrin smiled. "I'm not sure, either," he said. "You have my love and loyalty until death, brother, but my cock is another story."

"I don't need your cock. I have a perfectly serviceable one of my own."

"Couldn't tell by looking at you." Ferrin gave Dorand's limp member a meaningful look that nearly made him blush. Fuck. Dorand had always been the strong one, the rock that both Ferrin and Carantha could turn to in times of trouble, and he'd been reduced to blushing like a virgin on his mate-claiming night. It was ridiculous. Worse, it was no way to get in the mind to make the magic they would attempt in this place.

"Fuck you, asshole," Dorand said, reaching out to take Ferrin's slightly thickened shaft in his hand. His heart beat faster as he anticipated feeling uncomfortable, maybe even a little repulsed by the idea of sexual contact without a woman involved in some way, but the feel of Ferrin's cock was strangely soothing and familiar.

"If you try to fuck my asshole, we're going to have a problem." Ferrin smiled that wicked grin that had always made Carantha laugh and usually ravage him soon after.

With his shoulder-length ebony hair and dark coloring, Ferrin looked more like a pirate than a member of the usually fair-haired Amiantos coven. Dorand had always suspected that difference was why Carantha seemed to favor him at times. Ferrin had an air of danger about him that Dorand, for all his size and temper, knew he could never possess. He might be six feet four and out-weigh his clan brother by nearly fifty pounds, but anyone who knew him well knew that Dorand was a soft touch. Beneath his tough exterior, beat the heart of a peace-loving woodsman, not a fighter.

Until now. Now he was ready to fight, to kill. All he needed was a name.

"Let's do this, Ferrin. For her."

"We *will* reach her. We're going to find out who did this, and we're going to make them wish they had never been born onto this earth." Ferrin's lust for vengeance was clear in every word, and Dorand's body answered with lust of its own, his cock beginning to thicken between his legs.

"Yes, we will," he answered, stroking his hand up and down Ferrin's shaft, coaxing him to a state of full arousal. The night was cold, but the skin beneath his hands was burning, hot with need, with power. This was how their magic had always worked best, and Dorand could feel that old, familiar swell of potential energy begin to gather in the air between them.

"Close your eyes," Ferrin said, taking Dorand's cock in one hand and cupping his tingling sac with the other.

Dorand's eyes slid shut, and he immediately found it was easier like this, easier to imagine it was Carantha's hand caressing his sac, stroking the juncture of his thighs and groin. Easier to imagine Ferrin's shaft was thickening as he prepared to thrust into Carantha's ass while Dorand lost himself inside Carantha's sweet, tight pussy again and again until they were all spent, until their power reached a fever pitch and released itself. Until their spell was cast.

They'd raised spirits dead hundreds of years with the strength of their deathspeaking spells, making their coven famous again in the modern world. Amiantos hardly ever worked in threes, but no one could deny that they had been the most powerful force their clan had produced in years. That Dorand, Ferrin and Carantha were such a strong triad was a source of wonder to their people.

Had been a source of wonder until Beltane, when Carantha's broken and mutilated body was found in the woods. Here, in this spot. This was where she had died, where some bastard had tortured his lover, his friend, made her scream and no doubt beg for the release of death before he struck the final blow.

"Dorand." Ferrin's voice was thickening, taking on that lazy edge that it always had when the three of them had been together. "What are you thinking about?"

"Nothing,"

"Then why are you going soft, man?"

"Why are you mentioning it? Bringing attention to the problem is certainly no cure," Dorand barked, squeezing Ferrin's cock none too softly.

Ferrin grunted in response, but Dorand knew he would never say uncle. Ferrin was good with pain and at times actually seemed to enjoy a little mixed in with his pleasure. "How many times have our cocks rubbed together while we made love to Carantha, how many times have we kissed over our sweet girl's head? The fact that she's not here tonight means nothing."

"It means everything."

"Don't be a fool."

"Don't talk." Dorand's voice shook and he was glad he'd kept his eyes closed. He might have kissed Ferrin before, helped him make love to their woman, but there was no way he'd let the other man see him cry. Besides, the bastard was right. If he kept dwelling on Carantha's murder, they would have no chance to avenge her.

Ferrin's hands returned to his shaft, stroking Dorand's thickening cock, running up and down his stomach. Ferrin's cock was still hard in Dorand's hand, its burgeoning weight slowly becoming arousing. This was good but it wasn't enough. Before Dorand could second-guess the impulse he stepped forward, bringing their bodies into more intimate contact.

His lips found Ferrin's, tentatively at first, then with growing demand as their groins rubbed together, busy hands tangling as they started to stroke each other harder, faster. Little sparks of magic flew from them, tiny lights in the growing darkness of the forest. Heat flowed through Dorand's body, filling him with power that he could feel buzzing down into the earth beneath his feet. They were getting closer, almost to the point where they could begin to cast.

Dorand moved his hands away from Ferrin's cock, stroking down the muscles of Ferrin's back, down farther still to clutch his lover's ass, digging his fingers into the firm flesh. Ferrin was his lover, had been for years. His brother was right. This was a part of who they were, with or without Carantha. Ferrin groaned and moved his hands around to mimic Dorand's, grinding his hips forward until he drew a sound from deep in Dorand's throat. The sweet friction of their cocks rubbing together built the fist of power growing within him to a feverish point, a feeling he knew was echoed in Ferrin.

"Let the gods see this night," Ferrin whispered. The first words of the spell. Dorand faltered in his rhythm for a moment, but Ferrin urged him on with his hands, his hips.

Dorand continued. "Let this space be made holy by their presence."

"Let the spirits of the earth and sky stand guard as the dead rise to speak."

Power swirled around them, a faint breeze that grew as their passion rose. Dorand reached down to grip Ferrin's cock once more, stroking and pulling, his breath hitching in his chest as Ferrin did the same. The trees around them danced with energy, the few leaves left on them whispering as the wind whistled through them.

Ferrin's throat was salty under Dorand's lips, his pulse pounding beneath his skin. All feelings of awkwardness were gone. All feelings except the awareness of the desire burning between them had vanished under the strength of their need. Dorand wanted this. Wanted Ferrin's cock in his hand, wanted the other man's strong hands to bring him to orgasm, to watch his seed spurt across the smooth skin of Ferrin's stomach and chest.

He shook with it, his body tight and hot as they sank together to the dirt. "Let this, our offering, be accepted," Ferrin whispered, catching Dorand's eyes and holding his gaze before lowering his head.

"Let this, our offering, be accepted." Dorand groaned as Ferrin's lips parted around the head of his cock. His hips thrust upward of their own accord, arching toward Ferrin's mouth, the sensations as he was suckled deep inside the hot, wet place taking him higher. By the gods, if he closed his eyes he could almost imagine that he was sliding inside Carantha, that it was her pussy gripping him in its tight sheath.

He knew in that instant that this was what he needed, what they both needed.

Hands on Ferrin's shoulders, Dorand urged the other man onto his back on the cool earth. Ferrin went without a struggle, immediately taking Dorand's cock back into his mouth when Dorand straddled his face and leaned over to place his lips over the tip of Ferrin's shaft. The salty musk of the other man's cock invaded his mouth as he suckled and laved, and Dorand felt his own cock begin to leak in response.

"Let this, our offering, be accepted." Ferrin pulled away from his arousal and spoke the words for the final time, then brought his mouth back to Dorand's sex with merciless fervor.

Power shot through him, through them both. Dorand's back arched, his hips lifting away from Ferrin's attentions. It was too much, more than he'd ever felt. Ferrin's power had always run through Carantha before reaching Dorand, tempered by her sweet light. Now…there was only Ferrin. His energy rocketed through Dorand's body, buzzed through his mind. His muscles convulsed with the effort of controlling it, and he pulled away from Ferrin's member for fear that his jaw would clamp down against his will.

It was time, time to call for her and pray for an answer.

"Carantha," he groaned. Ferrin's mouth was still busy on his cock, bringing him rapidly to his peak. "Carantha, we call you."

"Carantha, we call you." Ferrin's voice seemed very far away as he replaced his mouth with his hand, fisting Dorand's slick cock. Dorand mimicked the movement and soon their hips moved together, thrusting, demanding satisfaction and an answer to the spell they had cast.

"Dorand…Ferrin…" Carantha's voice, so quiet it barely registered, drifted through the trees.

"Dorand," Ferrin gasped. "I hear her. Are you close?"

"Gods, yes. Don't stop. Faster…faster, Ferrin."

Ferrin groaned and quickened his pace, his hand squeezing Dorand's cock until Dorand thought he might pass out from the pleasure of it. He grounded their threesome and had always been the one most able to handle their power. But the physical sensations, combined with the almost feral nature of Ferrin's magic, was too much. If they didn't find release soon, he might fall apart, shattered into a million pieces from the pressure of channeling so much raw power.

"Dorand…Ferrin…" Carantha again, stronger now. Dorand thought he saw a glimmer of white in the trees, her pale form moving toward them.

"Dorand…now…oh Gods, now…"

The glimmer of white turned into a flash of blue, a blinding rush of pure light. Dorand's body screamed on the brink of orgasm. His balls tightened—his cock throbbed. Ferrin's cock swelled in his fist as Ferrin's groan turned into a scream. Just a moment…another moment. Dorand would come, they would come together, and the energy of their climaxes would give their beloved Carantha form and voice enough to speak. To tell them who'd killed her.

Dorand closed his eyes against the painfully intense blue glow. Shouts erupted from his open mouth, but still he hovered. His balls ached. His body screamed with the need for release, a release that did not come.

The light went out. It didn't fade, it simply disappeared, and with it the vague shadowy form of Carantha.

No orgasm. No Carantha.

"What the—"

Ferrin looked around, dazed. "What happened?"

"Did you come?"

"No. Did you?"

Dorand shook his head. "Fuck!" His body still throbbed and ached, but the intense pleasure was fading, leaving him sore, exceedingly dissatisfied and more than a little pissed. What the hell had happened? They'd never failed to cast once the power had risen. Not one damn time in over five years.

"God damn it." Ferrin pulled back, sliding out from under Dorand's body, panting hard on the ground beside him. "I'm still fucking hard."

"No shit." Dorand let out a roar of frustration that echoed through the silent trees, and jumped to his feet to pace the accursed space. All for nothing. It had all been for fucking nothing. They'd walked the five miles from the Amiantos settlement in the nude to prepare their bodies for the magic, they'd hung all their hopes on this ritual, and it hadn't worked.

He hadn't even managed to get an orgasm out of it, an orgasm his body still cried out for no matter that his mind had moved on to other things. He was going to have to jerk off, stand here in the cold air and find release in his own hand. It was pathetic.

"Something's not right. The power had risen. We were nearly there—I could feel it." Ferrin sat up, his breathing returning to normal. "I don't know—"

A scream interrupted him, a woman's scream. The sound made the hairs on the back of Dorand's neck stand up. In the pale washed-out glow of the moonlight he saw the same reaction on Ferrin's face.

Both men leapt to their feet. The murders had all taken place on Fire Festival nights. Samhain was still four weeks away, but that didn't mean the killer—or killers—couldn't change their pattern. Nor did it mean they wouldn't take advantage of the secrecy of the forest to kidnap a victim now.

Ignoring both his nakedness and his erection, Dorand started to run.

* * * * *

Aleeza set up her things in the clearing. The full moon sat heavy in the sky, smiling over her as she took out the large chunk of Queen Elizabeth root and placed it on the cloth in front of her. Her skin tingled just touching it and her pulse began to race. If this worked, she would get a lot more than just tingles. She would finally get what she needed, what she'd been needing for so long.

"Please." She closed her eyes and whispered the words, offering up a heartfelt prayer for the first time in way too long.

Hunting the worst of humanity while laboring under a centuries-old curse didn't inspire an abundance of faith. But Aleeza still believed, knew that the ancient gods were there and might just be listening to a witch whispering in this quiet wood tonight. The Amiantos had settled here for power, not privacy, though they defended their hermit-like ways with a vengeance that didn't fit with their nicey-nice image.

She was risking more than a lawsuit by invading their turf. Many of the Amiantos had the ability to magic meld, to give their magic away and to take magic from others. Her Aunt Sylvia's husband had stolen her magic before he left to return to the woods, and it had taken nearly three years of therapy for her to return to her full power. But sitting here in the midst of the ancient wood, Aleeza had no doubt that the risk was worth it. The air around her vibrated, even the trees seeming to move with an awareness of the supernatural.

If the spell was ever going to work, it would be here.

"There is no 'if'." Aleeza spoke the words out loud in the same tone she used to intimidate criminals three times her size. It had to work, failure was not an option. She couldn't go on like this anymore, at the mercy of the endless frustration or destined to marry a man from a clan she despised.

She would succeed, or suffer the consequences.

Either way, the best part was that no one would know. If she failed, her magic could take a serious beating from working a gray spell and failing. But she didn't rely on magic as much as others in her clan. She could still work the bounty hunting business without supernatural aid. And if she succeeded, she could behave as though the chastity curse bound her. She might have to watch herself in situations like the interrogation with Keller, make sure she didn't allow things to go too far unless she was prepared to finish what she's started. But she would know freedom. She would finally know how it felt to be held in a man's arms, to have his warm, bare skin pressed against hers. To be filled with not only his cock, but his power.

Lovemaking between witches was alleged to sate not only physical lust but to enhance magical ability as well. Not that she cared about enhancing anything at the moment. All she could think about was finding release from sexual frustration and from the dreams that had haunted her for the past year. Since Beltane, they had become almost unbearably frequent and wickedly vivid. Every night she was ravaged by some invisible lover who tormented her, driving her to dizzying pinnacles of desire and then leaving her to hang there, breathless, bruised and aching with a need so horrible that often she awoke with tears streaming down her face.

Just thinking about it made it difficult to swallow and sent sharp waves of heat rushing to her pussy. Hopefully, tonight that heat would finally find its climax.

Aleeza stripped off her jeans and corset, placing them neatly on the grass and dropping her bra and panties on top. Her nipples hardened in the night air, but the shiver that went through her wasn't due to the cold.

The moon gave enough light to see clearly, but she lit the candles anyway. She wasn't dependent on them for focus and usually left them out of her rituals, but tonight she needed all the help she could get. It had taken months to find this ancient spell, and the candles were listed as part of it. She wasn't taking any chances. If she failed, it would be because of a lack of personal power, not because she was too rushed to follow the spell to the letter.

"Goddess, hear me," she whispered, placing the candles carefully in a triangle on the ground in front of her, framing the root. She'd never seen candles in this pattern before, but the spell specifically designated that layout. "By flame and smoke, let my words be carried."

She stood up, grabbing a handful of earth and sprinkling it over the candles. "By dirt and tree, let my words be carried."

Next she sprinkled the blessed water over the candles, her words forming a soft mist in the magically charging air.

Aleeza knelt in front of the candles, her legs spread just enough for her hands to reach between them and stroke the soft, damp skin of her pussy. So many times in her life she'd tried this exact thing. She was an expert at finding the spots and pressure that pleased her most. She'd brought herself to the edge more times than she could count but had never been able to topple over. She would stroke herself until her muscles were strung tight and every inch of her body yearning, struggling toward that promised release, but she was always denied.

Celibacy shouldn't mean the Gunera shouldn't at least have the comfort of pleasuring themselves. But maybe that was a side-effect her ancient ancestor hadn't anticipated.

"My power burns," she whispered, knowing that she had never spoken truer words in her life. Her power did burn, just as her body burned for the basic human right of pleasure that had been stolen from her and her people. "My power calls. Great Venus, hear me. Feel my energy call to you."

The air around her changed, becoming heavier, thicker. Power pulsed through it, dancing against her raw skin. She felt exposed, exposed in a way she'd never been before, and she pulled her wet fingers away and reached beside her for the final spell ingredient.

The intense blue of her energy faded slightly as she picked up the bone. Robbing graveyards was not something she liked to do, especially not witches' graveyards. If she'd been caught, she could have been punished. Severely. This bone, from one of the oldest Gunera bodies in the cemetery, thrummed with power as Aleeza picked it up and passed it through the candle. The oil she'd rubbed on the end earlier caught the flame. "Bone of the ancestors, soul of the ancestors," she said softly. "Share your power with me."

The fire faded immediately, and the bone was strangely cool against the slick skin of her pussy as she rubbed it gently against her clit. Only for a moment, just long enough to anoint it with her creamy fluids. The blue light flared again and the bone glowed. She passed it over the flames and watched as her fluid caught fire. The bone burned, the reddish flames mixing with her blue energy. Purple, the color of dark power. It was working. She watched the flame for a moment, aware of the enormity of her actions but more strongly aware of her body's yearning. She was committed. If she stopped the spell now, it could be dangerous.

She didn't want to stop. Her body still tingled and itched, her thighs slick. She reached down to spread her lips and stroke her sensitive flesh. Her hips jerked in anticipation.

Her fingers were slick now, slick with the hot fluids of her reckless need. She slipped one fingertip into her tight channel. Her muscles squeezed around it. "Aphrodite, hear me." It came out as a moan. "Great Eros, take my energy and give me what I desire." Her thighs trembled as she continued sliding her finger in and out, adding a second. Her other hand kept its rhythm on her clit, in her folds, teasing herself. She could not attempt an orgasm until the spell was done, but the temptation…the temptation was always there. If she was able to finish, she could do it so quickly. Twenty-five years was a long fucking time, and she was more than ready.

"Herktar renula fazsia," she whispered. "Eros, Venus, Aphrodite, hear me. Herktar renula fazsia. Herktar renula fazsia." The words reverberated through her entire body, igniting her blood. The clearing brightened with her power, pure blue, making the trees look unreal. Her fingers quickened their pace, thrusting into her heat, rubbing her wet flesh. Her nipples ached and tingled, diamond hard in the cool swirling air.

"By these words," she cried out, her fingers working furiously now, her body twanging like a guitar string, "By my power, grant me my desire. Break this spell. Eros, break this spell. Harktar renula fazsia!"

The bone exploded in a shower of purple sparks. Her own power glowed so bright she closed her eyes. Pressure built inside her, a pressure she'd never felt before but knew instinctively was what she sought. What she needed. Her laughter bubbled over her lips, a triumphant cry, as her loins blazed with heat and her muscles trembled and ached.

Her hips pushed forward, the muscles of her walls clenching around her fingers. Something deep inside her swelled, and every nerve ending in her body sang as Aleeza finally pushed herself into the first orgasm of her life.

She screamed, screamed from the pure, breathtaking glory of it, but her scream turned into something else as the blue light of her power was replaced by a flash of white, pure and clean, bleaching the trees and her own sweat-damp skin. She came again as an energy too sexual and primal to be anything but male forced itself into her body.

For a moment it was as if the power had kicked her out. She hovered somewhere in the air, watching herself spasm in great, curious detail. The delicate skin of her nipples was now pebbled and rough, her facial expression one of pure savage ecstasy, the fluid making her thighs slick.

Then she was back in herself, crumpling to the ground as the final wave of her orgasm finally abated.

Or was it really hers? She hadn't been mistaken in feeling a man's presence in her body, the thundering rush of a man's savage release. Eros coming to take his due. She smiled.

Speaking of coming…

A sound half-laughter, half sob of relief pushed its way past her lips. It had been…indescribable, by far the most amazing thing she'd ever felt before in her life. No wonder orgasm had been cursed away from her coven. Why would anyone want to do anything else when they could do that? When they could feel so alive, so free, like a goddess?

The question was, could she do it again?

* * * * *

Dorand ignored the pain as his feet stumbled over rocks and sticks, ignored the scratches on his skin from wayward branches. Even as he forced himself to go faster, he knew it was likely too late. There hadn't been a second scream. Whoever she was—

He didn't want to think about it.

Off to his left he spied a faint blue glow. Without thinking, he turned toward it. It was evidence that another witch was in the woods tonight, probably Gunera coven. Their magic was tainted with color, usually blue, but more rarely green or yellow. Whatever their color, they were all dangerous and dabblers in magic too gray for his tastes. It wouldn't surprise him at all to find out that one of their gods-forsaken clan was responsible for the murders.

After all, the blue glow had come to him and Ferrin too. It had stolen their power, stolen their release, stolen Carantha. Even now their own power might be being used against another. All of the victims had been tortured with ritualistic black magic before their deaths.

"Not this night," Dorand swore under his breath. He wouldn't be too late, not for this woman. He would reach her in time and save her loved ones the pain he and Ferrin still suffered.

A soft laugh convinced him he was headed in the right direction. A woman. He had never stopped to think that the killer might be a woman but it was a definite possibility. Evil didn't discriminate between the sexes, and neither did black magic.

He suddenly wished Ferrin were behind him, that they hadn't agreed to split up their search. Dorand was powerful, but taking down a witch who wouldn't hesitate to call upon the black arts by himself, unclothed—and still partially erect— wasn't an ideal situation.

Another sound, more like a moan now. It was very close, and he stopped, his heart pounding in his ears, waiting to track it.

He didn't need the sound after all. When his eyes adjusted to the bright glow after the dim light of the trees, he saw her.

Only one woman, but his mouth still dropped open as his cock went from partially aroused to fully, screamingly erect, and his slowing heart sped once more.

She was completely naked, blue light playing softly over every luscious curve and plane of a body men would kill for. And Dorand could see very bit of that body, from her high, round breasts to the heaven lurking at her core because the woman was flat on her back. Her long legs were spread, and her fingers were playing gently in the soft crevice between them, sliding in and out, coaxing the blue and white light that flashed between her thighs into a bright, roaring flame.

A sex spell, she's stolen our magic for a fucking ecstasy spell.

Dorand started toward the bitch, suddenly as angry as he was aroused. He wasn't sure what he was going to do with the woman when he got his hands on her, but he *was* getting his hands on her—there was no doubt about that.

Chapter Three

∞

Almost there, god she was almost there again, and this time was going to be even better, she could feel it in every electric nerve ending in her body. Between her legs, sexual bliss and magic merged, sending her spiraling toward a height that felt almost dangerous. Would she survive the fall from that dizzying place?

She couldn't wait to crash and find out.

"What the hell have you done?"

Aleeza screamed and pulled her hand away from her pussy as if it had burned her, bolting into a seated position. The superstitious part of her had half expected the spirits of her ancestors to seek vengeance upon her for what she had done, but she had never expected vengeance to come in the form of a naked giant of a man. He towered over her, not simply because she was lying down. The guy had to be pushing six and a half feet, and all of it was pure muscle.

His body was masculine perfection, every inch of him sculpted and hard...every inch. She'd seen photographs of aroused men but never viewed one in the flesh. Goddess, it was achingly beautiful, a column of need with a tiny pearl of essence shining on top. Her pussy let forth a gush of cream simply from looking at it, and Aleeza could only imagine how she would respond if he were to touch her, to take her in his arms and press her against every hot inch of him.

"Answer me," the man snapped, eyes she couldn't quite name the color of flashing with rage. But his hair was sandy blond and his face a classic example of male beauty that would have done any ancient Greek statue proud.

Fuck. Her god was an Amiantos—he had to be. She'd been caught red handed. Or…wet handed. Her fingers were drenched with her own juices. She had no idea if that was normal and hadn't thought to give a shit until now. The man's eyes dropped between her legs, taking in the slickness there with a hard swallow and a twitch of his swollen member.

Ah-ha. It seemed perhaps not all was lost.

"I was working a spell. What does it look like I was doing?" She kept her legs spread as she casually tossed her hair over her shoulder, trying to ignore the racing of her pulse in her throat. She could practically feel his hunger caressing her flesh, warm herself on the heat burning in his eyes, and it was almost impossible to keep from reaching her hand back down between her legs.

He wanted her—that was clear, and Aleeza knew in that instant that she was going to let him have her. Not only was it her way out, but it would be the ultimate test. If the spell was truly broken, she might be feeling that thick cock working inside her body in the next few minutes.

She shivered at the thought and let her knees drop open even wider.

"It looks like you were defiling a sacred space to get a fix." His words were hard, but for some reason they excited her. But then, she always had enjoyed a good fight and Mr. Tall, Fair and Grumpy looked like he was spoiling for one. Well then, she was happy to oblige.

"What the fuck are you talking about, asshole?"

"You're an ecstasy addict. Look at yourself. Even now you want to get those busy little fingers back between your legs. Don't you?" He squatted down a few feet away and quickly snuffed out the candles with stiff, angry motions.

An ecstasy addict? She'd never seen a true addict be able to walk more than a few blocks without falling apart, let alone make their way all the way up into the woods of Amiantos nation bum-fuck. But if that was the conclusion he'd jumped to, it was fine with her.

"No, actually I'd like to get your cock between my legs. Wouldn't you?" She grinned a wicked little grin and reached up to caress her own breast, moaning and squirming as she plucked at her nipple. She'd brought in three ecstasy addicts on robbery charges—they always turned to theft when money ran out for the sex-bliss potion—so she figured she could fake an addiction good enough to satisfy.

"Stop it. Have you no pride? You obviously have a great power. It doesn't matter that your coven won't claim you. You could still do something with your life and your magic." He slapped her fingers away from her breast with a sharp crack of his hand that brought a real gasp of desire to her lips. Oh god yes, she wanted to see Adonis' forceful side. She wanted to see it very, very badly.

"So you're assuming I'm some homeless coven reject?" she asked, coming to her knees and running a fingernail down his cheek to trace the fullness of his luscious-looking bottom lip. He flinched but didn't pull away and the raging erection between his legs began to look a little purple. That couldn't be comfortable.

"If you were Gunera I might not, since they'll claim any sack of shit still capable of casting a first degree spell. But thankfully, one of their gods-forsaken ancestors had the sense to protect them from themselves."

"I don't want to be protected from myself." Aleeza leaned in close to whisper the words inches from the man's face.

"Stop it."

"Stop what?" She leaned closer, smelling the purely male scent of him. Musky, salty and something else, something that made her clit pulse hungrily and her mouth water for a taste of his lips.

"I'm not in the business of feeding addictions." He clenched his jaw and fisted his hands at his sides, as if to keep himself from reaching out and taking what he wanted.

"And what business are you in? Tree-hugging or sanctimonious spell casting?" Her tongue flicked out and teased his upper lip. His breath hissed out through his clenched teeth and his eyes turned decidedly stormy. They were blue. Up this close she could see the color as well as the icy fire that burned within him.

"You know nothing of me or my—"

"I know you're Amiantos—that's enough. I'm Onterantu, but let's not talk politics. In fact, let's not talk at all." She closed the distance between them quickly, wrapping her arms around his neck and pressing her bare breasts against his chest. The thick ridge of his erection was suddenly trapped between their bodies, pressing up against her belly. Aleeza sucked in breath, her heart racing from the combined thrill of the intimate contact and the very awake, very non-spell-affected man in her arms.

Holy fuck. It had worked, the counter spell had really worked.

"Onterantu don't usually have a color in their aura or your kind of power." His words were soft, almost calm sounding, but the look in his eyes was the scariest yet, by far.

"I'm not your usual kind of girl." Her racing heart skipped a beat as he came to his knees and slowly moved his hands to rest at the curve of her back, just above the twin swells of her ass. This time she didn't need to exaggerate the moan that ripped from her mouth as she squirmed into closer contact with her angry giant. The guy thought she was a liar, and she wasn't sure anymore if he was dangerous or not. She should probably try to run, but at this point common sense wasn't ruling her actions. "Please, please." She moaned the words as she lifted her leg and hooked it around his waist, tightening her grip around his shoulders to lift herself higher until she could grind her dripping slit against his thickness.

"Ah!" he cried out, his hands shifting to her ass, gripping her cheeks with fingers that dug into her flesh so deeply it was almost painful.

"Fuck me. Please…fuck me."

"You want me to fuck you?" He spoke the words through gritted teeth, then pulled her so tightly to him that Aleeza could only moan in response.

The skin of his cock was hot, but achingly soft, and her moan turned into a sob. She wanted him so badly. It couldn't be natural. For a split second the haze of lust left her as she wondered what she hell she had done. Had she simply exchanged one monkey for another, swapping the torture of denied satisfaction for the agony of knowing she would lose her mind, her will, and gladly spread her legs for any man with a hard-on?

But then he was rolling them both to the ground, pinning her beneath him and banishing every thought from her mind with a brutal kiss that made her entire body hum. Aleeza met his tongue, his teeth with the same relentless fervor. Her fingernails raked down the skin of his tautly muscled back, digging in deeply enough to break the skin as he reached down and wrenched her legs wide.

"I'll fuck you, but that doesn't mean I won't kill you afterward." He spoke the words against her lips, a threat mingled with a kiss and then he spread the lips of her pussy with rough fingers and shoved himself inside her body.

"Goddess!" Aleeza cried out. She'd been dripping wet from her first orgasm, but she still wasn't prepared for him. He was long, but that didn't seem to be the problem. It was his thickness. He was so thick, so hard that he stretched her virginal body mercilessly wide. The pain was immediate, a sharp sting that made her muscles seize.

"What have you done?" he asked, shock mingling with the lust in his eyes. It seemed he knew somehow, knew that he had hurt her, maybe even knew he'd taken her virginity, but that didn't stop him from pushing even deeper. He thrust forward until every inch of his cock was buried inside her, until his balls nestled in the crevice of her ass, and the tip of him felt it would bruise things deep inside her body.

"What do you mean, what have I done?" Aleeza said, struggling not to let the horrible stinging she felt show on her face. Tears pricked at the back of her eyes, but there was no way she would cry, not in front of an Amiantos. She'd eat her own hand first.

"Wait. Stop moving." He grunted the words, but the hands he placed on either side of her face were surprisingly gentle. And this time, when he kissed her, his lips were feather soft, stroking over hers, teasing with his tongue until a tingling sensation joined in with the stinging between her legs. "Please, you have to stop."

"Sorry," Aleeza breathed, not having realized she was still squirming beneath him.

He pulled his upper body slightly away, but didn't remove his cock from her pussy. Without the motion of his thrust, her body relaxed, the pain abating.

Or maybe she just didn't notice the pain because she was suddenly sucked into those baby blue eyes. Damn, the man was beautiful, and…kind. There was no way in hell she would admit it to him, but the caress of his aura against her felt like a hug from a good friend.

"What did you do?" he asked again. "You're not an ecstasy addict—you're a virgin. What have you been doing up here?"

Aleeza shifted her weight. Now the ache was subsiding, she longed to feel him move inside her again. Why did he want to talk? Didn't now seem like the perfect time to not talk?

She licked her lips and leaned forward, trying to catch his mouth with hers. He pulled away, his face telling her he wasn't moving again until she answered.

"Can't a girl do a little sex magic without an interrogation?" Ignoring his request, she pulsed her hips forward ever so gently. His eyes closed, but his hands lowered to her hips and tightened, holding her fast.

She squirmed against his fingers, the pressure of those ten digits digging into her flesh only building her need. Nice guy or not, he was really starting to piss her off. The least he could do was help her lose her virginity properly.

"It looks to me like you were doing something a little more serious than sex magic, though I don't think you're the witch I'm looking for."

"Does this mean you're not going to kill me?"

"No, but I can't speak for anyone else," he said. "This isn't a safe time to be up in these woods."

"I can take care of myself," Aleeza said, wishing she could fit her fingers in between their bodies and prove that fact to him with a little pressure on her clit.

"I'm sure you can. You know, most virgins aren't red-hot temptresses."

"So you admit you find me red hot? And tempting?" She smiled and wiggled beneath him. His cock pulsed inside her and she groaned. Fuck, he felt so good, even better than she had imagined. Now if only he would start moving again already.

"Why don't you tell me who you really are?"

Aleeza rolled her eyes. She wanted him forceful, not enforcing. If he was going to waste that beautiful hard-on by just sitting around and talking, she would find a man who could do it properly. She hadn't waited all her life for this.

"Forget it," she said, twisting in his grip, but his fingers only tightened.

"I'm not forgetting anything."

"You can forget about this," she said. "I wanted a man, not a magical cop." Focusing her power, she forced it outward, knocking his hands off her and allowing her to scramble away from him. Damn it. Her pussy practically screamed, and she noticed his erection hadn't abated either. They clearly wanted each other. So why this stupid stand-off?

She stood on shaky legs and started to walk past him, back to her bag. She could be back in the city within an hour and find a willing man in less than half that. He may not be as big or as handsome as Mr. Questions, but she knew he'd be more willing. "Thanks for the tease," she snapped.

"Wait just a minute." His hand wrapped around her ankle so fast she stumbled and nearly fell.

"Go fuck yourself." Too bad her anger couldn't overpower her treacherous body. Little waves of heat spread from his hand up her leg, to tingle between her thighs, and farther up still, sliding over her nipples with a velvet touch that took her breath away. Whoever he was, he was powerful. She hadn't felt it as strongly before, when she was so intent on having him inside her.

Now…her hair stood on end. Death magic. He communicated with the dead, and he'd been doing it recently.

"I think you did enough of that for both of us, lady," he growled.

"You've got balls complaining about my spell when you're out here raising the dead. Don't you need a warrant for that? Or at least consent from the surviving relatives?"

Why it was the wrong thing to say, Aleeza didn't know, but it certainly was. In a flash the man was on his feet, his grip changed from her ankle to her wrist with bruising strength. His body, so close to hers, radiated heat. She shivered and did her best not to wince as her bones rubbed together in ways that just weren't natural.

"That's right," he said, his eyes gleaming strangely. "I was trying to raise the dead. But funnily enough, my power was stolen. Now who could have done that?"

Aleeza looked down and turned away, suddenly afraid. Her mind raced. Maybe that alien male power that rushed through her body hadn't been Eros after all. She'd never stolen power from anyone, no matter that her father had been Amiantos and some witches of her own coven insisted she might very well have inherited the ability.

By the age of four or five it had been clear that her power would develop Gunera, not even the slightest doubt, as there had been with her two older brothers. Simon and Heath both had green in their auras, a sign that they might carry some of their father's Amiantos power. But not her. Sometimes she wondered if that's why her pop had left, if the shame of siring a pure Gunera witch was too much for him to handle.

"I didn't steal anything. I wouldn't know how."

"Why don't I believe you?"

"I don't care what you believe," she said, pulling at her wrist. He lightened his hold but didn't set her free. Shit. The flat-out denial wasn't going to work.

Think, Aleeza!

He'd run into her grove already naked and been semi-erect when he arrived at her side. So maybe *he* was lying. Maybe he hadn't been raising the dead. Maybe he had been doing some sex magic of his own.

Amiantos could share power when performing similar spells. Maybe she had stolen his? Goddess, as if she'd know what to do with it even if she had. Witches practiced for years to channel others' power. If she'd accidentally shoplifted his, she wouldn't know how to use it for good or evil. Hell, she wouldn't even know how to give it back to him without asking for advice.

And she would never ask for advice from a member of the undefiled coven.

"Any ideas?" His voice was low and hoarse now, his body so close she could feel his skin against her back. Her breath caught.

"Never had an idea in my life," she said, but her voice trembled. Smartass worked so much better without the tremble, but she couldn't seem to control her own traitorous body. She wanted him still, even more fiercely than she had a few moments ago when he had been buried inside her.

"I'm sure you don't." His hands slid up her arms, her shoulders, stroking forward and down over the slopes of her breasts. He cupped them, lifting their soft weight. Aleeza, unable to stop herself, leaned back into the heat of him with a moan. His cock was hard and a little sticky with their combined fluids against her ass, prodding at her soft skin.

Suddenly he pinched her nipples, hard enough to make her cry out. "I think I know someone who owes me an orgasm," he said. "And in my world, debts are paid."

"I don't owe you—" she started, but he turned her roughly around, forcing her to the ground. The second her ass hit the dirt, his lips covered hers, savage, ruthless.

"A little sex magic," he murmured. "I can do a little sex magic of my own."

She wanted to answer but couldn't. His large body rested between her legs, his cock butting against her entrance. His fingers slid down between them, teasing her clit. Aleeza's hips bucked upward. He chuckled. It wasn't a nice sound, but it was a sexy one. He had her completely in his power, and it thrilled her more than she could have imagined. "You were pretty far down the road when I got here," he said. "Had you finished your spell?"

Of course he knew she had. He couldn't possibly doubt it. She knew what the question was. He was making a point, telling her he knew she wanted to come at least as badly as he did.

"No," she lied.

Again the chuckle. "I don't think you're telling the truth." One thick finger slipped into her. Her eyes closed. "I don't think you're telling me the truth about what you were doing here, either. So I'll make a deal with you."

"I don't make deals."

"You'll make this one. Because I can do one of two things. I can fuck you until we're both limp from it, until we've both lost count of the number of times we've come…or I can keep you here all night, playing with you, teasing you, tasting you, and not let you come at all."

Aleeza bit her lip. Oh goddess, not that. After all these years, after those dreams that had driven her to risk the most dangerous spell of her life, she'd finally had an orgasm. There was no way on earth she could take another night of frustration.

It was almost as if the bastard knew.

"Do we have a deal?" His eyes bored into hers. He removed his finger and shifted forward so the tip of his cock just slid into her. This time there was no pain, only the hungry roar of the awakened beast inside her. She wanted him. Oh, she wanted him so badly.

His thumb rubbed her clit in slow circles. "You're not answering," he said. "I can wait all night."

"If you don't let me come…how will you?"

"Oh, I wouldn't worry about that. And if you tell me what I want to know, you won't have to."

For years Aleeza had used her sexuality to manipulate men, to get them to talk. Now she was getting a taste of her own medicine. Boy, did it suck.

Her hips moved again as his thumb increased its pace. Pressure built in her pelvis again. Oh, she was going to come— she was going to come all over his hand, and it would be glorious. Even better than doing it herself. Her back arched.

He pulled his hand away. "You play it pretty tough," he said. "But do you really think you can take a whole night of that?"

Part of being a bounty hunter, a warrior, was knowing when you were defeated. Aleeza sighed. "It was a sex spell to free myself of an old boyfriend's curse," she said, glaring at him. "And to find a man who could finally satisfy me. Think you're up to it?"

He grinned and thrust the entire thick length of himself into her. "Oh, honey," he said. "I know I am."

Chapter Four

ℰℭ

Ferrin stood at the edge of the trees, watching Dorand's buttocks contract as he shoved his thick cock into the woman beneath him. She cried out, a sound of passion that made Ferrin's own erection twitch painfully, and began to buck into Dorand's swift thrusts with wild abandon.

His large hands pinned her smaller ones to the ground above her head while his mouth attended to her full breasts, sucking, laving, nipping at them with his teeth. Ferrin's mouth watered as he imagined the taste of her skin—sweet, salty and something else, something so magnificent he knew he would never want to let her go. The smell of her wet sex drifted to him though he stood some ten feet away, intoxicating him, making his cock ache, burn with the wild need to go to her, to rip Dorand away from her body and bury his own shaft deep in her pussy.

He wanted to fuck her, to shove his rampant erection between her legs until he exploded, shooting his seed deep into her womb. Then he would stay buried inside her until he was hard once more, until he could ride her again, come inside her again, until their magic achieved the ultimate union and a child was conceived.

What the hell? A child? The idea was ludicrous and clearly not the product of his own mind.

"By the gods, I call…" Ferrin swallowed with difficulty and struggled to remember the rest of the words to the liberty spell, but his mind failed him.

His feet suddenly began to move of their own accord, but he wrapped his arms around the nearest tree, holding on tight to keep from running to join the couple still furiously mating in the glen. The rough bark scraped his skin but did nothing to banish the all-consuming lust that raged through his body. The sounds Dorand and the woman were making didn't help either. Moans, grunts, cries of ecstasy and the slap of skin against skin as Dorand fucked her with a rough passion unlike anything Ferrin had seen in five years as his lover.

If you'd asked him ten minutes ago if Dorand was even capable of that level of abandon, even in the midst of the greatest fuck of his life, Ferrin would have said no. Dorand was strong, steady, downright boring at times. Even when in the grip of high temper, he wasn't the type to give up his infamous control. Not like Ferrin…

That's why Carantha had called Ferrin to her bed when there was no magic involved. She loved to feel him ramming away inside her, lost to everything but the need to take his pleasure. She liked for him to hurt her, bruise her delicate tissue with the force of his desire, and he enjoyed the same. He had never come as hard as when Carantha scraped her nails down his back until he bled, breaking the skin on his shoulder as she bit him in the midst of her passion.

But he had an instinctive feeling that this raven-haired woman could make him come even harder. Just the touch of their lips would be electric, a wickedly sensual promise of how addictive the sex could be between them. Once they were skin to skin, his cock sliding into the velvet sheath of her pussy, there would be nothing that could separate them. They would meld together, a tangle of sweaty flesh, mating so furiously that they would both fear they would die from it—and know that they would welcome that sweet death when it came.

Get it together, man! You've got to stop this, got to stop Dorand before —

Before what? There was no danger out there in the mix of white and blue light that shone around the couple. There was only magic sharing, Dorand lapping up the azure power of the woman beneath him even as she glowed brighter and brighter with white Amiantos power.

No, the danger was here, inside his own body, pulsing through his veins. Whatever he was, whatever evil had spawned him and abandoned him in the Amiantos woods so many years past raised its horned head within him.

"No," Ferrin muttered, licking away the sweat that beaded on his lip. "Be gone from me by the gods of the grove. By the gods of the fathers and their sons, by the gods of those who would welcome man into the Otherworld, be gone from me. Let me see with the eyes of the common man, speak the words of the common tongue, and know the—"

Fuck! What was the last part of the spell? He'd chanted the damn thing a hundred times, a thousand. The seed of blackness had always been a part of him, of his magic, but it had been a part he could control. Don't give the damn thing water, don't give it food, and it will stay a seed. That had been his motto, and the only thing that had eased his mind when he realized how different he truly was from his adopted coven members.

He wasn't Amiantos by blood, but he had learned to be by magic. He was a deathspeaker, a witch who raised the energy to call the dead with a strength that rivaled any other in the known world. If he could learn to work a magic most could only claim through birthright, he could control the monster inside him, always so ready to come out and play.

"Yes, oh goddess, yes!" The woman screamed and arched into Dorand's body, the look of primal bliss on her face drawing a growl from Ferrin's throat. His fingernails dug into the tree bark until they tore and began to bleed. At that moment he knew that he would gladly kill his brother, his lover, the man he was closest to in all the world, if it meant he could take Dorand's place, feel Aleeza's pussy pulsing around him, drawing him into her, triggering his own release.

Aleeza...her name was Aleeza. It was almost as if someone had whispered the knowledge in his ear...someone with a forked tongue.

"Please, by the gods." Ferrin closed his eyes and sucked in a deep breath, groaning as the scent of Aleeza's pussy invaded once more. She was so sweet, so purely, amazingly what he'd been waiting for.

What you've been waiting for? What the fuck are you thinking!

Beads of sweat rolled down his face, despite the cold autumn night. This was it, as close as he had ever come to letting that "other" voice in. It was always there, offering up knowledge that Ferrin himself could have no way of knowing, promising power beyond his wildest dreams. But he'd always been able to ignore that quiet whisper, never been tempted to let down his shields and welcome the beast within. It was the woman who made him vulnerable, something about her, something that only the darkness could recognize.

"Ahh!" Dorand's cry broke through to his right mind, and Ferrin opened his eyes to see his brother coming with a magnificence that took his breath away. Dorand's hips were arched so powerfully that Aleeza's ass scooted across the dirt. His face was twisted with wonder and passion, edged by just the hint of that sweet, sensual pain that Ferrin had always thought him too closed-minded to appreciate.

The white light glowing around Aleeza suddenly transformed into a white mist as she came again, a mist that Dorand inhaled into his body with his next deep breath. A small ember of that pure brilliance still burned in Aleeza's aura, just as a small coal of blue burned in Dorand's, but the magic sharing had ended. In a few more seconds, both shades of magic faded until only the moon lit the nude bodies of the man and woman who lay panting in the glen.

"And know the truth of my senses to be the truth of the gods." The last part of the spell came to him, and immediately Ferrin felt his mind clear.

Whether it was the spell or the fact that he suddenly couldn't catch the musky smell of Aleeza's arousal anymore, he couldn't say. But he was more than grateful to be in control of himself. Now if he could get control of Dorand, maybe they could find out exactly who this Aleeza was, and why she called to the blackness within him so strongly.

* * * * *

"Goddess," Aleeza panted, running shaky hands down the strong, sweat-dampened skin of her lover's back. It was getting colder by the second, but somehow they'd made each other sweat as they'd mated with a furious passion that had turned her bones to jelly.

Sex. She'd finally had sex. With another person. And it had been…unbelievable.

"Am I a man of my word?" He breathed the words against the skin of her neck, his warm breath sending a shiver through her body and renewing the tingling between her legs. "Are you satisfied?"

"You were amazing, but I don't know if I'll ever be satisfied." Aleeza stiffened as soon as the words were out of her mouth. They were true, but she hadn't meant to speak so frankly. What was wrong with her? It was as if some wall had been broken down between them. She felt close to this man and strangely vulnerable as he pulled away to look down at her with smiling eyes.

"It's like any other new toy, addictive at first, but eventually the new wears off."

"You really looked like the new had worn off, big guy." Aleeza couldn't help but smile as his laughter filled the glen, a low, rumbling sound that made her wish it was tangible so she could rub up against it like a cat. But then, almost everything about this man made her want to rub some part of her against some part of him. He was undeniably magnetic, though his strong-arm tactics earlier left a lot to be desired.

"My name's Dorand Tedder, of the Amiantos coven."

"Who said I wanted to know your name? Maybe I like my one-night stands anonymous," she said, wrapping her legs around his waist and lifting her hips. The part of him still buried inside her began to thicken, pressing against the highly sensitized walls of her pussy.

"This isn't going to be a one-night stand." Dorand's smile faded as heat began to burn in his eyes once more. When he moved his hands to cup her breasts, rolling her nipples softly between fingers and thumbs, Aleeza was nearly ready to agree with him. Sure, she hated the Amiantos, but the way he worked her body, the way he coaxed her into a state of desperate arousal again in seconds was surely worth making a friend out of the enemy. At least for a little while.

"Don't speak too quickly, brother."

Aleeza yelped and jumped in Dorand's arms as a second man emerged from the shadows. Two times in one night she'd been taken by surprise. It wasn't like her to let her guard down so easily, especially when she knew she wasn't in safe territory. She'd known the risks when she invaded Amiantos lands, and Dorand could still decide to punish her for that invasion. She still had her magic, she could feel it vibrating within her with even more potency than usual, but she wasn't out of the woods until she was out of these woods.

"This witch has a few questions to answer before you set about fucking her again." The new guy had dark brown hair that fell to his shoulders and a wicked smile on his face that simultaneously softened his hard words and made them even more threatening.

He was shorter than Dorand but no less attractive. Though his was a rough-around-the-edges kind of sexiness. He looked like the type who liked to party too late and skip a shave the morning after, the kind of man who would concentrate every ounce of energy on a woman while he was making love but forget her name seconds after orgasm. He was…trouble. Something within her sensed it intuitively even as another, less reasonable part of her insisted that she meet his wicked smile with one of her own and invite him down to play in the dirt. He certainly looked ready to play.

"Now, now, Aleeza, don't look at me like that," Trouble said, his smile fading away. "I just might take you up on that offer, and the gods only know what we three would be in for then."

The words sent a spasm of pure passion through her. Was this normal? She'd never even considered such a thing before. It hadn't been possible for her to be with more than one man, but even if it was, Aleeza never thought she was that kind of woman. Now…she could picture them both touching her, teasing her. Two thick cocks to play with, two mouths and tongues to caress her body. She saw the two of them kissing, touching each other while she watched, Ferrin's mouth taking Dorand's cock while Dorand's tongue carried her into a place she'd never been. Involuntarily, she shifted forward, taking Dorand's erection deeper into her. He gasped and tightened his hands around her waist.

Wait. How did she know his name was Ferrin? *Was* his name Ferrin?

For that matter, how the fuck did he know *her* name?

He smiled. "I can read your thoughts," he said. "It's not a talent of mine, but your desire is so plain on your face you may as well speak it out loud."

Good try, bucko, and I suppose you can read my name on my face, as well?

"You don't need to say anything either." She gave his cock a pointed look just as a bead of moisture fell from the tip, deciding to keep his little slip to herself. Quickly she firmed up her mental shields. Her oldest brother, Simon, had some telepathic ability so she'd learned to shield before she could read. This guy didn't want to lay down all his cards. That was fine—she didn't like to give away her hand at the first meeting either, but it confirmed her hunch that she couldn't trust him as far as she could throw him.

Still she had to fight not to lick her lips. Ferrin was sex personified, and she couldn't help the way her inner muscles clenched around Dorand. He grunted softly, and slipped his right hand around to her front so his thumb could stroke her clit. He clearly wasn't embarrassed to have an audience, which surprised her. Amiantos weren't known for their kink factor.

"I don't think we need to ask her questions just now, brother," Dorand said. Aleeza watched the two men's eyes meet. Something passed between them, some communication she couldn't understand even if she tried.

Which she didn't because Dorand's solid thickness inside her was quickly driving her back to a place where nothing else mattered. Her muscles twitched. Neither of them moved, but there could be no mistaking the pressure building inside her. Her pussy burned. She wanted to move, to lift herself up and slide back down the glorious length of his cock. Every nerve ending in her body felt alive, itching with need, but she didn't dare allow herself to do so much as shift her hold on his shoulders.

Despite her desire for this Ferrin guy, despite the wonderfully filthy images in her head, she couldn't seriously do it, couldn't fuck him while Ferrin watched. She was actually shocked by how comfortable she felt sitting naked in front of two strange men with one of them buried inside her. Surely this couldn't be normal.Was sex really this addictive? Surely she couldn't be so completely shameless.

But she was. It was all she could do to keep still despite the rising tension in her muscles. She tensed her thighs, trying desperately not to start riding him the way she wanted to. Her back ached from being kept still, her fingernails dug into her palms. Power rose in her pelvis. Her body started glowing again, and her embarrassment started to fade as she fought not to move, not to explode. She was sure they could both see her agony but couldn't decide which was worse to share with these men—her agony or her abandon.

Soon she didn't have a choice.

Dorand said something else, quietly, but she couldn't seem to pay attention to his words as her pelvis flooded with heat and her muscles tightened in preparation for another amazing orgasm. This couldn't be happening. They weren't even moving.

"Aleeza." Ferrin's voice cut through her thoughts and she turned her head to him without thinking, shifting her weight. That one small movement made Dorand's cock twitch inside her, and the friction from that tiny change sent shockwaves through her system. There was nowhere else for the power to go, and now it was Ferrin's eyes into which she looked while she came, his impassive face that watched as her body flooded with a pleasure.

Aleeza felt her face twist with the violence of her orgasm, but her eyes stayed open. She couldn't tear her gaze away from him, even when Dorand groaned and his cock began to pulse inside her.

Ferrin waited until she stopped trembling before he spoke. "You might want to get off my brother if you don't want that to keep happening. Although I'd like to see it again."

"You're an—"

"Ferrin."

So that *was* his name, an answer that spawned another batch of questions. She'd never read anyone's mind, never had the slightest inkling that telepathic power was within her grasp. She'd obviously gotten more than she bargained for when she lay down on the earth and spoke the ancient spell. She shivered as she wondered what other surprises might be in store. If she knew the nature of magic, not all of them would be welcome.

"I don't think our little witch is used to this sort of thing," Dorand continued. "Maybe you could turn your back and let her get dressed?"

Little witch? Who the hell did he think he was? And why did she find his diminishing endearment strangely exciting?

Ferrin grinned. Damn it, she still found him sexy as well and couldn't help returning the grin. It was so…approving. Like he knew what she felt and was telling her not to worry.

"Do I have to?" he said. "Can't I even watch her bend over to pick up her clothes?"

"No, you may *not*," Aleeza said, with a glare she didn't really feel. Ferrin sighed heavily and turned around. She noticed the view of his back pleased her just as much as the view of his front although without the undeniable attraction of his cock.

"If you don't get off me," Dorand whispered in her ear, his breath against her skin making her shiver, "I can't be responsible for what I'll do. Or what Ferrin will do when he sees it. So unless you want both of us right now, it's best for you to get dressed."

What had she walked into this night? Two men throbbing with power, brimming with sexual energy. Two men obviously comfortable with their sexuality together. She wondered if those images she'd received in her head were her own wild imagination after all, or if she'd read them with her newfound power.

Dorand kissed her throat. "I'm not joking," he said, pulling her hips forward.

Aleeza hovered on the edge of indecision. Modesty and some vague sense that most women would have said no to sex with two strange men at once made her detach herself and stand up.

"Damn," Ferrin said, his back still turned. "I got my hopes up for nothing."

"You poor thing." She reached out and patted his shoulder. Her hand froze. Ferrin, too, crawled with death magic. What had they been doing here in these woods?

Something else made her shiver as well. Ferrin was not Amiantos. He used Amiantos magic—she could feel it on him—but something inside this man was older, darker than Dorand's people. It was something that made her heart race, but whether it was from fear or excitement she couldn't quite decide.

But wouldn't it be fun to find out?

"What are you?" she asked without thinking, responding to the quiet hiss in her mind. Wherever that thought had come from, it hadn't been her own subconscious, no matter that she might have wondered the same thing herself given time to consider her options with this dark, handsome man.

Ferrin's breath caught. He turned to her, and she caught one glimpse of the fear in his eyes before he blinked. The fear was gone. Instead, he gave her a slow smile. "Want to find out?" He reached for her, pulling her to him.

Aleeza gasped. The same kindness, goodness Dorand possessed was evident in Ferrin's aura, in his soul. But she hadn't been wrong. Something else lurked inside him, something that made her insides spasm with pure, terrifying desire. She'd come just from having Dorand's cock resting inside her. She thought she might be able to do it again simply from looking into the depths of this man's eyes.

"I can't—" she started to say, but the noise drove all thoughts from her head, sent her flying to the ground with Ferrin's warm body on top of hers.

No matter what sort of magic was being performed in the woods tonight, it shouldn't cause explosions.

The sound ended as abruptly as it had come, leaving the woods even more oddly silent than before. Fear crawled up Aleeza's spine. Some bounty hunter she was, so preoccupied with her sexual desire she hadn't even noticed someone, probably a human, setting off a bomb. This wouldn't be the first time a group of right-wingers had taken to the woods for a little illegal witch hunting. Nor would it be the first time the human authorities would show up too late to save some innocent witch's life. Time to get out of here, and fast.

Ferrin helped her up. "Are you okay?"

She nodded.

The two men exchanged another glance.

"I'll stay." Dorand nodded.

"I'll be fine," Aleeza said quickly. "Really. You guys go. I'll get dressed and come right after you."

"No, you should stay here, it isn't safe—"

Dorand was interrupted by another explosion, the fire glowing red-orange in the forest before blinking out. Whether it was a bunch of kids pulling a prank or something more serious, she didn't want to stick around to find out. Her two knights in shining armor could rush off to the rescue. She'd get her ass out of Dodge and live to see tomorrow. It was the Gunera way. Save your own skin first, then the skin of your coven mates. The rest of the witches could fend for themselves, just as they'd always left the Gunera to do the same.

"Go!" she shouted, relieved to see both of them rush from the clearing.

It was time to get her clothes on and get the hell out of here before they started asking questions she didn't want to answer…or before she took them up on their offer and let them both screw her senseless.

* * * * *

Raven smiled as she picked up her bag and once again became one with the shadows, heading back to her car. Fireworks. Who would have thought such a mundane thing could be so useful to a witch? It only confirmed her belief that a girl should never clean out her trunk. You never knew when leftovers from last year's Beltane celebration might come in handy for creating a distraction.

In a way, she was sorry to have created one at all. Watching her cousin and that Amiantos had been incredibly exciting. Watching her cousin and both of the men…now that would have made this damned trip into the woods even more worthwhile.

Raven had no doubt it would have come to that. If Aleeza's desperation had led her all the way out here to perform forbidden magic, it surely would have led her to take two men at once. Gavyn's little golden girl, the biggest wage earner for Gunera Bounty, had indulged in magic too gray even for their coven leader's infamously suspect tastes.

And Raven was the only one who knew about it. What an interesting situation.

She threw the bag of fireworks into the passenger seat of her car and turned on the ignition. Kali would be thrilled to hear about this. The only missing piece…a Gunera witch able to be fully penetrated by a non-Amiantos man…

Now they had it.

Raven shivered as she pulled out onto the rural road that led back to the highway, her nipples growing rock hard against her thin t-shirt. She was going to have to work hard to keep from speeding all the way back to Savior City. Just thinking about how Kali would reward her for her job well done made her pussy gush into her simple cotton panties. She'd worn pink ones tonight, with a little bow at the front.

Kali loved it when she played up the innocent little girl routine.

She was going to flip when she saw Raven's simple t-shirt and demure little skirt. Raven had even gone the extra mile and pulled her shoulder-length blonde hair into two braids. Kali loved to fist a braid in each hand, wrenching Raven's head back until it was nearly impossible to breathe, as she fucked her from behind.

Despite what she'd seen in the grove, Raven would still swear that Kali's dildo was every bit as good as the real thing. With each night they spent together, Raven became more and more certain that she would die if she were to lose favor with the woman who had once been nothing but a barely tolerated roommate. But that was before she'd known the wicked skill of Kali's tongue between her legs, or the pleasure-pain of Kali's teeth raking over her nipples as her lover slid a double-shafted vibrator into her pussy and ass.

Raven hadn't been sure initially if she would enjoy Kali's brand of kink, but she'd been so desperate for release that she'd leapt at each opportunity Kali offered to "help her get around the damned Gunera curse". A year ago that had meant a weekly blood donation in exchange for a spell that allowed Raven to find release in her own hand. A few months after that, she'd taken to spying on other members of her coven in exchange for a night with Kali in her bed.

After that, she'd agreed to anything, given in to every demand so long as it meant she would spend another night with her dark goddess. Raven knew she'd gladly sell her soul in exchange for the way Kali made her feel, the way she worked her body and her mind, withholding pleasure until it became pain, then agony and finally pleasure again. The power of her release after their sessions was the most intense feeling Raven had ever known. It was love, hate, lust, contempt and a little bit of torture, all wrapped up in the most extreme magical high.

"Better than cock any day," she whispered, something in her voice making her shiver. She rolled up the windows, cold for the first time that night despite the chilly autumn temperatures.

Was it really better than the real thing? She would never know because Kali wasn't strong enough to break the Gunera curse, only work around it. Raven still couldn't have sex with a man, only members of her own sex. What would it feel like for a real man—a man like that big guy in the grove or even the smaller, darker one—to shove his cock between her legs? What would it be like to feel hard muscle, coarse hair, rubbing against her breasts instead of Kali's soft, pliant skin? What would it feel like for the shaft working inside her cunt to swell, thicken, spill its seed inside her, growing limp with sated lust?

She would never know, not without marrying some damn Amiantos. But Aleeza did, and it made her hate her cousin even more.

"As if I needed another reason." Raven pulled onto the highway and smashed her small, Keds-covered foot down onto the accelerator.

Let some human cop pull her over—she was always able to talk her way out of a ticket or worse. She'd bat her big baby blues and be on her way in no time. On her way home to the woman of her dreams with the last ingredient for Kali's spell as well as the juicy gossip that they might not even need the damned thing. Just as Kali had planned, Aleeza had done the work for them. She was curse-free, and ready to conceive.

Kali's hard work had paid off. Now she just had to sit back and enjoy the ride with Raven by her side. The demon had promised he would take care of everything else. Once the vessel was in place, the rest would be gravy.

"It's all over but the crying," Raven said, turning up the volume on the radio and ignoring the voice inside her head that warned of trusting demon promises.

Chapter Five

⁊

"Wake up!" The volume her mother used was bad enough, but the feel of her hand, hot and stinging, on Aleeza's cheek was enough to make her bolt into a seated position on the cot where she'd sacked out for the night.

"What the fuck? Shit, Mona, stop hitting me!" Aleeza rolled to the floor to avoid another well-aimed smack from Mommy dearest, who looked like she herself had just crawled out of bed after a restless night.

Mona's hair hung in a tangled wave down to her waist, and her long, peacock-colored night dress was wrinkled and reeked of last night's cigarette smoke. Aleeza held her breath as she scuttled across the floor on her hands and knees, barely keeping clear of Mona's furiously kicking feet. Her mom might not have wasted time getting dressed before she ran out to the shed behind the house, but she had stopped to slide on her mud boots. The last thing Aleeza needed this morning was a kick in the ass or anywhere else from one of those. She knew she would lose what little she'd managed to shove down her throat before she passed out last night. Hell, she might lose it anyway if she had to keep moving this fast.

"Mom, please, stop it, I can explain," Aleeza said, crawling into the corner and cowering there with her arms across her face. She had no idea if she could explain or not but hoped the words would penetrate her mother's rage. Mona hadn't struck her in years, not since she was about twelve and tall enough to fight back, so whatever had pissed her off must be serious business indeed.

"If I'd thought you were going to try something like this, there 's no way in hell I would have given you the root. What were you thinking? Have you lost what little sense you were born with?" Mona ran a frantic hand through her hair, revealing eyes shot through with red.

"I don't know what you're talking about," Aleeza snapped. The sense she was born with? That must be from her father's side since Mona was about as sensitive as your average parole officer.

"You're in heat!" Mona screamed the words loud enough to stir the birds nesting in the old tin roof above the shed.

"What?" Aleeza laughed and immediately regretted it when her mother delivered another kick in her direction. It made contact with her shin, but Mona had lost the driving force of her anger so it didn't hurt—much.

"I'm betting you'll ovulate in the next few days, and you're practically vibrating with sex energy. If the sperm is still viable, you could get pregnant!"

"What?" Aleeza tried to smile, to pretend her mother had finally lost it, but the lump that had suddenly taken up residence in her throat made it difficult.

"Pregnant, and with goddess knows what," her mother said, sinking to the cot and dropping her forehead into her trembling hands.

Goddess…what had she done? Aleeza hadn't even thought about contraception, and especially hadn't bargained on Mona's particular breed of reproductive magic leading to her discovery. She'd thought she would be safe here or at least safer than she would have been at her own apartment.

The entire building had been touched by black magic, not enough to leave an obvious stain, but the slight stink of it had left Aleeza nauseous and more than a little concerned. Was the blackness new? Placed there by some force that knew what she had done and was eager to make contact? Or had it been there for months, going unnoticed until she approached the building with Dorand's borrowed power held within her? The white light had begun to glow the instant she set foot on her block and practically burned a knot in her stomach when she'd tried to mount the steps to her apartment.

It was already four in the morning by that time, so Aleeza had taken her Taco Hut takeout and driven across town to camp out in Mona's shed. She'd thought she'd be safe there, at least until morning when the hard light of day might offer some answers. But she should have known better. She hadn't been safe at Mona's when she was a relatively innocent little kid and she wasn't safe here now. She had to get out and find someone who might really be able to offer some help.

"Listen, Mona. I think you just had a hard night. I was out late and yeah, I did try to hook up with a couple of guys—"

"A couple?"

"But nothing happened," Aleeza continued, ignoring the shame that tried to rear its head at Mona's shocked expression. So she had considered fucking two men at the same time. So what? It wouldn't have hurt anyone. Could Mona say the same about all of her decisions? "We're cursed, remember? They were out cold before contraception could even become an issue."

"Do you think I'm stupid?"

"Mom—"

"No really," Mona interrupted, tears in her eyes. "Do you think I'm stupid? I know you've always thought I was a shitty excuse for a mother, and a bitch who ran away your precious Daddy, but do you actually believe I'm a fool?"

The question hung in the air, floating between them in the silence left as the angry finches that nested in the shed's roof flew away into the cold morning air. Aleeza shivered and pulled the old flannel she had found in her trunk tighter across her chest. Her mother never cried. Never. Not when her dad left, not when Simon was nearly killed on his first mission for Gunera Bounty.

"Mom, don't worry. Whatever I've done, I'm prepared to handle the consequences. This isn't about the coven, or you, or—"

"If you believe that, then you're the fool." Mona shook her head and let out a small, strangled laugh, smearing tears across her face with the finger and thumb she dug into the tops of her closed eyes. "Come in the house. Let me get you some herbs to help prevent fertilization. Then you've got to got see Gavyn."

"I'm off work today," Aleeza said, the lame excuse falling from her lips even as she rose to follow Mona back into the house. If there was one other member of their coven who might be able to sense what she'd done, it would be Gavyn. She didn't want to be anywhere near him until she'd had time for a shower and a nice, long shielding session.

"He called here looking for you this morning when he couldn't reach you at your place. He's got another private client lined up but Daniel is still out of town on another job."

"Right," Aleeza said, mentally cursing herself for being such a damned workaholic.

Only she and Daniel had managed to complete the sixty-hour correspondence course for their license in Special Supernatural Investigations. None of the other coven members had been overly enthusiastic about expanding Gunera Bounty into areas other than bail bond enforcement, but she and Daniel had seen the possibilities of Gavyn's idea immediately. If Gunera Bounty became Gunera Bounty and Investigations, there would be more work to go around and eventually better money once they built a reputation.

But right now, her ability to look to the future of her coven was working against her. If she was the only one in town licensed to take this big job, there was no way she could avoid Gavyn. She was going to have to head into the office…and pray her coven leader wasn't as sharply attuned to reproductive magic as Mona.

* * * * *

"Gunera Bounty and Investigations has its second job. At this rate we're going to need more people certified, pronto. I'm putting you in charge of finding volunteers. And don't tell me you can't find them. Let them know how much cash you're getting for this and they'll be jumping at the chance."

Aleeza hadn't even finished closing the door behind her before Gavyn spoke, waving a thick manila folder in her direction. "Here." The sunlight streaming in the frosted glass window behind him cast an odd whitish glow around his dark head, like the glow of Dorand's energy the night before had made his skin gleam. Aleeza shivered and hurried to take the file from Gavyn, making sure their fingers didn't touch.

"Good morning to you too. And how much money am I getting for this job anyway?"

"What's wrong with you? Are you sick?" Gavyn's smile faded and his green eyes narrowed. He held on to the file more tightly.

For a second Aleeza thought he might pull her over the desk into his lap and make her sit there and say "ah". Gavyn was their coven's strongest healer and had basically been her pediatrician when she was growing up. Aleeza had learned every healing spell she knew from him and had known he would be able to sense something off with her energy. She shouldn't have come here, should have made him fill her in over the phone and picked up the damn file later after she'd had a nice long nap.

"Nothing's wrong. Give me a break, Gavyn. I haven't been sick in ten years," she said, rolling her eyes and pulling the file from his grip with a firm yank. Play it off, she just had to play it off and get out of here ASAP.

"Don't bullshit me, there's something wrong," Gavyn said. "You seem different somehow."

Aleeza sat down in one of the cracked leather chairs and shrugged, keeping her eyes down, scanning the words on the folder without reading them. "Nothing. I guess I'm just tired. I had a late night."

"No, your energy feels off, like it's been tampered with. Maybe—"

"What's the case, Gavyn? The sooner you tell me about it, the sooner I can start, and the sooner we get paid."

"I like that you're eager." Gavyn gave her another hard look, then leaned back in his own, much nicer chair, and put his feet up on the mess of paper covering his desk. Every Gunera Aleeza knew had offered to help him organize the office at least once, but Gavyn insisted he had a system. "But this is a challenging job, and if there's any question about your health—"

"Cut the crap, Gavyn. You'd send me out while I was in the middle of giving birth if the job paid well enough."

Now why had she said that? Giving birth? Idiot.

Gavyn smiled and rubbed his own ever-rounding belly. "Funny you mention that, Al. I'm sending you up to the Pekora Forest for this one."

Only the powerful shields Aleeza had built up since heading for the office kept her from betraying her emotions. Did Gavyn know where she'd been last night? She wouldn't put it past the old man to fuck with her a little before he dealt out a punishment. But surely he wouldn't be so blasé if he'd known what she'd been up to in the woods. Best to keep playing dumb and give out as little information as possible. "Oh? What's up there, except a bunch of Amiantos?"

"That's right. The Amiantos have hired us for this one. I'm sure you can't wait to get better acquainted. Might be your chance to finally meet that special someone." The words were ripe with sarcasm. If Gavyn had ever been married, Aleeza didn't know about it, and he certainly knew how she felt about the undefiled coven.

"You know I don't want to meet any damned Amiantos. I'm surprised you even took a job from them. Are you sure it's not a trap? They might be working with the human police."

"No, the job is legit. The question is, are you? I don't want to send a frustrated virgin up there to be swept off her feet by some blond god and make our company, and our coven, look like a bunch of fools."

"What are you talking about, Gavyn? I still feel the same way I always have about them," Aleeza said, her heart beating fast in her throat. He knew. Shit, he had to know, and now she was going to be in the biggest trouble of her life. She might be kicked out of the coven or worse, she might be—

"Really? Because I've been hearing some things. Like maybe you're getting a little too frustrated with celibacy. I heard you ended up on your ass in an alley last night so desperate you were going to let that living dildo Keller into your pants." He stood up, all six feet of him looming over her from behind his desk. He was a big man in every sense of the word and the closest thing she'd had to a father since her own disappeared. Looking into his angry face and not spilling everything wasn't the easiest thing she'd ever done, but she met his green eyes with her dark brown ones and willed a look of complete innocence onto her features.

"Not to mention, you reek of male. How many guys were you with last night?"

"W-What?" Goddess help her, she'd almost said, "only one." "What are you talking about?"

"I think you know what I'm talking about."

Shit. Shitshitshit. "Fine, Gavyn. Yes. I tried to pick up two different guys last night. I thought maybe if the guys weren't supers I could make it work. It didn't. The experience left me drained so I did a spell to charge back up and it's made me a little high. Then my mom pumped me full of herbs this morning to 'even out my humors' and I'm about to throw up on your desk. I just need a shower and a nap, and I'll be ready to go. I don't want an Amiantos man any more than I ever did, and I've never, *never*, embarrassed this company."

He gave her a hard look, then took a deep breath and sat back down. He'd bought it, at least for now. "No, you haven't, but I'm warning you, Al—"

"Can we just get to the briefing so I can go home and clean up before I head into enemy territory?" All that training paid off. Lies came so easily to her now.

"They're not my favorite coven either, but they're the client and I expect you to treat them with respect. Amiantos might not be our friends, but neither are they the enemy."

"They might as well be."

"You can't really believe that, Al. Sometimes it works out between the Gunera and the Amiantos. Just because your father—"

"Damn it, Gavyn, are you going to brief me or not?" She stood up, anger suddenly boiling in her chest. How dare he, how *dare* he talk like this? Who did he think he was? She wanted to hit him, to punch him, to slice his throat with her nails and let his blood run—the desire was so strong for a minute she thought she'd done it. She saw Gavyn's limp body on the floor, saw herself standing over him, laughing, sucking his power into her body…

What the *hell*?!

"Aleeza? Aleeza! Are you okay?" Gavyn's hands squeezed her arms so hard it hurt. Her vision cleared and she saw that his face, only inches away from hers, was thankfully unmarked. Had she really seen that? Goddess, had she really imagined doing something so terrible to Gavyn, her coven leader, her friend?

Her legs shook as she sank back into the chair. "I'm fine."

"You don't look fine."

"I am, I'm just…I'm just tired. Could you get me something to drink, please? Preferably something with caffeine?"

"Caffeine might not be a good idea if you're unbalanced today," he said, actually looking as if he might regret having given her such a hard time. "I have—"

"Just anything. Please." Please, let him leave her alone for a minute. He needed to leave her alone for a minute. Because the image of his broken body still shone in her head like a bright new penny and she had no idea why, but the thought of hurting him made her pussy throb.

Something was definitely wrong, horribly wrong.

The feeling of foreboding didn't disappear when Gavyn brought her some orange juice and started briefing her on the new job.

"Three witches murdered," he said. "All on Fire Festivals. The first was Rimer Lorcan, at the Spring Equinox. Rimer was a loner, a petty criminal. He'd been covenless for years, and pissed off more people, super and human, than you can count on two hands. Everyone assumed it was a revenge killing until they did postmortem." The picture she pulled from the file was so lurid with blood Aleeza had to close her eyes for a second. "They found evidence of ritual murder. Magical symbols carved into his organs—the ones they didn't take, anyway." Aleeza swallowed hard.

"Next was Carantha Smoler, on Beltane. This one was better documented than the first, more pictures, close ups of the symbols in the organs." A picture of a woman's battered, broken body seemed to leap out of the file at Aleeza. Tears sprang to her eyes. The woman was lovely—had been lovely. For a moment it was almost as if she could see her smiling, laughing…Aleeza shook her head. She was more tired than she'd thought. She'd never had psychic flashes like these before.

Unless the sex spell had opened her up somehow. She didn't even want to think about that, couldn't think about things like that until she was far away from Gavyn.

Whatever that odd flash was, it didn't happen with the next picture.

"Lymera Brown." Gavyn shifted on the arm of her chair. "Lammas. The Amiantos have no leads. Since the murders all took place in the forest, they've been the ones responsible for investigating, even though only two of the victims—Rimer and Carantha—were theirs. Lymera was Phillias coven, but she was going to marry an Amiantos, so they feel she was theirs too."

"And now they want us to find the killer?"

Gavyn nodded. "Not only that. They want us to prevent the next murder, which if the perps follow their pattern will take place on Samhain…not quite a month away."

* * * * *

The leaves crunched under her feet as she made her way from the small gravel-covered parking lot and into Amiantos lands. For years they'd lived up here, separate from the other covens, separate from society. Tree-hugging freaks, she'd always thought, picturing Grizzly Adams with a lordly sneer and a rotten attitude toward women.

But her father hadn't been like that and neither had Dorand. She wondered if she would see either of the men and couldn't decide if she wanted to or not. She probably wouldn't even recognize her old man. She'd been six years old when he left, and her memories of him were more than a little fuzzy. Besides, what would she say to him? He'd abandoned their family, was good as dead to her, and it would probably be best if he stayed dead.

Dorand, however, was a more complicated issue.

Her body certainly wanted to see him, *all* of him, again. Just the thought of him, of his hard chest and even harder cock, made her panties wet. She'd fallen asleep thinking of him, and if Mona hadn't barged in, she probably would have woken up thinking of him too.

It was probably like this for every woman who lost her virginity. Surely that first man made an impression that was hard to shake? Or even every man. She'd read *Cosmo*. She knew how many women got upset when men they slept with never called again. And she hadn't even told him her name, though Ferrin had seemed to—

Hell. If Dorand saw her, he would know for sure. He would also know she was Gunera, and he would know exactly what kind of spell she'd worked last night. Dorand would know she'd danced the line, nearly executed black magic to free herself of the Gunera enchantment. He might even turn her in.

And what would her coven do then? What would they do to her? Banish her? Worse? Mona hadn't said a word after she'd given Aleeza the herbs, but the expression of impending doom on her face hadn't been comforting. Neither had her order for Aleeza to get her ass to Sunday afternoon dinner with the family, come hell or high water.

She'd been so busy shielding, and then so unsettled in Gavyn's office, she hadn't allowed her imagination to run wild. Now she stopped still, caught by a terrible urge to run, to run away from all of it and hide.

"Well, well. Look who it is." The voice came from the trees off to her left. She couldn't see the speaker, but she didn't need to. She knew that voice. A bolt of pure heat ran from her head down through her stomach and settled between her legs. It was Ferrin.

Raising her eyebrows and crossing her arms, she turned toward him. "Oh, it's you," she said, but the cool tones she'd intended turned into a gasp when she saw his bare upper body. Didn't Amiantos men ever wear clothes?

But then, he wasn't Amiantos, was he?

"I knew you'd be back." He smiled, a slow sexy tilt of the lips as he kept walking toward her. "I just had a feeling."

"I'm not here to see you," she managed. "I'm here on official business." Her nipples poked through the thin fabric of her long-sleeved t-shirt. Damn it, why hadn't she worn something heavier? The days were only starting to cool down and she just hadn't thought of it, but what she wouldn't give for a nice blousy shirt or a heavy cardigan right now.

"Official business?" He stood so close she could smell him. Salty-sweet, musky and pure male. He affected her just as strongly now as he had the night before. He'd barely said three words and she already wanted him to touch her, to stroke her. Wanted his fingers delving into all the places he hadn't gone last night, wanted the cock she remembered seeing so well to move inside her.

She hugged herself a little tighter. "I'm here to see the chieftain."

"On official business?"

"Yes."

He stared at her for a long moment, his dark brown hair curling down around his shoulders, his dark eyes staring into hers. He looked good enough to eat, and he was definitely offering her the chance to try. "You want to tell me what the business is?"

"No."

"You want to come to my place for a little while first?" He winked, and grinned until a dimple appeared on his left cheek. He looked wicked and adorable. Adorably wicked and more than prepared to follow up on all that promise in his eyes.

"No!" It came out as a whisper. Her face grew almost as hot as her pussy. Almost.

He raised an eyebrow and stepped even closer. "You sure about that? You look like you want to."

Aleeza didn't respond. His hands slid up her arms. It took all her strength not to gasp as the same electricity she remembered from the night before, the same connection, flooded her body. "I'm here on official business," she whispered.

Ferrin paused. "I'll take you to the Chieftain. He's doing some work at the dam. Follow me."

Aleeza stood still for a minute, shaking, watching his lean hips move as he walked away. Part of her knew following him was not a good idea. The other parts—specifically, the parts practically begging for his touch—didn't care if it was a good idea or not.

She followed.

The path he took wound over hills and through trees for what seemed like miles. Aleeza's feet would have started hurting if she hadn't been so distracted by the way his ass moved in his jeans. The sight made her heart pound, but it wasn't until the roaring in her ears grew so loud she couldn't ignore it that she realized it wasn't the sound of her blood.

It was a waterfall.

The path came out at the foot of it, where large rocks guarded the edge of the pool at the bottom. Aleeza opened her mouth, but before she could speak or gasp Ferrin covered it with his, and she fell into the pit of desire without a word of protest.

She'd never been kissed like this, not once in her life. Ferrin dove into her with more than his tongue and lips. He dove into her with power, making her weak and dizzy before a few seconds had passed. In the blink of an eye he mastered her. Some small part of her knew instinctively that when it came to personalities, when it came to life, she was the stronger one. But this—this was where Ferrin dominated—and he overpowered her as easily as she forced humans to get out of her path in a crowded store.

He tasted of the forest, clean and cool, but something else hid there. A hint of spice that Aleeza was too caught up to name, something as indefinable as the difference in his energy that told her he was not Amiantos.

Whatever he was, she didn't care because his lips and tongue were already sending her to the edge and he hadn't even taken his hands from her waist yet.

She tried to pull away. "We shouldn't—"

"Oh yes, we should."

His broad body edged her backward until she rested against one of the border rocks. Low and cool, it hit right under her bottom. She knew he'd chosen this spot for that very reason. She didn't care.

"You know what I did last night?" he asked, his breath uneven, as he tugged her shirt off over her head. His lips left traces of fire down the side of her throat and farther down to the edge of her bra. He slid his tongue just under the lace. A tiny cry escaped her throat.

"I thought about you." His skin was hot on hers as he took her hand and brushed her fingers down the muscles of his stomach to the open fly of his jeans. She clenched her fist. Eager anticipation so strong it shamed her coursed through her veins.

He was still talking as he inched her fist lower. "I thought about you all the way home, and when I got there, I took this in my hand." Her fingers closed around his cock, with his fingers clasped over them. Her head swam. "I moved my hand, just like this, and I thought about you, your eyes, your hair, your body. I thought about your pussy, Aleeza, and how badly I want to taste it." His eyes bored into hers as he took his hand away, leaving her to continue stroking him on her own, and reached around to unfasten her bra. "And I kept going, all night, and it wasn't enough. I knew I wouldn't be happy until I actually had tasted it. You're not going to deny me my only chance at happiness, are you?"

From any other man the line would have been laughable. From Ferrin it was an order. She could barely concentrate well enough to shake her head. Her body buzzed like a swarm of bees, and it was all she could do to keep up the slow, steady rhythm he'd demonstrated on his cock. She wanted to rip off her own jeans and force him inside her.

His hands on her upper arms held her still, her back on the large rock, while his tongue danced across her nipples, first one, then the other. He pulled them into the wet heat of his mouth and sucked, nibbled, tugged. At some point the pain of his teeth scraping against her delicate skin turned into pleasure. His pelvis pressed against hers, the ridge of his erection rubbing her pussy through her jeans. Bent over backward as she was, she couldn't see him. She could only feel him, and her body started shaking as she succumbed completely to his power.

She knew he felt it, the moment when her barriers fell, but he didn't indicate it. Instead he took his hands off her arms and stroked her breasts, squeezing them, twisting her nipples just hard enough to make her cry out. Seemingly satisfied, he unfastened her jeans and inched them down her hips, taking her soaking panties with them.

"Turn over."

She hesitated. Turn over? But wasn't he going to…?

He didn't slap her hip hard. The sound of skin on skin wasn't even audible over the rush of the waterfall behind them. But it still stung, and Aleeza's eyes flew open as she started to sit up.

Ferrin watched her darkly through hooded eyes, his brawny arms folded across his chest. "I said turn over."

She licked her lips. Something in the way her hip tingled made her say, "And what if I don't?"

"Then I'll make you."

She only had a split second to decide. What would he do if she refused? Would it hurt?

Part of her was certain he wouldn't hurt her. He was Dorand's clan brother. Dorand would never hurt her, would never hurt anyone.

But Ferrin was different. His energy wasn't like Dorand's, welcoming and sexy and smooth. Something dark lurked in Ferrin's soul, something dangerous, something that probably would hurt her if given the chance.

Aleeza had never thought of herself as the kind of girl who would enjoy such things. But she'd be lying if she didn't acknowledge there was some dark part of her own soul that reveled in the idea, that wanted desperately to play with Ferrin. To really play, to let him use his hands and teeth on her and to do the same back, to scratch him until blood flowed. To fight and fuck until they were both battered and bruised and flying off the furthest edge of pleasure because they were coming so hard from the glory of it all.

She hesitated that second too long. Ferrin grabbed her arms, yanking her off the rock. The hard stone scraped against the delicate skin of her buttocks. She fell forward into him, her legs still tangled in her jeans. The power in his skin leapt onto her, mingled with her own aura, and the glow it created was the sharpest, brightest green tinged with black and gold. A color she'd never seen before.

"What's—" she started, but he ignored her, spinning her around and pushing her slightly forward so she bent over the rock with her ass presented to him.

He spanked her once. This time she heard it as well as felt it. Something deep inside her roared with pleasure.

He lifted her legs one at a time, slipping her tennis shoes and her jeans off, then stood up. His cock pressed against her stinging buttocks. "Next time I tell you to do something, you do it," he murmured, his voice thick.

Aleeza nodded. She didn't trust herself to speak, but when he slipped his hand between her legs to caress her dripping pussy from behind, she moaned.

Keeping one hand on her ass, he kissed down her spine, nibbling at the two mounds of her buttocks. His tongue darted forward.

"You taste even better than I imagined," he said. "Turn back around."

This time she obeyed instantly. Part of her wanted to wait, to see what he would do, but the demands of her pussy won out. She wanted to feel that tongue again, in the places it would do the most good, and she didn't want to wait another second.

Ferrin hoisted her up on to the rock and spread her legs apart wide enough to make her thighs ache. The look in his eyes as he surveyed her made another gush of fluid drip from her already soaking slit.

Her arms trembled as she held herself in a sitting position on the stone, as upright as she could, so she could watch as he knelt in front of her and leaned forward.

His tongue touched her, lightly at first. Her muscles shook already, just from that tiny bit of heat and pressure. She was so ready, had been ready ever since he kissed her, ever since she saw him again. Aleeza looked down and saw the top of his head framed by the mounds of her breasts, her erect nipples burning and her skin flushed.

His tongue delved into her folds, exploring every inch of her tender flesh. Her own breathing was loud and harsh in her ears as she watched his head move, felt the incredible sensation of him laving her, tasting her, shoving his tongue inside her and circling it around.

Sounds came from her throat she'd never heard herself make, weeping, begging sounds, as he feathered the tip of his tongue over her clit again and again. Her hips tried to move on their own but Ferrin's hands held her fast, pinned against the rock like a butterfly spread open on a board.

He looked up at her, pulling his face away just enough for their eyes to meet, and just before she lost herself in them she saw his tongue pressed into her pink flesh, saw it moving against her. The image stayed burned in her mind as her eyes closed of their own accord and she came, pleasure thundering through her body like a runaway freight train. She trembled and shook, her throat raw from screaming his name. Nothing had ever felt like this. The knowledge that he was still there, nibbling and licking, swallowing the hot juices that flowed from her only egged her on, made her keep coming, harder and harder, until she was dizzy and fell back onto the rock.

Ferrin pulled away. Aleeza's eyes were still closed. She hovered alone for a second that seemed to last forever until with one quick, hard thrust Ferrin shoved the thickness of his cock into her.

She cried out again, both from pleasure and the shock of it. One moment she'd been empty. The next, full. It surprised her, and part of her still expected him to pass out, unable to complete the act.

He didn't give her any time to adjust. He pulled out and slammed back into her, grabbing her shoulders to hold her steady as he pounded into her body.

Her legs rose up, wrapping themselves around his waist as easily as if she'd been doing it for years. He grunted his approval and sped his movements, his hips jerking forward again and again. With every thrust he grunted, his fingers digging into her skin hard enough to bruise. With every thrust she cried out, lost to everything but the feel of his body inside hers, the feel of their energy melding and swelling around them. When she opened her eyes she saw him through a haze of greeny-gold.

He shifted his grip to her hips, lifting them slightly so his cock found a different angle inside her. Still he did not slow his frantic pace. Her back scraped against the rock every time he moved. She didn't care. The pain only added to the overwhelming sensations in her body, in her mind. She reached out for him, intending to hold his arms, but instead scraping her fingernails along the skin over his biceps.

"Oh, gods…yes…Damn it, yes," he gasped. She hadn't thought it was possible for him to go faster, to fuck harder, but it was. The man was a machine, an engine that never seemed to stop, and Aleeza dug her nails in hard enough to make blood run down his skin as her body tensed yet again.

This time she felt him swell inside her as she came, felt his cock jerk and twitch as he tugged her up to press her chest against his. His arms convulsed around her as her body convulsed around his. Her legs tightened, as if she could press more of him into her, and they clung together as their mutual orgasm thundered through their bodies and left them limp and gasping on the rock by the edge of the lake.

Chapter Six

Again, fuck her again. It didn't work. Fuck her again. Again!

Ferrin sucked in a deep breath and held it, the volume of the "other" voice louder than it had ever been. It roared through his mind, overpowering his true thoughts. The evil seed had begun to grow—it swelled within him, under the skin, threatening to take over. All he had to do was relax that last vestige of control, and its poison would swim through his veins, its shoots spread out into every finger, making him nothing but a vessel for the dark magic it would have him work.

But it will be a relief, really, to finally succumb to that black temptation. Haven't you always known it would end this way? Haven't you always expected –

No! No way in hell. He hadn't held the beast off for nearly thirty years to lose control now.

"Let go. Let go of me." He whispered the words as his hands feebly tried to pull the woman wrapped around him from his body.

By the gods, the last thing he wanted to do was let her go. He wanted to pull her so tightly to him that they became one person, to fuck her until neither of them could form words and then take her home and fuck her some more. She was the half that could make him whole, fill that empty place in him, that place that had always suspected he wasn't fit for mating. He had shared Carantha with Dorand not only because their magic worked better that way, but because he had known on some level that he would never be man enough for any woman.

He was "other", an orphan without a true coven, a man who could never give his heart the way he'd seen his Amiantos brothers do. He loved Dorand like a brother but not with a passion that would consume his soul. Not even sweet Carantha, with her ready smile and her love for playing the tart with him in the bedroom, had managed to touch him that deeply.

"Goddess, please. I want more. More of you." She purred the words as she took his face in her hands and guided him down for another taste of her lips, her sweet, wickedly addictive lips.

He fell to his knees in the leaves, and guided her down to the forest floor, moaning as her tongue tangled expertly with his. He could kiss her forever and never want for food. He could live on her magic, get drunk on the smell of her body, lose himself in the feel of her soft skin sliding against his with such previously unimaginable perfection.

"We can't. Stop—oh, fuck!" He cried out and thrust his hips forward, burying his cock deeper in her wet cleft as she dug her fingernails into his buttocks. He was instantly swollen and aching, as if he hadn't fucked her a second before and come so hard he thought he might lose his mind.

"Yes, fuck. Fuck me, fuck me now." She followed the words with a stinging slap on his ass, and he groaned and hastened to obey.

She knew somehow, knew what no lover he'd ever had could ever have guessed. He was the master in the bedroom, but he was a master who longed for a disobedient slave. He wanted to dish out punishment and receive his in return. He wanted to release the full power of his sensual fury upon a woman who wasn't afraid to keep fighting back.

"You aren't giving the orders here," Ferrin said, fisting a handful of Aleeza's hair and yanking hard. She cried out as her head snapped back, baring the white column of her throat, but then her cries turned to desperate pants as she struggled to breathe.

He'd gone too far, made it difficult for her to draw breath…but he didn't loosen his hold, only fucked her harder. A rush of fluid coated his cock as he tunneled into her pussy again and again. She liked it, liked knowing that he held her life in his hands, knowing that it was his job to decide whether she lived to feel her next orgasm or not.

"Gods help me," Ferrin called out to the forest, his words drowned out by the roar of the waterfall. He released Aleeza's hair and brought his hands to her breasts. He didn't want to really hurt her, let alone threaten her life. What was wrong with him? What—

Then it was his turn to scream as Aleeza's hands closed around his throat and squeezed. Her magic helped turn the pressure of those tiny hands into a vise that quickly cut off the flow of oxygen to his brain. His vision swam and gray flecks danced in front of his eyes, but still he kept pounding inside her. Her laughter filled his ears, louder than the blood thudding there, and he knew he would gladly take death at her hands, so long as he could spill his seed inside her—one last time.

"Stop this! Stop this now!" Ferrin heard Dorand scream, but it wasn't until he felt the massive hands of his brother on his neck that the words actually registered in his brain. Stop? The man must be mad.

"No, please! Dorand, I didn't mean to, I—"

Aleeza's words turned into a moan as Dorand ripped her hands away from Ferrin's neck and pressed them to the ground above her head. Ferrin looked up, seeing Dorand squatted above the woman beneath him, anger and confusion mingled on his face. A part of him wanted to comfort the other man, but another part, just wanted to laugh.

"Ferrin!" Dorand bellowed his name as Ferrin laughed and reached down to twist Aleeza's nipples in his fingers with a force he knew had to hurt. She screamed in response and stopped writhing beneath him, her body growing tense against his savage thrusts.

"Touch him, Dorand. By the goddess, touch your brother," Aleeza said, her eyes squeezing shut.

Dorand hesitated for the briefest second, then released one of Aleeza's wrists and reached out to clamp a hand down on Ferrin's shoulder. Ferrin's first instinct was to turn and bite the other man, but a second later the calming feel of Dorand's energy flowed through him, banishing the strange golden green light that had danced in front of his eyes the second he and Aleeza had touched. Immediately he slowed his bruising pace between Aleeza's legs, gentling his thrusts to a slow, deep penetration that had her lifting into him once more.

"Thank you, brother." Ferrin reached for the back of Dorand's neck, pulling him in for a kiss. The other man resisted at first but finally gave in to the caress, opening his lips to let Ferrin's tongue gain entry to the heat of his mouth. He tasted of the earth, of the rain, of everything safe and natural, and for some reason that made the bliss of being inside Aleeza even more intense.

"Yes, oh please, yes," Aleeza whispered the words, drawing his eyes down to where she watched him trace the line of Dorand's lips with his tongue. "Oh, goddess!" She cried out and arched into his cock, the hand still held above her head tangling with Dorand's.

Ferrin came a second later, pulsing into Aleeza with a long, wrenching orgasm that seemed to wring the soul from his body. It most certainly wrung his heart from his chest and placed it somewhere in the depths of the dark brown eyes that met his with such fearless pleasure.

He loved her. The realization hit him so hard it suddenly became as hard to breathe as when her hands had closed around his throat. It was impossible. He hardly knew the woman, but the truth of the emotion wasn't something he could deny. At least not while he was still balls deep inside her.

"Thank you," he muttered to Dorand, pulling away from Aleeza and standing quickly. His head swam as he hitched his jeans back up around his hips. He hadn't even bothered to take his pants or shoes off to fuck the woman, and he was imagining himself in love with her? It was insane. As insane as the fact that they'd both just tried to kill each other.

"Are you okay?" Dorand was gathering her into his arms, stroking his hand down the front of her body. Despite the obvious erection tenting his brother's khaki pants, the touch didn't seem to be sexual, but it still pissed him off more than he could say. He'd shared a woman with Dorand for years and probably would have seriously wounded Aleeza without his help, so why the jealousy?

Because you love her. She's yours, yours to mate with, no other man's.

"Is she all right?" Ferrin asked through gritted teeth, as he pushed the weakening voice aside and firmly slammed the mental door. He would hear no more from it…at least not for the rest of the day.

"She's right here and can speak for herself," Aleeza said, though she clung to Dorand, wincing as he gently slid a hand down between her legs. The fingers he brought up were bright red with blood, and the look he shot Ferrin black enough to kill.

"I'm sorry, I—"

"You don't have to be sorry. I wanted it. I was as mad for it as you were until Dorand touched me. I didn't even realize it was…hurting me," she said, her eyes on the ground as pink stained her cheeks.

There wasn't an ounce of self-pity in her strong voice, but still the words "hurting me" sliced deep into his chest. Ferrin wanted to go to her, to take her in his arms and kiss away her pain, to tell her that he would never do anything to hurt her.

But his brother was already taking care of that for him…

"Let me do a healing spell. I have a little gift for it. I can at least help mend the worst of the tear," he said, pulling Aleeza onto his lap, her blood staining his pants. Dressed in khakis and a light blue dress shirt, Dorand looked ready for coven meeting, not hiking, and Ferrin wondered what he'd missed by taking off to chop wood this morning without notifying anyone at the main lodge.

"No, it's fine. I can take care of it," she said. A second later, she began to glow, a deep midnight blue that seemed to draw night down into the bright morning sun. Seconds later, the blood stopped flowing from between her legs while various other scratches and bruises Ferrin hadn't even realized he'd delivered vanished.

"What a gift," Dorand murmured, obviously as impressed by the magical display as Ferrin himself. He had felt her power but had no idea she could do something like that, hadn't even known such instantaneous healing was possible.

"I can do you too," she said, meeting his eyes as she held out her hand.

"I know you can do me. You did me until I was ready to die with a smile on my face," Ferrin said, glad that the joke didn't sound as strained as he felt, and managed to bring a grin to her face. Squatting down by where she and Dorand sat, he reached out and placed his palm over hers.

Shockwaves of energy buzzed across his skin. There was a slight sting and then nothing but heat, a wonderful warm heat that took away every ache and pain. It was like a shot or two of whiskey mixed with an hour in the sauna, and when she pulled her hand away he felt completely relaxed and healthier than he had in ages.

"Impressive," he said, shifting a bit to conceal the raging erection her touch had also inspired.

"Thanks," she said, starting to look uncomfortable on Dorand's lap now that she was healed. "I'm sorry I ruined your pants."

"I'm just glad you didn't ruin my brother, or vice versa," Dorand said while Ferrin went to fetch Aleeza's clothes from near the rock where he had taken her the first time. The gods only knew how they'd gotten ten feet away from that rock.

"If she can heal like that, brother, I had no worries. She could have roughed me up all she liked and fixed me up after," Ferrin said, the look in Aleeza's eyes as he handed her the clothes revealing she'd just been having the same thoughts—and was just as uncomfortable about having them.

Whatever they could be to each other, it was something wonderful and terrible, and it seemed they both knew it. But what to do about it? Leaving her the hell alone would probably be the best option for them both. Too bad he had absolutely no intention of swearing off Aleeza or her sweet, dangerous little pussy.

"I don't think either of you should be allowed to test that theory. The energy was out of control. I thought you were going to kill each other. I didn't think I could ground that much raw power." Dorand stood up and politely turned his back as Aleeza began to dress. Ferrin stood there and watched her, meeting her dark eyes with his own as she watched him watching.

They would be trouble together, all right. Big trouble.

"But you did," Aleeza said, "and I can't thank you enough. I don't know what was wrong. I've never felt anything like that before."

"I'm sure you haven't." Dorand's voice was filled with some hidden meaning that Ferrin couldn't quite discern. But Aleeza evidently did. She hastily pulled her shirt over her head and turned to him.

"Listen Dorand, I know that you—"

"There's no need to thank me. You and Ferrin both have incredibly strong abilities for power generation. I doubt either have you have met your equal before and weren't prepared to handle the rush." Dorand turned back around but not in time to catch the flicker of doubt that passed across Aleeza's beautiful face. She wasn't buying that theory any more than he was but seemed grateful for his answer.

"I'm sure you're right," she said with a nod and then turned back to smile in Ferrin's direction.

It appeared she was fine with letting Dorand believe what he would. Good, Ferrin was fine with that too. The truth would be their little secret, a secret that might help whatever was between them grow into something bigger, something even more intense, something like—

"Are you all right, Ferrin?" Dorand asked. "You have the strangest fucking look on your face."

"I'm fine, just fine." Ferrin smiled and pretended he had missed his brother's flash of temper. It seemed Dorand didn't enjoy standing there and watching him and Aleeza making eyes at each other either. Interesting. For years they'd shared, completely, willingly, even lovingly. Now, a woman they'd each known less than a day was threatening their relationship.

And he didn't care one fucking bit.

"Listen. Is there anywhere I could go to clean up a bit? I'm late already, but I don't want to meet your Chieftan looking like...well what I obviously must look like," she said, running a hand through her long dark hair. It was tangled but not too badly, and if Ferrin had his way he'd keep her looking like this. Like a wild gypsy, fresh from her bed—no, scratch that, fresh from *his* bed.

"You can come back to my cabin. I have a shower and a bath. I could scrub your back and you could scrub—"

"I think the main bathhouse would be a better choice. It's on the way to the lodge and we don't have much time. Cato was expecting you several hours ago, and he's not a man who likes to be kept waiting," Dorand said with a glare in Ferrin's direction.

"You're really here on official business?" Ferrin asked, more than a little shocked. He'd assumed that had been a ruse, an excuse to come looking for him or at least for him and Dorand.

"I've been hired by your coven to look into the Fire Festival killings." Aleeza and Dorand shared a look that let Ferrin know he was definitely still missing something.

"You? Why you? Are you with law enforcement, as well as a witch and a healer?"

"She's allegedly the best her company has to offer, with a reputation for success unparalleled in her business," Dorand said, in his "we'll see" voice. He might like this witch, but he seemed more than a little doubtful that she would be the one to catch Carantha's killer.

"And what company is that?" Ferrin asked with a dubious laugh of his own.

"Gunera Bounty and Investigations. And I *am* the best—you can both be sure of it," she said, the determined set of her chin and the fire in her eyes telling just how little she enjoyed her skill being held in question. "Is the lodge this way?"

Dorand nodded.

"Good, I'll see you boys at the meeting." She turned and headed off toward the main building. Ferrin blamed the sight of her ass rolling in her tight jeans for his delayed reaction.

"Did she say Gunera?" he finally asked, turning to catch Dorand staring at him, obviously awaiting this very conclusion.

"She did."

"You fucked her last night."

"And you fucked her this morning," Dorand said, his voice tight, as if he disliked the taste of those particular words in his mouth.

"God damn fucking shit." Ferrin laughed, a wickedly pleased sound that bubbled up from his very core. "She broke the curse. She's strong enough to break a two-thousand-year-old fucking curse."

"Let's see if she's powerful enough to find Carantha's killer. That's all I care about," Dorand said.

"You say that as if you doubt I feel the same, brother," Ferrin said, letting his hurt, his anger be heard in the words. From the night of her death, Dorand had claimed the right to mourn more than he, more deeply than he. They had both loved her, both lost her, and his assumption that Ferrin didn't feel that loss was starting to wear on his patience.

"I'm sure you do. Let's go." Dorand turned to stomp after Aleeza, quickly disappearing from view, leaving Ferrin to the stand alone near the roar of the waterfall, and the softer, more sinister roar of the dark power, newly awakened, in his mind.

* * * * *

Aleeza wasn't sure what she'd expected an Amiantos coven meeting to look like, but this sure as hell wasn't it. She'd thought maybe they'd all be in long Druid robes, clutching gnarled wooden wands or other ancient, nature-themed symbols of magical practice. They were the hippiest of the hippies, after all, leftovers from a time that made the Amish look positively new wave in their tastes.

Instead, the ten men and three women who sat around the large, mahogany conference table were dressed in business suits or dress pants and shirts. Even Ferrin had apparently stopped off somewhere to change, for when he entered the boardroom, he was dressed in a black dress shirt and pants, with a bright red tie. His newly washed hair looked black in the soft light and was tied back in a low ponytail at the base of his neck.

He looked even sexier in clothes if that was possible, and Aleeza was grateful she hadn't been the one talking when he strode in and took his seat beside Dorand. She would have stuttered, stopped to stare, lost her train of thought as her pussy let out a primal roar, demanding that she get that man on top of her, behind her, inside her, as soon as humanly possible, no matter that her heart was starting to have other ideas.

When Dorand had pulled her onto his lap in the woods and touched her with such aching tenderness, a piece of her had melted. Somewhere in the recesses of her mind, she'd started to wonder what it might be like to have those strong arms and those kind eyes on her side on a more permanent basis. He was a magnetic man who brought her body to life even as he calmed the ragged pieces of her soul, making her feel inexplicably safe even before she'd realized he wasn't going to divulge her secret.

"I apologize, Cato, but I must respectfully disagree. It's true we've never let an outsider reside on Amiantos lands, even on a temporary basis. But then, we've never had a situation this dire on our hands," Ferrin said.

His eyes were glued to his chieftain, but Aleeza could feel his attention upon her, feel his magic curling around her ankles, reaching up for a naughty caress beneath the large table. No matter that Dorand might be able to claim her heart, Ferrin still claimed her pussy. Dorand was no slouch in the sack, but if forced to choose between the two of them, she wasn't sure she'd make the wisest decision.

"She'll have run of the land, freedom to come and go as she pleases. I don't see what difference it would make for her to have a cabin at her disposal." The woman's name was Freya, and she wasn't the only one of the thirteen who seemed to resent Aleeza's presence.

"It could mean the difference between another life lost or a member of our coven saved," Dorand spoke from the end of the table.

"And her father was coven, right? She's at least half "undefiled", Freya, which truthfully gives her more right to be here than yours truly." Ferrin grinned his wicked, dimpled grin after he said the words, but the bite was still there. The look Freya gave him in return was positively arctic, leaving little doubt that the animosity between the two was completely mutual.

"The brothers are right. Aleeza will have a place to stay if she chooses to spend the night here during her investigation. And I expect the full support of all of our coven members. The decision passed to approach the Gunera coven for aid in this matter. Whether you were one who voted for or against that decision, I know all of you will put forth your best effort to ensure the mission is a success." Cato let his eyes linger on each of the coven members at the table as he spoke. The smile on his face was kind and the look in his pale blue eyes gentle, but there was still something intimidating about the leader of the Amiantos coven.

He was handsome in a middle-aged sort of way, the light brown of his closely cropped hair streaked with gray and his tanned face creased with smile lines. His well-muscled shoulders filled out his suit nicely, but he was barrel-chested rather than possessed of flat, six-pack abs. He looked strong, solid and friendly, like a retired athlete, but his energy was strong enough to slice through skin at ten feet.

Aleeza had considered asking the man about her father on the walk up to the lodge, but had rethought the decision within seconds of meeting him. If Cato had something to share with her, he would share it. If not, she wasn't going to do anything to attract his attention. She was absolutely sure none of the people in the room were blood relatives, and that would have to be enough…for now.

"Thank you, chieftain. The cooperation of the coven will be vital and extremely appreciated," Aleeza said, using her most formal voice, hoping to make up for the fact that she was hideously underdressed. At least she'd taken the time to clean up a bit before heading up to the main lodge and was quite a bit tidier than she'd been half an hour ago.

Cato nodded and shot her a wide smile that should have been super-friendly but wasn't. It was a heavy look, in which Aleeza imagined she read all the myriad consequences she would suffer if she were to fail this man. "Of course, Aleeza. It's wonderful to have you here. Anything you need, I'll be available in my office, or you can reach me via the yellow phones located throughout the coven grounds. In the meantime, I'll leave you to Jillian. She'll show you to your cabin and give you full access to any files related to the investigation as it has been conducted thus far."

The second Cato stood, every other person at the table, male and female, shot to his or her feet. The room cleared with amazing swiftness, as if every Amiantos were in a desperate hurry. Must have a lot of tree-hugging to do…or maybe they were just eager to get out of their dress clothes. Dorand and Ferrin did pass her way as they exited, however.

"We'll be seeing you soon, Aleeza. Let us know if there is anything we can do to help." Dorand reached down and squeezed her hand in a friendly caress that she never would have imagined could send such a rush of heat straight between her legs.

"Absolutely anything," Ferrin said, shooting her a devilish wink she knew would always make her sex burn, as he followed Dorand out.

She'd gone from being a virgin without prospects, to a woman torn between two lovers in less than a day. Not to mention her strange new taste for violence, or the little voice that seemed to whisper information in her ear, information she never would have been able to guess before she'd worked that spell in the woods. Her world was changing rapidly, but she prayed she'd be able to come back to herself enough to succeed in catching a killer. Those photographs had been more than gruesome—they'd been magically terrifying. Whatever or whoever was committing the atrocities, they had to be stopped before another innocent died and before they completed whatever black magic they were about.

"Aren't they wonderful? They're the sweetest men." Jillian smiled down at her with guileless blue eyes. With her long blonde hair and legs that stretched on forever, she looked more like a supermodel than an old-school witch. Thankfully, she was also much nicer than the other two women who had attended the meeting.

"They do seem very nice," Aleeza said with a neutral smile. She'd shielded with a vengeance throughout the meeting, so was fairly sure Jillian could have no clue just how nice she thought the clan brothers.

"All the girls have a soft spot for them. It's been so hard to watch them grieving," she said, picking up a large collapsible file.

"Grieving?" Aleeza asked, following her out of the room.

"Their third clan mate was the Beltane victim. Carantha. Such a sweet girl and so loved by her husbands and by our clan." Jillian's voice was thick with sadness and the look on her face genuinely tortured. There was no way she was telling anything but the truth.

"I'm so sorry for your loss," Aleeza said, even as her mind began to race.

Shit! Dorand and Ferrin had a personal stake in her investigation. Hell, they might *be* the investigation. What had they been doing in the woods last night? And why would two grieving widowers be so eager to fuck a complete stranger?

One of them is a liar—one of them wants to frame you for the murder.

The thought startled her enough to stop her dead in her tracks. Where the hell had that come from? She had no evidence to support that theory. Hell, she didn't have enough evidence to support any theory.

"Are you okay?" Jillian asked, turning to look over her shoulder.

"I'm fine, just fine." Aleeza hurried to catch up, hoping that if she repeated that phrase to herself enough times, it might actually become the truth.

Chapter Seven

℘

Kali's olive skin shone in the candlelight, the oil she'd rubbed into her flesh making her gleam like a goddess. Black hair tumbled in a midnight wave nearly down to her knees, and her honey-colored eyes reflected the dancing flames with inhuman magnificence. The only thing more stunning than her eyes were her breasts, natural D-cups that were a rare find on a woman so thin. Women paid millions of dollars to look half as good as she did. It was the one thing that bastard of an ex-husband of hers hadn't been able to take away from her—her beauty, and she made the most of it.

Thinking of him made her smile. Things were falling into place even faster and more smoothly than she'd expected. A month from now…he'd be the one begging *her* for help.

"You're smiling, mistress," said the young man in front of her, some of the fear in his eyes fading. "Do I please you?"

"What? Oh." Kali looked him up and down, hiding her approval from him. It never did to let one's slaves know how much you wanted them. Let them think it was a favor, bestowed only as a reward, and sex got you much further. Monven, her bastard ex had taught her that lesson, and she'd learned it well. "I suppose you do," she said, letting a slight frown twist her thin red lips. "But use a different soap. I can smell that cheap stuff from here and it makes my nose itch."

"I'm sorry." The young man—Withley? Yes, Withley—looked down at the floor. Kali's smile broadened. The soap didn't bother her in the slightest.

"You should be," she snapped. "Now come here."

Hope shone in Withley's blue eyes as he stepped closer to her. His erection made her mouth water. She didn't often get slaves as handsome as this one. It was a shame, actually, that she'd never tell him that. What was the point? She never allowed them to touch her more than once. That way she didn't get attached, didn't give that soft part of her the chance to start getting ideas about some mythical happily ever after.

Kali didn't want anyone getting any ideas, least of all herself. She'd lived in service to Monven for years. Now she lived in service to another, far more powerful, and she was under no illusions about the nature of their relationship. They shared a goal—that was all. He could not touch her soul, could not satisfy her…nobody could. Not the way she needed. Only another of her race, another Daiesthai, could, or a Gunera.

There were no other Daiesthai. And the Gunera…were under that stupid curse.

Withley's reverent hands were hot on her bare skin as he stroked her. She could almost hear his heart beating. Some small part of her that still cared about other people, other supers, warmed. Withley was a sweet boy, and she'd busted enough balls in her little coven to know when she told him what to do to her, he would do it. He might not like it, but he would do it.

His tongue on her hardening nipples was exquisite. "Bite them," she murmured.

His teeth scraped her skin. She shook her head. "Bite them. Hard."

Doubt flickered behind his eyes, but he obeyed. Pain seared through her body, pain and pleasure combined. Withley grunted softly.

She reached for him, her fingers curled like claws, and scratched his shoulders. He pulled away.

"Withley, do I need to find a different slave?"

In response he slid his hands behind her and squeezed her ass hard enough to bruise. Good. The trickle of moisture that had started between her legs increased. Her lips found his, nibbling and teasing. Withley sighed, his comfort level obviously increasing.

She couldn't have that. So she bit his lip. The taste of his blood quickened her pulse. If he pulled away again she didn't know what she would do, but luckily for him he did not. He continued the kiss, his fingers still digging into her flesh.

It was good, all of it. But, as was usually the case, the fire wasn't there. Her body responded, and she would allow this slave to fuck her on the floor, but his heart wasn't in anything else. So hers wasn't either. Kali focused on that thought, let the rage build in her chest. If she couldn't have passion, true passion, fury was almost as good.

She drew back and slapped Withley with all her strength. For a moment his blue eyes clouded with pain and fear. She stayed where she was, challenging him, daring him to leave and suffer the punishment of displeasing her. Punishing him would be almost as good as fucking him.

They stared at each other for the space of a few heartbeats. Kali was just about to send him to the chains on the wall when his eyes darkened. She didn't have time to react before he slapped her back.

Perhaps Withley wasn't such a bad slave after all.

* * * * *

He finally left about an hour later, rewarded by a black eye and several deep cuts on his body. They would heal, but until they did he would be treated like a king by the other slaves. It was a fair trade.

The heavy silver clock on the wall told her Raven would be by in ten minutes. There was just enough time to heal herself before the girl arrived. Raven was a necessary diversion, and not an entirely unpleasant one. Too bad she wasn't a man.

Kali didn't know why it was possible, with enough power and the right dark magic, to break the Gunera curse—or ease it—for women but not for men. Raven's poor little cousin wasn't the first Gunera woman to break the curse. There had been two others over the centuries, women for whom the famous sex drive of the Gunera had proven too much.

But she herself hadn't been there to help them along. And she certainly hadn't been there to take advantage of it. Instead, they'd been killed, destroyed by members of their own clan, cowards who were too afraid to seize their true destiny. But not this time. The Gunera coven had grown lax in its teachings. They hadn't bothered to instill the proper fear in their members for generations. Now they would pay the price. By the time they realized what magic had been wrought, it would be too late.

Kali smiled through the screaming of her sore muscles and torn skin as she shifted position on the couch, reaching for her healing bottle. She didn't have the healing abilities of some of the other bloodlines, but she had magic more powerful than all of them.

Reglanus had given her this potion as a sign of his gratitude. He gave her many things, knowing the great service she was performing for him. It wasn't often demons got any help from witches, especially not witches of her blood. Once, before the Fallout, the two races had worked together. Now demons were a rare find on the earthly plane, and witches of her coven all but extinct. She was the last, the last chance to rebuild one of the most powerful races the world had ever known.

The bitter potion made her wince, but the sensation of light and heat spreading through her body was worth it. By the time Raven showed up, Kali would be perfect again and ready to reward her best little slave. At least the girl was Gunera, and thanks to that, Kali wouldn't need to use more of the potion to heal up afterward. Raven wasn't as gifted a healer as some, but she could get the job done. And Kali was all about getting the job done, no matter the cost, no matter the sacrifice.

Even if it means losing your greatest source of power?

The thought invaded her mind unbidden, but she knew it was her own, not the familiar hiss of Reglanus whispering in her ear. Her eyes drifted to the mirror in the corner, a Victorian affair with smoky glass and gold plating that emphasized her eyes and the warm glow of her skin. Now it reflected the image of an achingly beautiful woman, lounging on her settee. What would it reflect in a few weeks' time, however, once she'd given herself over to Reglanus completely? She knew there was a chance the transformation would ruin her forever.

No matter what power she might gain, without her beauty, would her victory be a hollow one?

The knock at the door told her Raven had arrived.

"Come in," she said, pushing away her dark thoughts. She leaned back on the cushions so the restored perfection of her naked body would be displayed to its best advantage. Casually, she settled her left heel on the edge of the cushion and her right on the arm of the couch. Watching Raven maneuver herself to get a good look at what Kali knew was a beautiful pussy was always good for some amusement.

Sure enough, Raven's eyes widened dramatically when she walked into the room, her hair in braids just the way Kali liked it. Destroying the girl's innocence again and again was more delightful than she'd thought it would be.

"Kali," Raven began. "I can't thank you—"

"Shhhh." Kali moved her left foot onto the floor, spreading herself open wider. Raven licked her lips. She'd never been allowed to pleasure Kali before, and Kali knew the girl might be expecting to as part of her reward. She'd put her off last night, insisting Raven continue tailing her cousin until they learned how the reversal of the spell might be affecting her. "Is there any more news of your cousin?"

Raven shook her head, but her gaze stayed focused between Kali's long, slim legs. "I haven't heard anything."

"What do you mean you haven't heard anything?" Kali sat up, snapping her knees together. "Does anyone know what she's done? She didn't go home last night. I couldn't reach her mind in the dream state. Where was she?"

"She went to her mom's house. I followed her there."

"And you let her go inside?" Kali felt the anger within her begin to burn into a rage. A fool! The girl was a fool and she should never have trusted her to handle this job alone. Aleeza had made their work easier by breaking the curse on her own, but she'd also further complicated the situation. They needed her fertile, yes, but not until the final kill was complete and Kali ready to perform. Now they would need to watch her every move.

They couldn't let her tell anyone in her coven what she'd done, or start fucking everything that moved. She would be no good to them dead or pregnant with someone else's child. They had to make sure her mouth and her legs stayed shut, or that she at least used some sort of birth control until they were ready for her. Raven had said there had been no change in Aleeza's energy after she fucked the Amiantos in the woods, so no conception had taken place, but they might not be so lucky next time.

"She went to the shed out back. She didn't even let her mom know she was there. And she was there alone—I swear it."

"You promise me that she didn't tell her mother, that she hasn't told anyone?"

Raven shook her head. "No, nobody but us knows—I promise."

"Make sure it stays that way," Kali warned. "We'll be ready to perform the ritual after Samhain. Until then, we can't afford to relax our guard for a moment."

"I know. I'm watching her. This morning she went to work at the same time as usual. She met with Gavyn and then went back to her place."

"And where is she now?"

"Still at home, I guess. She didn't get much sleep last night, so she must be tired."

"You guess? You don't know?"

"I had to go home and get some sleep, Kali. I was exhausted and…I thought maybe you'd be back at the apartment waiting for me." The hopeful look in her eyes made Kali want to slap her. Affection was only a commodity if it made Raven more useful. If it made her weak, then fear needed to replace desire as the girl's primary motivation.

"Take off your clothes," Kali said quietly, knowing by the stricken look on Raven's face that she realized there would be no reward for a job well done today.

"Come on, Kali, please. Even if she's not at home, she's probably at work, so we're safe. She isn't even—"

"You're the one who told me she nearly fucked Keller in the back alley. Now that the curse is lifted, what's to stop her from following through on a tease like that? Or to keep some frustrated man from raping her if she doesn't want to deliver?" Kali rang the bell beside the settee, summoning the slaves on watch. "You've failed, Raven, and now I need to clean up your mess. Take off your clothes."

Her wide blue eyes grew even wider, shining with unshed tears, but she did as she was told. At least she was thoroughly broken, so dependent on Kali for pleasure that she would do anything she was asked…absolutely anything. Her obedience had been amazingly useful the past several months, so Kali wouldn't destroy her completely, just take her to the edge of destruction and let her peer down into the abyss.

Kali was laughing as the two watchmen rushed into the room and bowed before her feet.

"Ammon, Luke, I'm putting both of you in charge of watching our Gunera. Make sure she keeps her secrets, and no sex without protection. Even if you have to take her into our custody sooner than we planned, make sure of it. Do you understand?"

"Yes, mistress." They spoke at the same time and immediately sprang to their feet to make their way back into the slaves' quarters. They would need to dress before heading into the outside world. The loft Kali had rented for their makeshift coven was located in the largely abandoned warehouse district of Savior City, but even the bums and coven rejects took notice of a man walking around the streets in nothing but a leather thong.

"Kali, please. I've done everything you asked. I'm only one person. I did the best I could," Raven pleaded once the men were gone, falling to her knees in supplication.

"Your best wasn't good enough." Her voice was casual, breezy, but Raven still whimpered as Kali rose from her chair and walked toward her toy cabinet. Some of her toys she kept out in plain sight, but the really wicked ones she kept safely locked away for special occasions such as this.

"Please, mistress, please. I'm supposed to work tonight. I have to follow Pierce and he'll know what I've done if I'm damaged. Please….please." Tears flowed down her face as she watched Kali pull one particular vibrator from her collection. It was enormous, easily three times the size of a man's dick, and heated to a scalding temperature when plugged in.

"Well then, we'll have to get going, won't we? Make sure you have time to heal yourself before you go," Kali smiled a peaceful little smile and plugged the device into the outlet in the center of the floor. The buzzing sound filled the room, a pleasing accompaniment to the sobs of the girl now crawling toward her on her hands and knees.

This afternoon was turning out to be more fun-filled than she had anticipated. And as long as Ammon and Luke did their job, she was going to enjoy the next few weeks. She was going to revel in her femininity, indulge all of her sexual whims and maybe even have some photographs taken. When the spell was complete and she had a cock between her legs rather than her pretty little pussy, the pictures and the memories would help her to accept her new body.

"Open yourself," Kali ordered, her cunt responding as she watched Raven, still on all fours, rest her cheek on the floor so she could reach behind and pull apart the pink lips of her pussy. She was newly shaved, showing just how certain she'd been that Kali would be pleased with her today. Kali only ate her out when she was clean and bare.

"Please, Kali, mistress, please." Raven's whimpering turned into a howl of pain as Kali thrust the head of the massive dildo into her unprepared entry. The sound brought a bolt of excitement shooting between her own legs, and Kali quickly brought two fingers between them, stroking her clit as she pushed the instrument deeper.

Not bad really. She might actually enjoy having a cock, especially if she made sure to ask Reglanus for a big one. A really big one.

* * * * *

The demon Reglanus hovered near the ceiling, his body a thin mist that neither of the women would notice unless they were seeking him out. His naughty little witch was being even naughtier than usual, a sight that normally would have brought him great pleasure. He liked her taste for blood and violence. It had made it so much easier to work a bargain. He'd needed her so badly at the time of their magic-fasting. He'd been certain the other child had been lost, abandoned to die alone in some forsaken place, especially when the boy's own mother had admitted to destroying him.

Elise had known that her boy child was the true danger. Daiesthai women could not conceive, something within them unfit for creating more of their own kind. Only a Daiesthai male and a female from one of the three demon-tainted covens could successfully birth another Daiesthai. Of those three covens, only the Gunera remained, and they had been placed beyond Reglanus' reach by their ancestor's magic. Elise had been the last of the Pandoranian coven, and when she slayed her husband and then herself, Reglanus had known the death of a dream.

There would never be another demon coven. His people would never again know solid form or the power of the magic-fast.

But then Kali had matured with Daiesthai magic, and her husband's betrayal had made her ripe for Reglanus' influence. He'd eagerly entered into their agreement despite knowing the magic they would work might not achieve his goals. Even with four human sacrifices committed on the most powerful days of the year, they might fail. Transforming a female into a fertile male was no easy task, but Reglanus had seen no other chance for the resurrection of the Daiesthai coven.

Until now.

He lived. The boy child lived and each second drew him closer to his destiny.

The spirit of the male had always been within reach, and there were times when Reglanus had spoken within his mind, trying to lure the child to some deeper communication. But the contact had never gone further than the barest whisper of connection. Reglanus had assumed the boy child had passed into another plane and was simply a soul waiting in the afterlife. Until the night the Gunera woman had broken her curse less than a mile away from the very alive man that boy had become.

The hand of fate was with Reglanus. The Gunera had already mated with a Daeisthai male once, and she would again. A child would be conceived sooner or later. Then they would both succumb to Reglanus' power and fufill their destiny, no matter what lies he had to tell or trickery he must use to force their hands.

"Oh goddess, please stop. Mercy!" The blonde screamed and clawed at the ground in front of her, but Reglanus could see the slight tilt in her hips. She was enjoying this little game nearly as much as his wicked Kali.

When Kali had first recruited the younger woman, Reglanus had thought perhaps she might be their vessel. She was Gunera and willing to do anything to break the curse. Unfortunately, her power hadn't been strong enough, though she had proved herself more than useful. Without her help, he and Kali might not have been able to reach into Aleeza's mind to plant the seeds of her liberation.

He might spare the blonde's life when it came time for the reckoning. As far as his dear Kali was concerned, however, it would be up to her to choose what kind of life would she would live. The winds of change were upon them, and she would be forced to adjust or suffer the consequences. He no longer needed her as desperately as he had before, and that would affect the particulars of their bargain.

"Thank you, mistress," the blonde sobbed as Kali withdrew the burning length from her pussy. The sensitive flesh was bright red and would torment her terribly until she was allowed to perform a healing spell.

"You're most welcome, slave. And since that has pleased you so much that you speak without permission—" Kali's words were cut off by a howl of agony as she shoved the instrument into the younger woman's ass.

Reglanus smiled. Kali was Daiesthai through and through, and soon there would be more of them, enough to accomplish their purpose on this earth for the first time in centuries. It was going to be a good year for demons—there was no doubt in his mind.

Chapter Eight

ઙ૭

Aleeza walked the shore near the lake where the first body had been found for the fiftieth time, searching for some answer in the strange energy that still throbbed throughout the place. Rimer Lorcan had been a coven outcast, an embarrassment to the Amiantos people. He hadn't set foot on coven lands in over ten years, but he'd died here, and what had been left of his body was now cremated and interred in the Amiantos coven tomb.

Sad. So fucking sad.

It was a depressing homecoming if there ever was one, and Aleeza had initially assumed the energy she'd felt in this place was simply that, the sorrow of a soul who'd departed this earth with no one. No one missed Rimer Lorcan. He'd had no wife, no children, no friends and hadn't even been reported missing. No one had cared where the man disappeared to until his body was found in this spot, anchored in the shallow water with an iron stake through the center of his chest.

"Two inches to the right of the heart." She mumbled the words out loud and gripped the folder in her hands a little tighter. She had its contents memorized at this point, for all the good it did her.

Rimer's folder was by far the thinnest of the three. There was little information on his life before the murder, and his body had been cremated within days of his discovery. The pictures the Amiantos had taken left a hell of a lot to be desired and gave her little to work with.

If they'd done a more thorough autopsy or at least taken more photographs, she might be able to discern what kind of magic was still afoot. But without close-ups of the symbols she could faintly make out carved across his stomach, without detailed descriptions of what had been carved into the remaining organs, she was left to make leaps in logic that might or might not lead her in the right direction.

It was an ancient spell at work—that much was clear. The writing was in runes but none she had ever seen, even in the oldest of spell books. The photos from the other two scenes and, blessedly, the autopsy reports, were more clear but the runes were still unidentified.

If the forensic witches had never seen such things and none of the clan elders had...Aleeza was at a complete loss. There wasn't even anything about it on that bastion of human information, the Internet.

Heedless of the damp, she sat down on a log by the water's edge and opened the file again. The runes leapt out at her, seeming a bit clearer than the last time she had searched the picture. Without thinking, she traced her fingers along the pattern. A double X with lines up and down and across, and a half-circle around it. The image grew in her mind, sending tendrils of something, some kind of energy, twisting and sliding through her every nerve ending. It was as if her body knew what this symbol was, could read it, though her mind had no idea. It had happened earlier too, this pulsing sensation as she examined the pictures. Maybe if she looked at it here, in the place where the black magic had been wrought, she could make sense of it.

Maybe the atmosphere by the lake would enable her to...what? She wasn't a psychic, despite the odd flashes she'd been getting lately. There was no way she could read the vibrations of this place or communicate with the dead...

But she knew two people who could. Goddess, how stupid was she?

A rain-scented breeze blew tendrils of her hair over her face as she sat, stunned. She didn't deserve to be a certified investigator. Dorand and Ferrin had been doing death magic— trying to do death magic—here in the woods when she met them. Their third mate was one of the dead. Murder victims were often beyond the reach of the death speakers, due to the violent energy surrounding the departure of the soul from the body, but that must have been what they were attempting last night. If she hadn't been so sexually enthralled, she would have seen it sooner. At least that's what she told herself.

They'd failed in their spell because she'd stolen the energy of their release. Had she somehow stolen part of their power as well, some of their ability? She and Dorand had shared magic when they'd had sex and she had assumed he'd reclaimed what he needed, but how could she be certain? At least some of his power still rode within her body. The white glow warning her away from her apartment hadn't been her energy, not at all.

Not to mention the first time she'd seen the photos of their mate, Carantha Smoler, she'd thought for a minute she was seeing the girl as she'd been in life. She must have seen through Ferrin and Dorand's memories.

So was it possible she was also seeing Ferrin and Dorand through Carantha's memories? The thought made her blood run cold. Only two days, only a few hours really, she'd known the men, but already she felt so close to them. Hell, if she was honest, she was already nearly obsessed with them. She wanted them, both of them, so badly. Seeing them kiss over her head earlier…she shook her head.

No point in thoughts like that now, not unless she wanted to come in her pants without even touching herself.

She'd sworn never to mate herself with an Amiantos. Why would she suddenly change her mind and start wondering how long it would be before she saw them again, before she felt them move inside her body? A pang of purest longing zinged through her at the very thought. Even now, with the closed file full of horrors resting in her hand, if Dorand showed up—or, goddess help her, Ferrin—she'd have her clothes off before he could blink.

Some madness had possessed her or maybe some magic. Or maybe, just maybe, she was being haunted by the soul of their murdered lover. That voice in her head…could it be…

Her legs shook as she grabbed her bag and stood up. Back to work. She wasn't going to find any answers sitting here, scaring herself half to death. She'd taken on murderers, rapists and even a serial killer last spring. If she was being haunted, she wouldn't let it frighten her into fucking up this case. She'd listen to the spirit if that was indeed what it was, but the conclusion she came to would be based on cold, hard fact, not the whisperings of a tortured soul in her ear. And not from two men who were too close to the investigation to be trusted.

Dorand and Ferrin might have been attempting to contact their lover's soul to find out the identity of her killer. Or they might have been trying to banish her soul from this earthly plane so that no one else could do the same. The whisper she'd heard at the lodge had insisted one of the men was responsible. She didn't want to believe that it told the truth, but she didn't know either of them well enough to exonerate them as suspects. She would do well to remember that, no matter how they affected her body.

Goddess, her body, just the word brought to mind visions of Dorand sliding inside her, Ferrin pulling her hair. Gritting her teeth, she forced the thoughts away.

Lymera Brown was found in the opposite direction from Rimer, and Aleeza left the lake and its ghosts behind as she headed for that scene. The positions of the bodies made a loose circle, with each victim found at one of the four directions. Rimer was east, Carantha south, Lymera west. It gave her a rough idea where she might expect to find the next body, but since they still believed the murders had taken place elsewhere and the bodies brought here after death or close to death, that wasn't as helpful as it seemed.

That's good, Aleeza. Focus. Think of the murders. The throbbing between her legs slowed. Think of the very real possibility that this desire you feel is simply a combination of years of celibacy and the sex memories of a murder victim. The throbbing almost disappeared.

Only to come roaring back when she saw the bare back of a man walking through the woods ahead of her. It was Dorand—she knew it instantly before her eyes even focused. What was he doing here, moving silently as a shadow through the trees?

She ducked behind a tree, certain her feet moving through the leaves sounded an alarm, but she could not hear it over the roaring in her ears. Just seeing him brought it all back, the musky clean scent of him, the feel of his hands on her body, his magnificent cock stretching her, filling her with such perfect pleasure…

Her bag fell to the ground with a thud, its sides hanging open. Aleeza gripped the tree behind her, digging her nails into the rough bark in a vain attempt to keep from unbuttoning her jeans and pulling down the zipper. Her pussy demanded satisfaction but it was a satisfaction she was afraid to give. What if she called him, asked him to come here? He would hear her—she knew he would, especially with the forest so quiet today.

She knew he would come. Knew he would be only too ready to remove his clothing too and make her scream and cry with delight.

But she couldn't let him. Maybe later, but not now, not when her mind was still full of horrors and her heart still pounding with panic. If she'd somehow managed to collect the memories and feelings of his dead love, then these feelings weren't real. Even if that wasn't the case, how could she keep sleeping with a man, or men, she considered suspects?

A better question was, how in the world would she be able to resist?

Her panties were so wet she was certain her jeans would soon be soaking as well and the musky scent of her desire would be plain to anyone. She might have a spare pair in her bag. She could quickly slip off her jeans and panties and put on a fresh pair—without touching herself in any way—and no one would be the wiser. Perhaps the mundane act of getting dressed would pull her out of this pit of lust.

She bent her knees and slid down the tree, the rough bark scratching her back as it lifted her shirt. The movement brought the inner seam of her jeans into contact with her desperate flesh and she bit her lip to keep from crying out. This couldn't be normal, could it? To want someone this badly, so badly that you fell apart in the woods and couldn't even think?

Aleeza fumbled in the bag with her right hand, digging amongst the jumble of weapons and files and various packaged snack foods, looking for her spare panties. Her fingers felt silk and she grabbed at it, only to close her fist over not just the panties but something else as well. Something hard and smooth and cylindrical.

Her leather billy club.

No, no, no! Something deep inside her howled, but at the touch of the black leather Aleeza's pussy screamed louder. As if in a dream, she picked the weapon up and inspected it.

It was about a foot long, the tip slightly bulbous, with deep ridges running all the way down its length. About an inch and a half wide, it was heavy and solid in her hand. She'd rarely needed it but bought it because she liked the look of it. It could be useful for intimidation purposes if her perp wasn't properly intimidated by imagining what a little Gunera magic might do to him if he didn't obey orders. It was dangerous and strong, even sexy in a way she'd never analyzed before.

No!

YES! The voice screamed through her head, overpowering her will to resist, sweeping her under like a black wave.

Her fingers tore at her jeans, yanking them and her panties down to puddle at her feet. Her own scent assaulted her, made her moan involuntarily as she slipped her fingers over her mound and down to touch her burning clit. That light touch was almost enough to send her flying.

Crouching down with her back against the tree, she spread her legs wider, wide enough to make her slick thighs tremble. She was so wet, so hot, her fingers sliding easily over her sensitive flesh.

Holding the billy in her right hand, Aleeza spread her lips with her left and butted the blunt, slightly rough leather tip against her opening, then pulled it away. The leather was already soaked, shiny in the dim light from the overcast sky. Experimentally she brought it to her lips, let her tongue play over the top, tasting her arousal on the thick, hard tip. She shuddered, then slid the wet leather up the inside of her thigh and drove it into her tight channel.

Her eyes closed, shutting out the dull greens and browns of the trees in front of her. She could not focus on them, could not focus on anything but the ridged thickness of the club as it rubbed against her walls, making her nerves sing and her body tighten. She was almost ready to come after just that one thrust, her legs trembling as she dug her heels into the soft dirt and pushed her back more firmly against the tree.

The club wasn't as big around as Dorand's cock or Ferrin's, but the ridges more than made up for it as she pulled it back out and thrust it in again, soft moans escaping her lips. Faster she moved and faster, rubbing her clit with the fingertips of her left hand.

The wind around her blew harder as she fucked herself with the club, her hands dripping wet, the leather hot and pliable now. Her muscles ached from tension and the need for release, a release she instinctively knew would not be enough but that she urged herself toward anyway. Later she would try to understand why this raging need had overtaken her here. For now she only wanted to feel the club's rings stimulate her nerves, to tighten her inner walls and grip it, forcing more friction between her skin and the black club working inside her.

It wasn't enough. But it would do for now.

* * * * *

Dorand headed up the hill, his arms aching. Rot had set into a few of the oaks, and as much as it pained him, the trees needed to be destroyed. Using the chainsaw made the process shorter but still required enough strength to tire him out.

Drying sweat made his chest and back itch as he took off his t-shirt and used it to wipe his face. He didn't particularly enjoy swimming in Potter Lake—once his favorite spot—after the body of Rimer Lorcan was found there months ago, but it wasn't far, and he was desperate for a dip to rinse the sawdust and dirt from his skin. Besides, it might be the last swim of the season. The nights were getting colder and soon the water would be too cold to tolerate, even for a man who enjoyed feeling his extremities numb.

Focusing on how good the cold, clear water would feel and not on what had once rested there, he reached the top of the hill and turned. To get to the lake he had to go in a half-circle around it, avoiding the clump of poison ivy growing in his path. The increasingly cool nights and the coming of winter frost would take care of it soon enough. Right now he just wanted to clean off before heading home for a real shower.

A sound in the trees now behind him made him stop. The rustling of leaves, like someone was walking past. A soft thud. His skin crawled. Potter Lake hadn't been eerie before. Now it was, the energy there as responsible for his aversion as the memory of Rimer's lifeless form floating in the water. It was almost as if the air around the lake was thicker, ripe with a potential for evil that was never there before.

Isn't there enough to be worried about without spooking yourself, man?

Dorand shook off the feeling and started walking again. Cato had cleansed the area himself, burned the smudge stick and banished the black magic. He was the most powerful witch Dorand had ever known. If his spells weren't good enough, nothing would be.

Another sound, the soft cry of a woman. Aleeza.

He knew it was her as surely as he knew his own name or where he kept the glasses in his small kitchen at home.

He turned and headed for her, moving as quickly as he dared while still being silent. If someone was hurting her, he wanted the element of surprise in his favor. His fists clenched. If someone was hurting her, he would kill them.

I won't let it happen again. Not like with Carantha.

He knew it wasn't his fault, the death of his mate. He hadn't been there—neither of them had. The impending wedding of one of their friends had taken both men into the city that night. The other covens might think them hopelessly old fashioned, but even the Amiantos had bachelor parties. They'd stayed out late, drinking a little too much beer and having two o'clock breakfast at the Waffle Shoppe. When they got back, she was gone.

He and Ferrin took turns reminding each other it wasn't their fault. Nobody knew what Rimer's death had started in these woods. Everyone assumed it was personal, a vendetta, a revenge killing. If they'd known, they never would have left Carantha alone the night before Beltaine.

Hell, they never would have left her alone, period. She was a part of them, a sacred part that deserved to be protected at all costs.

When he'd started thinking of Aleeza in the same way he thought of Carantha, when she'd become so important, he had no idea. It bothered him a little, but there was no time to think about it now. Another sound, louder than the first, came through the trees, and Dorand swung around in that direction.

He'd been right. The voice was Aleeza's.

He'd also been wrong. She wasn't in danger.

Unless she really was turning into an ecstasy addict, which was entirely possible. She was so focused on herself and what she was doing, she didn't even notice him standing there, dry-mouthed, with a cock that instantly sprang to attention as he watched her masturbating against a tree.

Her top was still on, her jeans and panties still hugging her calves. It was as if she couldn't wait to get whatever that object was inside her. She had a cabin—it wasn't even that far away. Couldn't she wait fifteen minutes to get there before scratching her itch?

Even as he watched, her back arched, her hips pumping forward as her face contorted. She was coming, her hard nipples poking against the fabric of her shirt, her thighs trembling. Dorand ducked back, hoping the sounds of his movement would be hidden by the wild cries escaping her throat. He would give her time to collect herself, to get her clothes back on…his cock throbbed at the very idea of letting her go. She was ready, she was naked…he could probably have her on her back and begging within seconds.

The idea was so tantalizing it made him dizzy. When had he started missing her, wanting her so badly?

Gritting his teeth, he leaned over to steal a look at her, hoping she would be dressed. She wasn't. Instead she was running the soaking wet tip of whatever she'd been using—it looked like a club of some kind, it was too thin to be a dildo— over her now-exposed nipples as she held her shirt out of the way. The sight took his breath away. Never had any woman looked so erotic to him, so overtly sexual and just the slightest bit…dirty. Her eyes were closed. The tip of her delicate tongue protruded from between her lips as she focused herself so fully, so completely, on the sensations coursing through her body.

She was Gunera. She was experiencing those feelings for the first time in her life…but this still wasn't normal, couldn't be normal.

She slid the club back down her stomach, back between her legs. He watched as she slipped it between them, rubbing the ridged implement over her clit, pulling it back and forth while she rode over it with small, smooth movements of her hips. She was going to do it again. Her skin was flushed, her mouth open now as she gasped for air. He took a deep breath and focused on her. Something was wrong, something was missing, but he couldn't for the life of him—

Wait a minute. It was her aura. It wasn't right. He'd seen her aroused before. Hell, he'd been with her. He'd fucked her and tasted her power on his lips while he did. She should be glowing blue, that bright hard blue that made her look like an angel. Instead, all he saw was a faint tinge of turquoise hovering in the air by her now rapidly moving hands.

No longer caring if it upset her, he stepped out of his hiding place and covered the distance between them in a few seconds. He smelled her arousal in the air, the heady, musky scent of her need. It filled his nostrils, his head, and he had to fight to keep coherent thoughts.

"Aleeza," he whispered.

Her eyes flew open. "Dorand. No, Dorand, you shouldn't—leave me alone." Her fingers and hips didn't stop moving, despite the look of shame that crossed her face. The night before, they had. She'd been in the grips of the very first orgasms she'd ever had in her life—he could only imagine how powerful that must have been after twenty-five years—but she'd still stopped. Now she didn't, her lust-glazed eyes begging him somehow to help her.

He reached for her, meaning only to still her movements, but she shook her head. "Just go. I can't let you touch me!"

"Why?"

Tears rolled down her cheeks. She looked away. "I just can't. Please…please…" The last words came out as a moan. She was coming again, her left hand twisting and pulling at her right nipple. Dorand could hardly breathe. He wanted to help her, the gods knew he did, but he didn't want her to stop. He wanted to watch her again, wanted to see her face as she brought herself to another orgasm and another. He wanted to bury himself in her and feel her throb around him. Something was wrong with her, and he knew it, but being so close to her that her gasps of breath were hot on his face made it hard as hell to think clearly.

A sob escaped her throat as she pulled the club out of her pussy. He watched, amazed, as she moved it back, tilting her hips forward and placing the sodden leather tip at the small, puckered entrance of her ass. Her hand snaked down to her clit, plump and exposed to him in that position.

"Aleeza," he said softly, unable to take his eyes off her hands. "Let me touch you. Let me help."

She sobbed again, her face contorting as she started working the club into her ass. Dorand thought the buttons on his jeans were going to explode open as he watched it disappear. He couldn't wait anymore for her permission. He reached out and grabbed her, wrapping his left hand around her thin wrist, taking whatever power possessed her into himself.

His head flew back. He screamed, his throat already aching, just as his entire body ached and burned. It hurt, oh goddess how it hurt. His skin crawled. He thought he was going to be sick. How had she been able to withstand this at all, this raging, greedy black lust thundering through his body? Desperately, he tried to ground the energy, to send it away, but it didn't work. Somehow he knew nothing would work but to let the power go where it wanted to go, but at the same instant knew he could not allow that to happen.

Aleeza's sobs stilled. Through the reddish haze of want and pain he saw her hand slow, her back straighten a little. It was working. He was helping her, but at what price to himself?

He had to banish this energy, find a way to release it. Only one method came to mind.

"Help me," he managed, not daring to take his hand off her as he fumbled at his jeans with the other. Her fingers, slick with her juices, covered his, tearing at his fly and finally freeing his swollen length.

He was so hard he was dizzy, so hard his cock looked almost twice the normal size and dark purple. It twitched and shuddered in the cool air.

Her wet hand closed over it. "Dorand," she gasped. "Dorand, come here." The club fell to the leaves below as she started to kick off her shoes and jeans, struggling with the heavy denim.

"No. No, I could give it back to you," he managed. He'd never heard of such a thing happening. Usually when Ferrin or Carantha or both got too carried away, when that blackness that sometimes invaded Ferrin reared its ugly head, he was able to ground it within himself. Whatever this was, he could not ground it, could not hold it. He could not risk releasing it back into her.

Her dazed expression gave him no clue that she truly understood, but she stopped trying to remove her clothing. Instead she moved her hand, sliding up the length of him and back down, her juices making his skin slick.

He gasped and leaned forward, taking one of her hard nipples into his mouth. It tasted of her arousal. He pulled it in between his teeth, pressing it against the roof of his mouth, sucking as hard as he dared to keep from crying out.

Aleeza had no such compunctions. Her back arched toward him, one hand snaking around to tangle in his hair and pull him even closer. Her grip on his cock twisted, almost painfully.

He let go and licked a path to her other breast, teasing it with his tongue. Out of the corner of his eye he saw her hips pump forward, and so reached down to the incredible slick heat between her legs. She cried out again, the pressure of her hand speeding.

Dorand thought his head would explode. He shuddered and twitched, his hips jerking forward in time with her inexpert rhythm. Making sure to keep his skin in contact with hers, he shifted his grip so he could run his hand up her arm to cup her breasts, lifting them each in turn and feasting on the puckered skin at their tips. His other hand was coated with her juices, his fingers making circles over her clit.

She was almost hot enough to burn him. The feel of her soft wet folds under his fingertips sent him flying, made the alien blackness burning across his skin scream. Whatever it was, it wanted to be inside her. He could not let it. He had enough presence of mind to remember that although he didn't think he'd be able to tell someone his own name if they asked at that moment.

Keeping his fingers buried in her pussy, he slapped her hand away from his cock. He needed to finish this, finish it now before he lost control and gave in. "Keep your hand on me," he gasped. "On my shoulder."

She obeyed, her hand a soft, familiar weight on his skin.

For another minute there were no sounds in the forest but his own frantic growls and her softer moans, which grew louder as she swelled under his fingers. His balls tightened—his cock grew even larger. The thing screamed to thrust into her, to take his hand away, to come inside her. He fought it as hard as he could, but deep down he was terrified he could not win.

At the last second, his body twisted toward her, against his will, but still too late. She cried out, arching toward him, and his own orgasm rolled through him, expelling the force within him as he shot his seed all over the bare, tawny flesh of her stomach. His howl of ecstasy and fury echoed through the trees around them.

They were still for a long moment, drawing great gasps of cool misty air. Dorand's eyes focused on her skin, on the drops of his ejaculate decorating her torso. "Shit."

His legs and arms like rubber, he bent down, hunting in the fallen leaves for the t-shirt he'd discarded, and picked it up. Leaves and sticks clung to the damp fabric and it smelled of his sweat, but he didn't care.

Aleeza jumped when he started scrubbing her off with the cold, wet fabric. "Wait." She tried to twist away, but he grabbed her arm and held her fast. "It can wait until I get a shower, can't it? The cabin is close and—"

"No. Whatever…infected you, whatever that thing was, it might try to get back in through your skin. I don't want that to happen."

"But I don't…" her eyes widened. "You think it could be transmitted by fluid?"

"Many of the ancient magics are, especially black magics." He finished cleaning her and stepped back, balling the shirt up in his fist. "What the hell happened to you, anyway? What were you doing before this happened?"

"I was doing my job," she snapped, stepping away and yanking her shirt back in place. Her cheeks were bright red. "I was investigating."

"Yes, but what were you doing?"

She pulled up her jeans and fastened them. "I was looking at the runes, the ones found on Rimer Lorcan. I tried tracing—" She stopped, her lips still moving but with no sound coming out. "I traced the rune."

He stared at her. "You traced a rune when you didn't know what it meant? What the hell is the matter with you?"

"I didn't say any words, I didn't cast with intent!"

"Yeah? So what? You don't know what this rune needs to activate it. How could you be so stupid? How could you put yourself at risk like that?"

"What do you care?"

The words stung more than he'd thought they would. "What's that supposed to mean?"

"It means why do you care if I put myself at risk? You don't know me. You don't know anything about me."

"Yes, but I—" Why was she looking at him like that, like she suspected he would make some sort of declaration? Like she *expected* he would? Something haunted that look, something scared. He didn't know what it was, but he wanted to find out.

Chapter Nine

✂

"We're almost there. Once I find a place to park, we'll be walking up the steps to the apartment in ten minutes." Aleeza swallowed hard and pushed aside the nervousness that had plagued her from the moment Dorand settled into the passenger's seat of her Vesta.

So she was bringing a man—a man she'd slept with—home with her for the first time. So what? He probably thought she was some kind of sex pervert at this point and had absolutely no intention of trying to take advantage of her. There had definitely been some dark magic afoot in what had possessed her in the woods, but she still couldn't keep from feeling ashamed of herself for the fact that she should have sensed the power moving within her if nothing else.

"I'm not in any rush. I don't have any responsibilities on coven grounds until tomorrow evening," Dorand said, his voice completely calm and at ease.

"Oh…good." Aleeza tried to ignore the possible implications of that statement. Did that mean he wanted to spend the night? That he planned to stay with her as she followed whatever leads they might uncover in her apartment?

She hadn't planned on letting anyone help her on this investigation, especially not a potential suspect, but it seemed she needed Dorand. If the vibrations of this black magic were subtle enough to take her over without her knowledge, it would pay to have a member of the undefiled coven, and his magic, by her side. Dorand was the only one who knew her secret at the moment, making him by far her safest choice. The fewer people who knew, the better. Not to mention he had connections in the demonology department at Savior City University. They needed to know the meanings of the runes, the sooner the better.

It might still be three weeks to Samhain, but some sort of black power was already afoot. The only good thing that came from her possession in the wood was that now she and Dorand knew for certain they were dealing with demon-based magic. Only demon spells could live in the atmosphere, lurking in wait until they found a proper host. Like an "impure" witch. Aleeza swallowed. The thought brought to mind the question that had been plaguing Aleeza since they left the woods.

"Do you think it's because I'm Gunera that the rune was activated?"

"Any witch could have activated it, but if it's demon-based—"

"Only one of the three impish covens could host it."

"Impish?" He turned to look at her and raised an amused eyebrow.

"The phrase 'demon-infected' does roll off the tongue, but…"

"Right." He laughed, and it made her smile. The sound was strangely, achingly familiar, bringing a rush of melancholy that wiped the smile from her face. "Perhaps. It could be the reason the murderer placed the victims on Amiantos land. We can't serve as conduits for black magic, and we've never allowed non-Amiantos in our woods, not even Gunera spouses. So they could be fairly certain the spell would lie dormant until they wished it to become active," Dorand said, echoing her thoughts exactly. "But that doesn't explain why I was able to take the power from you and release it. I shouldn't have been able to do that if it were pure-demon."

"Maybe a hybrid? A magic-fast spell?" Aleeza asked as she cut in front of an aging station wagon to grab the last parking space at the end of her block. The car honked its horn, and the driver cursed a blue streak before he pulled down the road. For some reason the interaction was comforting. Amiantos men, sex, demon spells, they were new to her, but she'd been pissing off human drivers for years.

"By the gods. It's a wonder you haven't been killed before now." Dorand looked a little pale and actually winced when she nudged the car in front of her with her bumper to help the Vesta wedge itself into the space.

"I'm an excellent driver."

"You're an aggressive driver."

"I thought you liked aggressive women," Aleeza said, the words flying from her mouth before she could think twice. Dorand paled further, and she wondered again where this instinctive knowledge of the man had come from. Stolen magic, lost soul or something else entirely, she planned to find out.

"It could be a hybrid spell, I suppose, but then you have to ask the question: Who has the ability to magic-fast with a demon?"

Dorand ignored her question, shooting her a pointed look that made her mind race to follow his line of reasoning.

"One of the impish covens."

"One of the impish covens who can perform the fasting ritual," Dorand corrected.

"They would have to be able to have sex," Aleeza said, a horrible sinking feeling in her stomach. The Pandorian and Daiesthai covens had been extinct for centuries. That left the Gunera…

Dear gods, she wasn't the only one. Someone else in her coven was free of the curse and they were aiding a demon in ritualistic death magic. The sinking feeling in her stomach shifted into full-blown nausea, and the shame she'd been feeling a moment ago grew even more profound.

"There could be another answer. It might not be one of your coven." Dorand placed a comforting hand on her arm as she shut off the ignition.

"The other covens are extinct, Dorand. It's a Gunera. Hell, I would be a suspect if I had freed myself of the spell sooner," Aleeza said, trying to pull away from his touch. It affected her too deeply, bringing to the surface a need more than sexual. She wanted to lean into his arms and bury her face in his chest, wanted to take comfort from him in a way she had never let anyone comfort her. It scared her nearly as much as the demon magic.

"No, you would never willingly aid that kind of black power. That's why you did what you did in the woods. You were trying to free the spell from your body with sexual release. It's more Amiantos magic than Gunera, but that's the instinct you were choosing."

"Right," Aleeza said with a bitter laugh, wanting to believe him but no longer sure who she could trust. If one of her own coven, her family, had become a cold-blooded killer, and she'd had no clue, her instincts were complete shit.

"I am right, and I could teach you how to work that magic more effectively. You might even be able to ground your own power in time."

"Thanks for the offer. Maybe after I figure out which of my coven members is killing your people, we'll talk." Aleeza finally succeeded in pulling away from him and leapt out of the car before he could reach for her again. His touch soothed her, but she didn't want to be soothed right now. She didn't deserve any peace of mind.

"I told you, it might not be your coven." Dorand slammed the passenger door behind him and easily caught up with her as she set a swift pace down the street. It was nearly sunset and the air had grown much colder, cutting through her thin shirt and making her shiver. "A few years ago, Ferrin, Carantha and I were hired to raise a spirit that was causing trouble near the docks. We succeeded in raising a Pandorian man, but we couldn't make him speak."

"The spirit was too ancient?"

"That's what we thought at first, but he was dressed in jeans, and his hair was cut in a style that Carantha said looked straight out of the 1970s." Dorand's voice caught slightly as he said Carantha's name, but Aleeza tried not to notice. Criminals, magic, and violence were things she dealt with every day, but she had no experience with comforting the grieving. Gunera were experts at pretending grief didn't exist.

Instead, she focused on the story he was telling.

"A modern Pandorian? That's not possible, is it?"

"His magic was clearly Pandorian, and he even had part of the coven tattoo on his chest, the part that wasn't shot up with bullet holes."

"So he was a murder victim. That's why you couldn't get him to speak."

"Maybe, maybe not. It was a strange case." Dorand slowed his pace and put a hand at her waist, pulling her closer to his side. "Wait. There's something wrong here. Your building—"

"Someone's been working black magic. I felt it last night for the first time. The…piece of your magic left inside me started to glow, and it burned when I tried to walk up the steps." Aleeza moved closer to Dorand's side, melting into him, letting herself enjoy the feel of his strong hand squeezing into her hip.

"We call it a remnant. It's not a permanent exchange, fades after a day or two."

"So that's why it's not glowing now?" Aleeza asked, instead of the hundred other questions his statement brought to mind. Did that mean what she felt for him was real? It wasn't some leftover from his magic, the magic he shared with his dead lover, moving within her?

Dorand nodded as his eyes drifted from the steps up the length of the five-story building. "It's an old spell, but it's been active within the past week. How long have you lived here?"

"Since I moved out of my mom's house when I was seventeen."

"It's not that old…maybe a year, maybe two. I'm going to have to go inside to know for sure."

"Okay." Aleeza started up the stairs, but Dorand pulled her back, wrapping his arms around her and squeezing so her breasts pressed into his chest. "What are you—"

"You can't go with me. If that spell has been working on you, you'll be vulnerable. Stay outside and wait for me or go back to the car if you get cold." Then Dorand whispered a few words too softly for her to hear before he dropped his lips to hers. She parted for him immediately, melting into the feel of his tongue sweeping through her mouth with tender strokes that made every inch of her, inside and out, ache to be closer to the man. Whatever fears lurked in her mind seemed to disappear when he touched her, kissed her, like this. It felt much better than she wanted it to.

"What was that?" she asked, when he finally pulled away.

"A spell of protection, I don't want you getting hurt while we're separated."

"Does all Amiantos magic involve sex in some way?"

"No, the kiss was completely optional." He grinned, a sexy smile that would have been equally at home on Ferrin's face, and released her, heading up the steps to her apartment with her keys in his hand.

"I can protect myself, Dorand."

"I know you can, but now I'll worry less while I'm inside."

Worried about her, the man was worried. That meant he cared, didn't it?

Aleeza's heart did a strange, aching little flip as she watched the door swing closed behind him, and then she turned and ran back toward her car. She wasn't cold, but she needed to move, needed to run until she was out of breath, until she forgot how wonderful it had felt for a moment to imagine herself as a person Dorand would truly care for.

* * * * *

Ferrin pulled the navy blue sedan into a red zone across from Aleeza's building. The message on his machine had been brief, but when Dorand said he was going into town with Aleeza, Ferrin had assumed they would be heading to her place.

He'd been right.

Your brother, your clan mate, so eager to get the woman alone that he's taken her off Amiantos lands. He won't rest until she's bound to him, and then what will become of you, what —

Ferrin shook off the voice and muttered the liberation incantation for the tenth time in less than a few hours. Something was wrong—there was no doubt about it—and a part of him ached to go to Dorand, to tell him about the black power and seek his aid. The other part of him, a part that had nothing to do with the wicked voice in his head, was too angry with his brother to ask for help.

He'd gone inside alone, it was true, but not before he'd kissed Aleeza like she was the last breath of air left in the world. Dorand didn't kiss anyone that way. He was falling for her, hard and fast, and if Ferrin knew his brother, it would be forever. They'd both loved Carantha, but neither had ever given her his whole self. It wasn't the nature of their threesome for any of them to lose their heart so completely, but Ferrin had always suspected that was how it would have been between Carantha and Dorand if he had been out of the picture. Dorand was a man who had been waiting to give his heart and soul to a woman for a long time, and it looked like he'd chosen Aleeza as that woman, whether he realized it just yet or not.

Stolen her is more like it.

The voice was faint, but it was still there, mere seconds after the incantation. If it continued like this he would run mad. Run mad or give in, sink into that voice and let it guide him to whatever dark purpose it would have him serve.

"No way in hell." He spoke the words aloud, giving himself a stern look in the rearview mirror just in time to see the two men slip between his car and the one behind and run across the street, following Aleeza.

They were witches, but of what gods-forsaken coven he had no clue. Their aura was a faint, sickly yellow, their hair shaved to within an inch of their heads. Something about their clothing bothered him as well…too new, too…what was it? Ferrin emerged quietly from the car and slipped his black leather jacket on as he crossed the street behind the pair.

Too identical, that was it. Their jeans were the same brand and even looked to be the same size though the men themselves were vastly different heights. One was barely taller than Aleeza while the other was pushing six feet. The smaller man had cuffed his jeans, and the taller one's ankles showed between the bottom of his pants and his cheap black shoes. They both wore black hooded sweatshirts that still held the creases from the factory, never even been washed.

They disappeared around the corner of the building and Ferrin followed at a trot. If the men had been human, he still would have followed. Aleeza's building wasn't in the safest part of the city and muggings were a regular occurrence. The fact that they were witches, however, brought his suspicions to a different level. Had the Fire Festival killer already learned of Aleeza's investigation? Could he or she have sent these two thugs to make sure she didn't get any closer to the truth?

"Shit." He cursed as he rounded the corner and found no sign of Aleeza or the two men. He broke into a run. If the two men were out to stop her investigation, an investigation she'd only been signed on to run for a few hours, that created an entirely new set of problems.

There had to be a leak somewhere. Whether it was on the Gunera side or gods forbid one of his own coven mates, this was starting to look like an inside job. Someone had tipped the killer off, someone close to the Amiantos coven. Someone he would kill swiftly, as soon as he could wring a name from the men's throats.

Ferrin reached the end of the building where the road turned into a bridge over the river. Nothing, not a sign of them on the bridge or the street that stretched beyond. He was getting ready to run back to the front of the complex to find Dorand and tell him what had happened when he heard someone cry out. The sound came from behind the building, down the sloping hill that led down to the river itself.

He darted down the hill, slipping on the wet grass in his damned dress shoes. He hadn't bothered to change after the coven meeting and now regretted the choice not to change into his hiking boots. Not only would they give him better footing, but they would hurt more when they connected with the other two men. He hadn't fought hand to hand with another witch in a long time, but right now he was spoiling for a fight and certain that rage would more than make up for his lack of practice in the ring.

Ferrin made it down the slope in time to see Aleeza twist free of the taller man's grip in a move that made him stumble and nearly lose his footing.

"Ammon! Come back!" The man screamed the words to the back of the shorter one, who was already making swift progress down the trail that ran beside the river. He was limping and holding a hand to the side of his head, but his injuries didn't keep him from hauling some serious ass.

"Yeah, come back, Ammon. We're not done playing yet." Aleeza followed the words with a wicked roundhouse that connected solidly with the taller man's chest. He grunted and flew backward at least five feet. She was packing a magical punch as well as a physical one, and the weaker witch was no match for her despite his larger size.

"Who are you?" Aleeza asked, stalking toward the man who scuttled away from her in a backward crab walk. "What do you—"

Her words ended in a gasp, her hands flying to clutch the sides of her head. The man at her feet took advantage of the shift in her attention and struggled to his feet. He turned to run but she caught the back of his sweatshirt in her fist.

"Wait, you're not going anywhere until—"

This time she cried out and fell to her knees, releasing the man who immediately fled in the same direction as his friend. Her cry turned into a moan and she clutched at her head as if she would pull the offensive thing off her body and hurl it into the river.

Ferrin reached her side in seconds. He couldn't pursue the men until he knew she was all right. If she'd sustained a head injury from her scuffle with the other witches, she might be in need of immediate medical attention. She had healing skills, but he hadn't a clue if could she heal herself from something as serious as a possible concussion.

"Aleeza are you—"

As soon as he knelt and touched her arm, he knew he'd made a very serious mistake.

Eternity. You will have eternity, sitting at the right hand of those who hold the reigns of the world. Power, such power, the power of blood, the power of the ancients, never again to fear the pain of death or the abandonment of those who you hold dear.

The voice crashed through his head with crystal clarity, no longer a mere whisper that could be shoved away. Even more powerful than the words themselves were the images, images of him and Aleeza, nude and anointed with oil, the power of the gods themselves shimmering across their skin. There was a babe at her breast and a little boy by Ferrin's side, and somehow Ferrin knew these were real children, the real offspring Aleeza would bear for him, for their clan.

The children fairly glowed with power, their dark eyes fathomless, holding ancient knowledge that no mere mortal or witchling could possess. Around their heads hung a vapor of pale gray, a mist that was as much a part of them as their very skin. Ferrin and Aleeza had the same halo around their temples, a sign of the magical union they had made with each other and with their Protectors.

The Protectors. They had waited so long, aching to join with a mortal witch, to give them the gift of everlasting life and unheard of power, as well as enjoyment of the thousand different pleasures of the mortal realm. It was the perfect arrangement, a magnificent exchange, a blissful way of life that had been driven to the edge of extinction. But he and Aleeza had brought it back, could bring it back. They only needed one more. One more of their kind must be born into the physical realm, so there were two generations existing at once, and then the magic could be wrought. The second coming of the most powerful coven the world had ever known. The most—

"Ferrin, please, you have to let go. Please." Aleeza's thin voice somehow reached him through the roaring in his head. He opened his eyes and found her beneath him on the ground. Their clothes were still in place, but his hips were between her spread legs, grinding against her as if they could find a way to fuck through the fabric that separated them.

The bright green-gold that had shone around them in the forest bloomed around her face, so bright he could barely see the grass beneath her. Her eyes glowed as well, gold mixing with the dark brown in a mesmerizing play of color. Ferrin felt himself being sucked into her gaze, and suddenly knew he would die if he didn't kiss her lips, didn't rip away their clothes and push inside her, getting as close to her as was physically possible while still in separate skins.

"Stop. No, Ferrin. Fight it, don't you feel it, can't you—"

Her words ended in a moan as he shoved up her shirt and captured her nipple in his mouth, sucking hard. The smell of her was achingly familiar, the taste of her everything that he had ever hungered for in his entire life.

"Please," she begged, but he couldn't remember what she begged for. Satisfaction, that must be it, and he would satisfy her. Again, and again, and again until the child was conceived, until —

"Please!" she cried, but this time it was different. Her fingers twisted in his hair, pressing his head to her breast while her other hand scratched at his back through his shirt, yanking it from his waistband. Her palm was hot on his skin as she slid it down into his pants to cup his bare ass.

The sound that came from his throat was unlike anything he'd ever heard himself make, a dark, triumphant growl. This was what they were meant for, what they'd been born for. He growled again when her fingernails dug into the bare skin of his ass and up his back, leaving trails of hot, sharp, blissful pain.

Her legs wrapped around his hips, pressing herself against his raging erection. The heat of her came through their clothing and for a moment he could see her, see her pussy pink and burning for him. The mental image couldn't have been clearer had it been a photograph.

Ferrin took his mouth from her breast to kiss her, his hands fumbling with their pants as if he could unfasten them both at once. He felt strong enough, powerful enough, to tear the fabric from their bodies if it didn't give way to him. Just as he would tear and rip anyone or anything that dared to interfere between himself and his mate.

She pulled her mouth away to gasp his name. He found the slender column of her throat and bit, hard, hard enough to feel her veins pumping against his lips. A little more pressure, just a little, and he could taste her blood, make her scream in pleasure and pain as he shoved himself into her.

He could smell Dorand on her body, on her skin, in a way he never had before with Carantha, but he didn't care.

Dorand was nothing, meant nothing. Dorand would bow before them, just like the rest of them would…once the child was born, once the children came and Ferrin and Aleeza were honored above all others.

"No…no…"

Just hurry up, fuck her, make her scream! She wants it, you both want it! Hurry up!

"Gods help me!" Ferrin forced his mouth from her addictive skin and struggled to think. The voice was so strong now, it was nearly impossible to tell which thoughts were his and which the "other's", but he knew these thoughts of conception were not his own. No matter how much he suddenly longed to see those children in the vision become a living, breathing reality, he knew that the desperate drive to force them into existence wasn't coming from his mind. Nor were the thoughts of Dorand bowing down to him, being a slave to his whims.

"Goddess, I call upon you, bring aid to your daughter. Reach me now in the time of my…"

Aleeza continued the prayer-spell through her sobs, but Ferrin could no longer make out the individual words. The screaming, howling in his head filled his entire world. With a gut-wrenching cry he threw himself from Aleeza and fell hard onto the concrete of the river trail. The second their skins separated, the screaming quieted, and Ferrin found the words of the liberation incantation on his lips.

By the time the last of the spell was spoken, he could breathe again, and the voice in his head was silent. In fact, for the first time since last night in the grove, he felt completely free of that foreign presence, blessedly alone in his own skull.

Chapter Ten

∽

"Ferrin, are you all right?" Aleeza sat on the ground near him, carefully not making contact. Her hands shook and she looked as scared as he felt, but she wasn't glowing anymore, and the wide eyes that met his didn't shine with that strange power.

"I'm fine. You?"

"Fine. Well not fine, not fine at all, but—"

"But we fought it off, whatever it is." Ferrin finished her sentence, and had to stop himself from reaching out to pull her into his arms. He wanted to hug her, to hold her close and feel their hearts beat in time. They had survived something together and it made him feel closer to her, deepened the feelings he already had for this amazing woman.

"That's the question we have to answer. What is it? And why me and you? Why now?" She struggled to her feet and took a shaky breath. "I have to go, have to see if I can catch up with those men. They're connected to this in some way. That strange voice, it was stronger when I touched them. I have to find them—"

"Wait, don't go. You can't go after them by yourself, and I can't be trusted to go with you. I hear the voice too… I've heard it for a long, long time." Ferrin watched as she backed away from him another step, as if she feared him, and he felt a strange, squeezing sensation in his chest. Of all the emotions he wanted to inspire in her, fear was nowhere on the list. "Never like this, but it's been there. It wasn't until last night, when I saw you and Dorand in the glen that it became stronger."

"That's when I heard it for the first time," she said, then paused as if considering how much truth she could trust him with. "It told me your name."

"It told me yours." Was that relief in her eyes? "It also told me other things."

"What kind of things?"

"Things…I don't think I can share with you." She stared at him and the uncomfortable silence stretched between them, but he knew she still felt drawn to him. It was taking all of her willpower to keep from crossing the few feet between them and pressing her lips to his. It took all of his not to do the same. "You're right—we can't go after them alone. Dorand's back at my apartment."

"I know. You were both standing outside when I pulled up."

"You saw him kiss me." The look in her eyes was challenging, as if she were daring him to make some sort of confession.

"I did."

"You didn't like it."

There was no doubt about that dare now, which was fine with him. He'd never been afraid to take a risk, and right now the truth seemed the best course of action.

"I didn't."

She took a deep breath and nodded, letting her eyes fall to the ground. The heat between them, even at ten paces was stifling. He didn't know how much longer he could stand here and not make any move to close the distance between them.

"Let's go find Dorand. Those two are long gone by now anyway." He walked up the hill and heard her follow.

"I think we're going to have another chance at them. They didn't try to hurt me. They wanted me to go somewhere with them. If whoever is controlling them wants me badly enough, I have a feeling they or someone else will be back."

They cleared the hill and were back on the street in time to see the streetlights flicker on. The sun had set while they were dealing with the men and the psychic attack and now the air was much colder. Aleeza shivered a bit, hugging herself, and Ferrin wished he could put his arm around her and warm her up.

Too bad with them there seemed to be no "warm". Only "red hot".

"I'm betting someone else. You kicked their ass." She returned his grin, obviously hearing the compliment in his words. Her smile was so beautiful he almost hated to finish his thought. "Their boss will send someone tougher next time."

"I know. I'll contact my boss, see if he can spare some muscle to help me out until I figure out why I've become a target."

"Dorand and I will be here to help you, you don't—"

"I appreciate the offer, but that might not be the safest idea. No one in my coven knows that I've broken the curse, and I don't want them to find out. At least not until I've figured out who else managed to do it."

She filled him in on what she and Dorand had discovered. Even before she finished, he knew they were both thinking the same thing.

"The magic fist. That's what I saw in the vision, when we—"

"When you touched me. I know. And there were…children." She stopped and turned to face him at the corner of the building, as if she wanted this talk to happen between the two of them before Dorand was involved.

"Two of them, a little boy and a baby girl. They had your eyes." He couldn't stop himself, he reached out and brushed a strand of her hair from those eyes, back behind her ear. There was no dark power this time, only a twisting sensation in his gut, and a strange certainty that he would never love another woman. There was only Aleeza, for now, for always. "They were beautiful. It made me want them to be real."

"Me too." Her eyes were wide and she leaned toward him. She was going to kiss him, and he was shocked to find that simple act of affection meant more to him than their fucking in the woods. In that instant, he knew he would trade in casual sex forever if it meant he could make love to this woman for the rest of their lives.

"Aleeza, I—"

"None of this makes any sense," she said, breaking the spell between them as she stepped away. "The way we all feel about each other in such a short time. It's not natural, Ferrin."

"I don't care if it's natural. I care for you, Dorand cares for you, and we're not going to leave you to fight whatever this is alone. If those men were really after you, then there's a good chance we've got a leak, either on your side or ours. Which one doesn't matter. We just have to make sure—"

"Somebody's been attacking you magically. There was a hex portal right underneath your bed."

Ferrin and Aleeza leapt apart like guilty children at the sound of Dorand's voice. The expression on his face told them he'd noticed that, just as he'd noticed the intensity with which they'd been speaking. People didn't have to physically touch in order to be deeply connected. Their auras still mingled and glowed faintly around them, a testimony to just how intimate they'd been down near the riverbank.

"Hey, Dorand, I came to—"

Dorand silenced him with a look, then turned back to Aleeza. "It felt like what we experienced earlier in the woods," he said. "Nowhere near as strong, but the same kind of energy."

"The woods?" Ferrin asked. Neither of them looked at him.

"So that was deliberate? It was an attack?"

"What happened in the woods?" Ferrin clenched his fists. They were keeping secrets from him. Aleeza was shutting him out, when just a second ago they'd been sharing their darkest secrets. Again in his mind he saw them kiss, and something deep inside him roared.

"It looks like it was," Dorand said. "I managed to ground some of it out and neutralize it, but I don't think it's a good idea for you to stay the night."

"I'll stay with her." Ferrin resisted the urge to put his arm around her and pull her close. Aleeza wasn't even looking at him now. Maybe she didn't want to risk looking at him in front of Dorand.

Or maybe she didn't really care about him the way he did her. She was looking at Dorand like he was some kind of genius. The way Carantha had sometimes done. Ferrin knew Dorand was smarter than he was. Not by much, but he knew it was there. It hadn't bothered him to let Dorand take the lead with Carantha. Now…he wanted to punch his brother in the nose.

"I don't think it's a good idea for you to stay with her alone," Dorand said, his eyes serious. "I don't think it's a very good idea for the two of you to be alone together, period. Not until we figure out what's going on here."

"So it's okay for you to be alone with her but not me?"

"Don't I get a say in this?" Aleeza stepped forward, effectively blocking the glares Dorand and Ferrin were sending each other.

"No." Dorand spoke to Aleeza, but he shifted his body so he could watch Ferrin. "I don't think either of you are thinking straight."

"Why, because she wants me?" Ferrin snapped, at the same time Aleeza said, "Don't tell me what I'm thinking. I can take care of myself."

"I don't think you can," Dorand said. Again, speaking to Aleeza. Apparently Ferrin didn't deserve a reply. He gritted his teeth as black rage filled his vision.

He'd always thought Dorand was his brother, his best friend. Now it seemed that was a lie, had always been a lie. Dorand was just using him, keeping him around for comic relief or maybe simply to satisfy Carantha's taste for a little violence with her sex. He didn't respect him, didn't care that with one word, one flick of his fingers, Ferrin could send him reeling into blackness, *into torment, and he will scream and beg but no mercy will be shown —*

He tried to open his mouth, tried to get the words of the incantation to form in his head, but they wouldn't come. Instead he only saw darkness, saw Dorand's blood, and before he could take another breath he leapt forward and attacked.

The crunch of bone beneath his fist felt wonderful, brought a grim and terrible smile to his lips even as he aimed his other hand for Dorand's midsection. Aleeza screamed. The sound filled his ears as the sight of Dorand's shocked face filled his vision.

Another punch. Dorand doubled over, then lunged forward, clasping Ferrin around the waist and knocking him to the ground in a tackle worthy of the NFL.

"Stop! Stop! What is the matter with you two?" Aleeza's screams cut through the haze of anger. Dorand's hands tore at Ferrin's shirt to touch his bare skin, igniting a cold fire that seared his chest when he made contact. Ferrin screamed, his back arching off the damp, rocky ground beneath him.

The incantation formed in his head, but before he could speak it he heard it around him, in Dorand's rich, authoritative voice. By the time Dorand got to the last line their voices rang and echoed together.

"Thank you," Ferrin whispered. Anger still burned in his gut. But it was just anger, not rage. Just jealousy, not the desire to wash his hands in his brother's blood.

Dorand must have recognized the change in his face because he let go and stood up, shaking his hands fastidiously as if he'd just touched some kind of slime. Which maybe he had.

"That's why it isn't a good idea for you two to be alone together," he said, helping Ferrin up. Blood still streamed from his nose, and he wiped at it with the hem of his shirt.

"It's infecting him too," Aleeza said softly. Her eyes were wide as she stared at Ferrin. "It's all my fault, isn't it?"

"It's neither of your faults. It's the demon magic. You can't be—"

"What demon magic? Will one of you please tell me what's going on here?"

Aleeza and Dorand looked at him. He could practically see the wheels turning in their heads.

Finally Dorand nodded. "I need to try and see Walter before he starts his evening ritual. We can talk on the way."

"He does magic every night?" Aleeza asked.

Dorand shook his head, smiling a little for the first time since he'd seen Ferrin talking with her. "He watches TV and drinks White Russians, but he gets very angry if someone interrupts him."

Aleeza smiled too. So did Ferrin. Some of the tension surrounding the three of them eased.

"Come on," Ferrin said. "Dorand can drive my car. I'm parked illegally anyway."

* * * * *

She hadn't been to this part of Rothschild University's Savior City campus before. Her classes had all been in the new buildings, squat, plain edifices of cement and glass that watched the roads with blank, dull eyes.

The Demonology Center was different. Towers and garrets jutted willy-nilly from the roof, and the building

143

sprawled and shifted like a drunk across the grass. Aleeza knew immediately, before she even stroked the stones surrounding the door, that this building likely predated the city itself. "How did it survive?" she asked softly.

Dorand heard her. He always did, didn't he? "Demon magic," he said. "The spells protecting it aren't dark, but they're powerful."

"Is it dangerous to go in?"

"No. They study demons here. They don't house them. It's been clean for centuries, and they clean it again every year. Just do me a favor? Both of you?"

Ferrin tensed slightly beside her but nodded.

"If something says 'Do Not Touch'…don't touch it. Don't even look at it hard. We don't know what we're dealing with."

"We're not stupid," Ferrin said, his voice tight. Aleeza wanted to reach out to him but didn't dare.

"I know you're not," Dorand replied. "But whatever this thing is it seems to have targeted you both, and I don't want to take any chances. Aleeza wasn't being stupid by the lake either, but she was still nearly taken over."

Ferrin nodded, his face flushing. She knew he hadn't liked hearing what happened between her and Dorand earlier. Even though they'd given him a version as clean as they could make it, there was no way to explain without admitting he'd caught her masturbating, that she'd jerked him off while he did the same to her.

She didn't know why it bothered him so much. Hadn't he and Dorand been a threesome with Carantha Smoler? He should be used to this kind of thing now, used to sharing.

Instead he'd wanted to kill Dorand for kissing her, for talking to her by her apartment building, and she'd seen that part of Dorand seemed to want the same thing.

What was happening to them? All of them?

They'd explained briefly in the car about the voices Ferrin sometimes heard, but that didn't explain his reaction to Dorand. It didn't explain what had happened after those goons attacked her either. Ferrin hadn't been in the path of the spell her attacker flung at her. Why had it affected him too?

She sighed while they waited for Dorand's friend Walter to come to the door. Hopefully he'd have some answers for her, for all of them.

This hope flagged in the face of Walter's uninspiring appearance. He was short and slight, with sandy hair and a pale, pinched-looking face. He looked like every victim she'd ever seen, the kind of guy kids picked on in school and muggers jumped on the street. He was weak, an easy target.

The impression lasted until he shook her hand. A wave of power surged over her, almost knocking her flat. Whoever this guy was, he could probably have her dead before she had a chance to react if he wanted to.

"It's nice to meet you," she said as firmly as possible.

Walter smiled, a broad, confident grin. "And you too."

She watched him shake with Ferrin, saw the same flush come to Ferrin's cheeks as had come to hers. Only Dorand seemed unaffected by his friend's power. Made sense, really. He was probably used to it.

The three of them followed Walter into the building, down the shiny marble hall. Glass cases shone against the walls as they walked past, too quickly for Aleeza to see what rested inside. Walter set a brisk pace, and after a minute she gave up trying to look around and focused on keeping up.

Of course, watching Dorand and Ferrin's tight asses as they walked in front of her was quite pleasant too. She resisted the urge to grin. Only a woman who'd been sex-starved for years would be thinking of such things while in a demonology center waiting to find out how severe the danger to her life was.

They turned down one hall, then another and another until Aleeza had lost track of lefts and rights. She had the vague sense they were descending, but there were no stairs or obvious slopes so she couldn't be sure.

Finally they came to a wooden door so old it was starting to petrify. Walter pulled an elaborate iron key, incongruous amid the small, shiny silver modern ones on the ring, from his pocket and inserted it. He muttered something under his breath and turned it. Aleeza shivered as the force of his magic slid over her skin.

The door opened on one of the biggest rooms she'd ever seen. Shelves heavy with books, trinkets, statues and various objects she couldn't identify at all covered the walls from floor to impossibly high ceiling. Light filtered in through tiny, dusty windows set in the rock.

They picked their way across the cluttered floor, past large statues and desks, past more stacks of books. Aleeza sneezed.

"Bless you." Ferrin and Dorand said it at the same time. She smiled her thanks. If she'd been a different type of woman, watching them jostle each other to stand closer would have made her feel great. As it was, it only reminded her what kind of situation her anti-celibacy spell had put her in.

She'd just wanted a man. Just wanted to try and put to rest the dreams that haunted her, the restless yearning of her body. Now she had two men, both powerful and sexy, both of whom wanted her and didn't seem eager to share.

Both of whom she cared about more than she'd imagined possible, especially in such a short time. But as she stood amid the clutter of the room, she realized that living without either of them might just feel like living without air.

In other words, like not living at all.

"What?" The men had been talking while she woolgathered, and now they looked at her expectantly. "I'm sorry."

"I'd like to see the rune, please." Walter's voice was as pleasant and unassuming as his appearance. She reached into her bag.

"I'll get it." Dorand took the bag from her. She started to protest, then thought better of it. Maybe he was right. The room was clean—magically, of course, physically it was so filthy and musty she half expected Jimmy Hoffa might be hidden there—but with demon artifacts around, it was better not to take a chance. Amiantos didn't have to worry as much, despite what happened earlier in the woods. If Dorand was re-infected he wouldn't need help to expel the curse.

He pulled the picture out of the file and handed it to Walter.

"Hmmm. It's demon, all right. I don't remember seeing this one, but it looks like an amalgam."

"Amalgam?" Ferrin bounced gently on the balls of his feet. Aleeza didn't like the way his eyes glittered.

Walter's eyebrows rose "A rune overwritten by a personal rune. I can figure out the base rune in a few minutes, but knowing what the caster intended with the new one will be guesswork."

"So there's no chance?" She tried to hide her disappointment.

"No, there's a very good chance, once we know what the original rune is intended to do. We know who the victim was. We can probably deduce a lot from the rune's meaning and manner of death."

"But we don't really know the manner of death. He had a stake through the chest, close to the heart, but the postmortem wasn't detailed enough to know if that was the cause of death or placed there afterward."

"For this case. But you have detailed autopsies for the others?" Walter adjusted his glasses and peered at Dorand. "You know how Carantha died, right? And the other victim?"

"Lymera Brown," Aleeza said quickly, seeing the shadows pass over Dorand and Ferrin's faces. "She and Carantha…different methods of death."

"May I see their rune photos please?"

Dorand handed them over, his face expressionless. Aleeza's fingers itched to reach out and stroke his cheek, to relax the stiff muscles of his clenched jaw.

She didn't, though. After the way Ferrin had attacked him earlier, she didn't dare.

"Hmmm." Walter, still examining the photos in his left hand, shoved some books sideways on a desk with his right, clearing a space for the pictures to rest while he grabbed a chair. He glanced up. "I'll probably be an hour or so. You guys can amuse yourself until then."

"Here?" Aleeza asked.

He shrugged. "You can wait in the hall if you want. Make a left out the door and you'll go straight to the armory. There's some interesting stuff in there, old demon weapons, things like that. We keep some books on their history too if you want to read."

"Can we go back outside? Maybe get ourselves something to eat?" Her stomach rumbled as she spoke. When was the last time she'd actually had anything to eat, anyway?

"I'd rather you didn't just because it's a pain in the ass for me to lead you all the way back out and come get you again." He glanced at his watch. "*Celebrities Behaving Badly* starts in an hour and a half, so I'd rather not waste any time."

"Of course," Aleeza said. Nice to see a man who had his priorities in line.

The three of them left Walter with his nose buried in his books and made the suggested left turn out the door. Aleeza's pulse quickened. An hour alone with Ferrin and Dorand. It was just what she wanted—and what she knew she shouldn't have.

Chapter Eleven

ഔ

"Look at this." Ferrin pointed toward one of the larger cases. Behind the thick glass was what Aleeza could only describe as a mace on psychedelic drugs. The enormous spiked ball had razor-sharp tips, each gleaming cold silver. The chain was as big around as her thigh.

"What would have carried that thing?"

"A giant." Dorand's breath stirred the back of her hair as he laughed softly. Aleeza fought the urge to arch her back, to see if her ass would come into contact with the man who stood behind her. Call her crazy, but museums had always done something for her, enough of a something that she'd made sure to avoid them while still under the Gunera curse.

"Giants didn't really exist, did they?" she asked instead.

"No, but giant demons did." He stepped forward to stand beside her, his upper arm brushing her shoulder. Just that slightest touch comforted her, made her feel warm inside. "It could have been a Trevero, or a Liguiran."

"Or a Viotoni," Ferrin said. "Like it says on the tag in the case."

He said it lightly and Aleeza considered laughing, but then Dorand tensed. "I didn't see that," he replied. The tinge of cold in his voice made Aleeza shiver.

"It's scary, anyway," she cut in, moving away to look at something else. This was not the way she'd pictured this hour going. She hadn't expected the men to keep sniping at each other.

Weren't they friends? Brothers? Could she really be coming between them like this?

It was the last thing she wanted to do. Nothing could be worth that, not even Dorand's thick cock or the way Ferrin made her blood feel like it was going to boil right out of her skin. She didn't want to hurt either of these men, and the last thing she needed after the gray magic she'd performed in the woods was any further stain on her karma.

"Guys, I think…I think it's not fair of me to have you both here."

They stopped glaring at each other and turned to her, identical looks of surprise on their faces.

"Yeah," she said, her words coming faster. "I mean, this is my job. I'm not even really authorized to bring other people into the investigation, especially when neither of you are Gunera. And you're witnesses, in a way, too, so…maybe you two should go now, and I'll—"

"Are you crazy?" Ferrin growled. His voice echoed in the cold room.

"Have you forgotten why we're here?" Dorand's voice was calmer but no less intense.

"Or about the guys who attacked you earlier?"

"I managed to beat them on my own," she said, crossing her arms defensively over her chest.

"And what about next time?" Dorand stepped forward then stopped, as if he wanted to cross the room to her but changed his mind. "What about the spell on your apartment? The runes on the bodies?"

"I'll know next time not to even trace the images," she said. "And Walter's going to decipher them, right? So he'll—"

"He's going to decipher them for me," Dorand said. "As a favor."

"And if you hadn't been here, I would have found my way here to get him to decipher them for me. It's part of my job."

"What are you really saying, Aleeza?" She didn't want to look at Ferrin when he spoke, but she couldn't help herself. The pain in his voice made her ache.

"Just that I don't think this is a good idea, I mean—"

"She's saying she doesn't want to see us anymore," Dorand cut in. "Either of us. Whether you want to 'break up' with us or not, Aleeza, you need to think of your safety. And about the success of the investigation."

"Please, that isn't what—that's not what I mean. This is official business, and your coven is paying me to do this. So I think it's best if you guys go now and let me talk to Walter alone."

"Our coven chieftain asked us to help you. This is helping." Dorand crossed his arms across his chest and widened his stance, the very picture of an immoveable object.

"Yes, Dorand, you're helping. But Ferrin and I are trouble. You said it yourself and—"

"So it's me. You want to get rid of me. You should have just said so in the first place, Aleeza. I'm a big boy," Ferrin said.

She opened her mouth to reply but couldn't think of anything to say. Ferrin stared at her for a long moment, then turned. She and Dorand watched him leave the room, slamming the door behind him.

Dorand sighed. "I'd follow him, but I think he'd kill me if I did."

Tears sprang to her eyes. "I didn't want to hurt him," she said. "I don't want to hurt either of you. That's why, don't you see, you guys have been so close for so long, and now it seems like—"

The last words were spoken into the soft fabric of his shirt as he closed the distance between them and circled her in his strong arms. "Don't cry."

"I'm not crying," she said, aware that in another minute she would be and desperate to make it stop. The warm comfort of his energy wrapped around her, giving her strength. "I just don't understand what's going on here, and I think I'm only making things worse by staying in such close contact with you two."

"I don't think there's anything you can do. That magic targeted you and Ferrin. Pushing us away isn't going to change that."

"But staying together it isn't making it better either."

"You don't know that." Dorand hugged her more tightly.

"I'm a good guesser."

"Not good enough. You never would have figured out we were dealing with a demon magic-fast spell without me," he teased.

His words brought a faint smile to her lips. "I just don't want anyone to get hurt."

"We're big boys. We can take it."

She lifted her chin, and their eyes met. A blaze of heat ran through her body. "So you're saying you want to get hurt?"

"No. But I think if you shut us out it will hurt more."

"But—"

His lips took hers, cutting off her words, turning the banked flames in her body into an inferno. Even thinking of Ferrin somewhere outside did nothing to cool the raging desire taking hold of her.

Together they fell against the wall, their mouths devouring each other. Her hands dove under his shirt collar, desperate for the feel of his smooth skin. Nothing existed but their need, their lust turning into a blue-white blaze around them. He slid his palms down her back, over her bottom, lifting her in his strong arms so she could wrap her legs around him and feel the ridge of his erection press against her pussy.

Her already swollen breasts ached for his touch. She hooked her arms tightly around his neck and strained against him, urging him to lift her shirt and stroke them, stroke her. He felt so good. She wanted him inside her, wanted to feel their bodies and energies join. She wanted his calm to overtake her and lose herself in the soothing ocean of his power even as her pulse raced.

"Aleeza," he whispered against her lips. His hips rocked forward, pinning her to the wall. She cried out in pleasure.

Bracing her against the cool stone behind her, he reached down to fumble with his jeans. She tightened her thighs on his hips, helping to keep herself up while he pulled the zipper down as far as he could.

Without breaking their kiss, he pulled away enough to set her feet back on the floor. Together they tore at her jeans, at his, tugging them down. She couldn't get her shoes off fast enough, and her jeans caught on them, leaving her barely able to stand.

"What the hell is this? I leave you alone for two minutes and this is how you decide to occupy your time?"

Ferrin's voice was like a swift slap on her ass. It surprised her, scared her, but only heightened the desire pulsing in her veins. She looked up at him, his face filling her vision. That dark hair, those perfect lips. Without even thinking, she reached out to him.

"Ferrin…Ferrin come on."

He didn't move, watching while Dorand stood gasping next to her, his cock pressing into her thigh, his hands still clasping her waist.

She pulled away, finally tugging her foot free so she could walk. She was naked from the waist down, and she didn't care. In fact she was pleased. She wanted Ferrin to see how badly she wanted him, cared for him. Maybe after this she would have to leave them both. But perhaps she could heal their fracturing relationship before she did.

His gaze threatened to swallow her whole. She could fall into it, into his eyes, and live so happily. She *would* be happy if he would touch her and be hers. Forever. She needed him so much. She just didn't want her need to be the ruin of a long friendship.

After all, it was partly her need—her need and her decision to break the celibacy spell—that was causing all of this, wasn't it?

Ferrin's hands hesitated before touching her. "I don't want to be your mascot," he said.

"You won't be." It was Dorand who spoke, not her.

"Please, Ferrin," she whispered. This time she couldn't fight the tears. "Please."

His kiss, like everything about him, was so different from Dorand's, but just like Dorand's it made her want to scream in delight. His fingers clenched her arms so tightly she knew she would bruise, and she didn't care. It felt good. It felt right when he bruised her, when he yanked her forward so her breasts crushed against his chest.

He kissed her so hard she could barely breathe, and she didn't care. He wouldn't let her die. He would protect her always, and when their time came and their children were born…

The children, there was that thought again. She'd never wanted children—her childhood in Mona's house had assured that. So why this horrible compulsion to make babies every time she touched Ferrin, every time that green-gold magic began to glow between them?

As if on cue, their auras collided and exploded around them like fireworks, green sparks raining down over their heads.

"What? What is that?" Aleeza pulled away from Ferrin, wincing at the noise.

Something was screaming, shrieking, its echoes in the almost-empty room deafening. Ferrin took his hands off her arms to cover his ears while she did the same.

"It's an alarm!" Dorand shouted, He grabbed her clothes and threw them at her. "What the hell—"

The overhead lights started flashing, lending a further air of unreality to the scene. Aleeza took her hand off her ears and tugged her jeans up as quickly as she could while Dorand did the same. Something was about to happen—she sensed it intuitively, and she wanted to be ready. Her bag was on the floor in the corner. The club was gone, but she might have a blade of some kind. Maybe she should smash one of the cases and take a demon weapon?

No, that probably wasn't a good idea, but there had to be something. Any minute that door would open, and they were only three witches against…what?

They all tensed as the door handle turned, looking jerky and terrifying in the strobe light effect. Aleeza grabbed for their hands, needing their strength. Together they could make trouble for an army of witches. And they would.

The door opened. She felt Ferrin and Dorand get ready to leap forward and meet their adversary.

Walter stepped into the room, holding some kind of remote. He pressed it. The lights steadied and the siren stopped.

"So," he said, looking at Ferrin who still glowed slightly green with that gold light dancing in his eyes. "I wondered what you were."

* * * * *

"The Pandorians were never completely gone. There are several clutches of them, some off the coast of Greece, a few near the Taiwanese islands, and one of the largest settlements six miles west of the Savior City harbor. They own an island out there, run eco-tours and the like," Walter said, muting the small television in the corner when the program once again went to commercial.

Dorand could see the frustration clearly etched on both Ferrin and Aleeza's faces. They'd activated a several-hundred-year-old demon alarm when their auras had touched, but Walter had still insisted on watching his show while he explained how the hell such a thing could have happened. Dorand would have been frustrated as well, but he knew it wouldn't do any good. Walter had an addiction, plain and simple. He needed his reality TV fix, and nothing was going to keep him from it short of the world catching fire and burning the building down around him.

"Then why does everyone assume they're extinct?" Aleeza asked, shifting on the couch beside him.

She was sipping the White Russian Walter had made for her and munching on green olives and cherries, the only food Walter had, coming from his fully stocked bar. Just watching her eat was an extremely sensual experience, and Dorand had to fight to keep his cock from thickening. He'd never been so wildly attracted to a woman. It would have been disturbing if holding her in his arms didn't feel so amazingly right. He knew it would be the same the next time they were in bed together. That sense of connection, of completion, would transform fucking into lovemaking.

Lovemaking. He was falling in love with her. The knowledge hit him hard, and for some reason made his eyes jump to where Ferrin sat on the edge of the chair he'd pulled up next to Walter's. But Ferrin wasn't looking at him. He was watching Aleeza slip a cherry into her mouth with complete absorption.

"Because they want people to think that. More importantly, they want the demons to think that. The Pandorians were victims of demonic possession for thousands of years. They couldn't fight them off."

"But I thought they were one of the impish covens? Doesn't that mean they could magic-fast with demons?" Aleeza asked.

"That's a bit of mythology. Only a Gunera or a Daiesthai has the power to magic-fast with a demon and form a symbiotic relationship. The witch gets power and longevity while the demon gets to experience the world as mortal flesh."

Ferrin and Aleeza shared a look then that made Dorand suspicious. Why hadn't they told him about this?

"The Pandorians, on the other hand, would simply get taken over. They wouldn't have to enter willingly into a contract with a demon. Their souls would just get kicked right out of their bodies. Even if they managed to maintain soul-body connection, the demons would be able manipulate them more than they would another, stronger-magicked witch. So they went underground a few thousand years ago and only a handful of demon-slayers know of their existence. They need to stay in contact with us, for those times when a demon does manage to sniff them out."

"You're a demon slayer?" Ferrin's tone was respectful, but Dorand could hear the disbelief under his words. It was true Walter didn't look like he could slay much of anything, but he was one of the most powerful supernaturals Dorand had ever known.

"Most demonologists are. We're the only people who can deal with the prolonged exposure to all these relics and not lose our minds."

"So the Pandorians exist but have been in the demon-possession protection program," Aleeza said, earning a short bark of a laugh from Walter. "Forgive me, but I don't see what this has to do with Ferrin and me setting off the alarm."

"You're a very impatient woman." Walter smiled as he said the words and Aleeza smiled back.

"Very impatient, especially when I've got a crime to solve and a demon trying to worm its way into my head."

"You're sure it's a demon, not the witch who's fasted with the demon?" Walter asked the question as if he already knew the answer.

"Um…yes."

"Because…" Walter prompted.

"Because it wants Ferrin and me to have a child, another generation for whatever spell it wants to work. If it was another witch, he or she would want to be part of the equation, wouldn't they? Either the impregnator or the impregnatee?"

"Not necessarily. If your witch is a Daiesthai woman, she might not be able to conceive. They're supposed to have fertility problems. She would need a Gunera or a Pandorian woman to carry the child. The only imperative is a Daeisthai male, or a Pandorian male whose soul had been completely possessed by the demon host. Or, in rare occasions, there were tales of Gunera men being able to impregnate Gunera women with a Daiesthai baby, but there was some complication. I believe that's the reason for the Gunera curse in the first place—something was wrong with their offspring. But I could be— Wait a second, we're back. Hold that thought until the next commercial." Walter hit the mute button again, and the theme music for *Celebrities Behaving Badly* filled the room.

"I'm sorry, Walter, but we can't wait." Aleeza stood and crossed the room to hit the power button on the television. She then stood in front of it, as if to block the signal if Walter decided to use his remote to bring the set back to life. "Three people have been killed and there's a demon strong enough to violate the protection spells on this building on the loose. It was talking in my head in the Armory, and from what Dorand told us, that shouldn't be able to happen."

"The protection spell is on the building, not on the people inside the building," Walter corrected, looking more than a little irritated.

"Please, Walter, I'm begging you. We need to know why we set off that alarm, and we need to know now, not at the next commercial break. Lives are at stake." Aleeza ran a hand through her long, dark hair and flashed wide, liquid brown eyes at Walter. Dorand watched Walter soften as he met those eyes and began to wonder if Aleeza had this effect on all men.

"Dorand's brother isn't Amiantos," Walter said, setting down the remote with a sigh and turning his attention fully to his guests. It was a minor miracle that Dorand knew neither Aleeza or Ferrin could fully appreciate.

"We know that. I was taken into the coven when I was a few months old."

"Ferrin was found in our woods. Someone had tried to use him in a spell as a sacrifice, but his adoptive mother found him before he died of exposure. He was adopted officially into the coven when his power showed signs of being Amiantos," Dorand explained.

"He's no Amiantos," Walter said with a laugh.

"I know I'm not, but I can work their magic like one of them. Better than most of them even." Ferrin's voice was calm and even, just stating the facts. Dorand was glad to hear it. Whatever insecurities had been plaguing him of late, they hadn't affected his confidence in his magic.

"Of course you can. Daiesthai can mimic the magic of any coven—that's why they're so dangerous. They can also assimilate the power of witches."

"So can Amiantos," Dorand said.

"No, Amiantos magic meld, give or receive, but at the end of the day there's only so much they can get from another witch. The rest they have to ground or release. Now Daeisthai can actually increase their power by absorbing the magic of the witches they kill, drink it up as the other soul leaves the body. They were notorious for slaying hundreds of other supers in their heyday. Killing until they had the strength of tens or even hundreds of individual witches. Take a witch with that kind of power, fast them with a demon, and you've got a recipe for serious mayhem."

"That's the second time you've mentioned the Daiesthai. So I'm assuming they're not extinct either?" Aleeza asked.

"See, now there's the interesting part. I thought they were until I met your friend here. I couldn't read his magic when he shook my hand. It was different, but I couldn't place it. It wasn't until you set off the alarm that it made sense. The color of your auras together confirms it. You're a workable, fertile Daeisthai union. We know you're Gunera, so that means Ferrin had to be either Pandorian or Daeisthai."

"So why do you say Daeisthai? Couldn't I be Pandorian? Or even Gunera?" Ferrin asked.

"You're not Gunera. They can't mimic others' power to the extent you do. And no to the Pandorian too. That wouldn't work unless you were completely demon possessed. That's the only way you'd be fertile for a Daeisthai union."

"He has been acting strangely," Dorand said, wanting to do something to wipe away the shame on Ferrin's face. His brother had been a pain in the ass lately, but he was still his brother and their fates were bound together whether either of them liked it at the moment or not.

"Demon-influenced and demon-possessed, two totally different things. I'd know if he were possessed and so would you. Besides, I don't think the influence is pure demon. There's a witch involved, a female witch I'm betting. It's the only way to make sense of the runes."

"You managed to read them? What did you find out?" Aleeza asked, her face changing subtly as she slipped into work mode.

She was doing her damnedest to find Carantha's killer, but somehow in the process she'd become a part of whatever black magic was behind the killings. It made Dorand's chest ache. He'd already lost one woman to this evil, and now another was in danger, a woman he knew could mean more to him than even Carantha ever had. He wanted to protect her, to do whatever it took to put her beyond the reach of this darkness, but that wasn't within his power. She'd been a part of this even before she'd freed herself from the Gunera curse, was as mixed up in all of it as he and Ferrin.

Whether fate or something more sinister had brought them together, they were all bound to each other until they stopped this evil from achieving its goals. After that…well there would be time to think of what they might be to each other in the future if they survived the present.

"The runes are an ancient demonic spell of transformation, probably originally intended to draw forth a demon from the ether into solid form."

"But they can't do that, can they? Isn't that why they have to magic-fast with a witch in the first place, because that's the only way for them to experience a physical form?" Dorand asked.

He'd always been fascinated by demonology. That was how he'd met Walter in the first place. Dorand had been curious to find out why the Amiantos were the only coven to survive the ages without any demonic history. Even the non-impish covens, those that couldn't magic-fast with a demon, had traces of demon, were still "defiled" in the eyes of the Amiantos elders. Dorand had never found the answers he sought, but he had made a powerful friend in Walter, a friend he was more than grateful to have now that people he loved were falling victim to demon magic.

"That's true now, but it wasn't a few thousand years ago when the demons who carried the weapons in the armory walked the earth. The spell would be useless to a modern-day demon, but a witch could still use it for a transformation spell if she was magic-fasted to a demon."

"You keep saying 'she'. Why?" Aleeza asked.

"The rune written on top of the ancient rune is sexual in nature, a yin to yang spell of transformation if I'm guessing correctly. There could be other explanations, but reading the three runes in order of the killings, that seems to be the best bet for what this witch is up to. And it would make sense if she really is a Daiesthai female. She wouldn't be able to create the next generation as a woman, but she might be able to swing it if she could change herself into a male."

"You're kidding. That's not even possible is it?" Ferrin asked. Not even magic could fuck with biology so seriously, at least none that Dorand had ever heard of either.

"I don't know. Maybe. At least this witch and her demon thought there was a good enough chance of it working to kill a few witches to work the magic." Walter said the words with a casual shrug, and Dorand tried to ignore his attitude. One of those witches had been his lover, his friend, his clan mate. But sensitivity had never been Walter's strong point.

"So why is the demon or witch after Ferrin? If she plans to become a man, wouldn't she just be after Aleeza, or another Gunera woman who could carry the baby?" Dorand asked.

"She didn't know about Ferrin." Aleeza chewed her bottom lip and began to pace the tiny corner where Walter had set up his bar and television lounge area. "He had to have been a surprise the night that I broke the curse. That's when Ferrin and I started hearing the voice, but I'd been having dreams before that. Shit! The hex portal under my bed, gods, I'm an idiot. It all makes sense now."

"What makes sense? You've lost me." Walter leaned forward, elbows on his knees, eager to catch up on the missed information, testimony to the fact that really smart people aren't at all shy about admitting when they don't have a clue.

"I'd been having graphic sexual dreams for months, but they got worse and worse after each of the Fire Festivals."

"As our witch got more power from killing the other witches. She *has* to be Daiesthai," Walter said with a grin, obviously excited by the news for some strange reason.

"She or her demon was attacking me in my sleep, driving me nuts until I—"

"Got frustrated enough to break the curse, making you able to conceive a Daiesthai child. She's trying to rebuild the coven." Ferrin finished her thought and made a move as if he would reach out and take her hand but stopped himself.

Aleeza stopped short. "And I played right into her hands. Oh goddess, this is all my fault."

She looked so lonely standing there Dorand had to grip the seat of his chair to keep from going to her, holding her. If Ferrin hadn't been sitting, tense and pale, at the other end of the table, he would have done so instantly. But why rub it in?

Dorand could touch her, make love to her for the rest of their lives in perfect safety. Whereas Ferrin…could never do so again. Not unless they wanted to attract demonic attention.

"What happens if we catch the demon and the witch? If we stop all of this?" He knew Aleeza and Ferrin both wanted to ask the question but were afraid to. Trouble was, he knew the answer they hoped for and the answer he hoped for were different. He felt like a jerk, but he couldn't help it. If Ferrin and Aleeza could never touch, never be together, that left the door wide open for him.

Walter shrugged. "I don't know. It would put a stop to this spell and hopefully save some lives, but I don't know what happens if a Gunera and Daeisthai mate without demon fasting. You'd need to ask someone schooled in reproductive magic. I know of one woman, probably the only one who'd be able to help. If there's something about reproductive magic or Gunera history she doesn't know, it's not a fact anyway…hold on…" He crossed the room and started digging around in a giant Rolodex.

"Never mind," Aleeza said. Her voice was hoarse, and Dorand caught Ferrin staring at her in confusion, a confusion he felt as well. Why wouldn't Aleeza want to solve this problem?

"No, it will only take a minute," Walter said.

"No, really. Never mind."

"Here it is." Walter beamed as he lifted the little white card. "Mona Perkins. She's Gunera too, and — what?"

Dorand cleared his throat in the silence. "Mona Perkins? Any relation, Aleeza?"

She nodded and licked her lips. "My mother."

164

Chapter Twelve

ॐ

"She's going to want to help you," Dorand said for the fiftieth time that evening. They sat in Aleeza's kitchen at the small, cracked-topped table, the remains of takeout Chinese spread before them.

"Sure. She'll be thrilled to help when she finds out her only daughter lied to her, robbed a grave and performed seriously gray magic in order to get herself laid. She'll be even happier to help when she finds out there's demon shit involved in all of this. But I'm sure her unconditional love for me will shine through, and she'll be delighted to do what she can."

"She's still your mother."

"She won't be after this, I bet." Feeling like her skin was about to crawl off her body, Aleeza stood and started picking up empty cartons with shaking hands. Not only had she lied to Mona to get the Queen Elizabeth root, she'd lied to her this morning—goddess, was that just this morning?—about doing the anti-celibacy spell. Mona would kill her. No, first she would scream and yell and probably set fire to Aleeza's pictures. Then she would kill her.

Why this brought tears to her eyes, she didn't know. But she'd almost rather be possessed by a demon than admit to Mona what she'd done. Not to mention having to drag two men with her and tell Mona she'd already had sex with both of them.

Several times. In a day and a half.

She could feel their eyes on her as she tidied up. Neither of them offered to help—typical men—but then, she didn't want them to and maybe they sensed that. She didn't even want to look them in the eyes, much less have to feel their broad, warm bodies bumping against hers in the tiny kitchen as they moved.

Just that thought was enough to make her flush. What she needed most right now was oblivion, the chance to lose herself even for a few minutes in the ballet of their bodies merging.

And it was the one thing she couldn't have. She and Ferrin shouldn't even think about making love again until they knew what the potential consequences were. And she didn't dare bring Dorand into her bed while Ferrin sat alone outside the bedroom. She couldn't do that to him. She cared about him — she loved him too much to hurt him like that.

She loved them both. She had to admit that much to herself, no matter how crazy it might seem.

Aleeza flung the last paper plate into the trash and pressed her face into her hands. Her head pounded. All she wanted to do was go back, go back to the night before and stop herself, to erase everything —

No she didn't. Despite wishing she didn't have these problems, she couldn't, not even for a second, wish she'd never met Dorand or Ferrin. Couldn't wish she was still a virgin, couldn't wish she'd never experienced the bliss they'd given her. Which made her a selfish shit of the highest order. A wave of self-loathing rolled over her, mingling with her desire and causing tears to spill down her face.

"Aleeza." Dorand's hands were warm and solid on her arms. His breath stirred her hair. "Don't worry, Aleeza. It will be okay."

She sniffled, wiping her eyes as surreptitiously as she could with him standing so close. "Yeah, it's going to be great. You're right."

"We'll just go over there in the morning and tell her everything. I'm sure she'll —"

"Okay." She nodded and turned around, avoiding his eyes. "Of course. Look, I'm a little tired. Long day and everything. So I'm going to go lie down. There are blankets and extra pillows in the hall closet. I'm sorry I only have one couch but you guys can flip for it or something, okay?"

"Stay out here, please—"

"The hex portal is completely neutralized, right?"

Dorand nodded. He'd checked out the entire apartment when they'd arrived and his counter spells were holding strong.

"So I'll be fine. I think I have some extra toothbrushes in medicine cabinet. Feel free to dig around."

"Aleeza." She'd been so caught up in her own misery she hadn't even noticed how pale Ferrin was, how his eyes sat in haunted shadows. "Please stay out here and talk to us."

More than anything she wanted to reach for him, to hold him. What he must be experiencing was beyond anything she could imagine. To suddenly discover you were a magic vampire of some kind, to learn you were a member of a cursed race…she wanted to be there for him. She just couldn't trust herself to touch him. Not now and maybe not ever again.

Something inside her broke, and she turned and ran into her room.

* * * * *

Not being permitted most sensual pleasures, Aleeza had turned her bedroom into a hedonistic cave. Silk sheets whispered against her skin as she slid between them naked. They hadn't compensated for the lack of a man's touch over the years, but they'd helped her feel good, sexy. She lit the candles on the bedside table—much better than a nightlight, especially when she spoke the words that would keep them burning safely while she slept—and buried her face in the pile of soft pillows.

She had a feeling one of the men would come in here soon enough. She just wasn't sure which one it would be. Or which one she wanted it to be.

Or if she wanted it to be both of them.

"What do you mean 'if'. Of course you want them both." Aleeza spoke the words aloud, finding some peace in finally admitting that truth to herself.

Even if she had wanted one man over the other, she couldn't choose just one of them. Ferrin's outburst in the museum earlier proved that. She couldn't have Dorand without breaking Ferrin's heart—and her own. She couldn't have Ferrin without losing Dorand. Not to mention whatever consequences she and Ferrin would face due to their ancestry. In her mind she pictured those two beautiful children, children who could never be allowed to exist. It suddenly didn't matter that she'd never wanted to have kids. She'd seen the little boy, felt the baby nursing at her breast and known the profound connection she supposed was what "mother love" was all about. To realize they would never be born was enough to bring the tears.

She rolled over and turned the stereo on with a wave of her hand. She liked soft music in bed, classical and baroque. She never listened to such music anywhere else, but here in her sensual cave it felt right. She turned it up. She didn't want the men to hear her crying.

The music rolled through her head. The tears poured down her face. She huddled under the covers, more lost and alone than she'd been before all of this started. Not to have something was bad enough. To have it so close yet be unable to grasp it was worse. And to know that her yearning had been manipulated by a murderer left her feeling tainted, weak and ashamed.

The hand on her shoulder made her jump, but not far. She knew it was Ferrin before she even turned around, so familiar was the feel of his skin, his energy.

She turned the music down enough to hear him.

"I need you to talk to me," he said, beautiful in the candlelight. His skin glowed, his eyes only a sparkle of reflected light in the depths of his face. "I know we can't do anything. I know I shouldn't even be touching you, but you have to talk to me. Don't leave me alone like this."

Aleeza took a deep breath. "It hurts to talk to you."

He nodded. "But it helps too."

"Where's Dorand?"

"In the living room. He says if he senses anything, he's coming in. But he told me to come talk to you."

"I don't know why." She adjusted the pillows so she could sit up, holding the sheet in front of her breasts. Already her nipples were hard. If Ferrin saw that, the fight would be over. Neither of them was strong enough.

Ferrin sat on the edge of her bed, careful not to touch her even through the sheets. "I think he figures we have some things to work out between ourselves, stuff we might not feel comfortable talking about in front of him."

"Like the voice. And how good it feels to hear it."

"Yeah."

"Like the kids in the vision, the baby…"

"How it feels like they've died." He swallowed hard, looking as tortured as she felt.

They stared at each other for another minute. Aleeza's body hummed with tension. Desire, shared grief, love…it all muddled together in her head, in her heart until she was fisting the sheet in her hands in an effort not to reach for him.

"Maybe this wasn't such a good idea," he said.

She shook her head. Her throat was too dry to speak.

Whether he moved first or she did, she couldn't be certain. All she knew was that one minute they were staring at each other, not touching, and the next she was in his arms, the sheet tangled beneath them as their lips joined with enough force to shatter her soul.

Together they crashed across the bed. Ferrin's hands tangled in her hair, pressing her face to his. Their teeth ground together through their lips. She tasted blood and something inside her roared. But for once, that something was all Aleeza. The spells Dorand had cast to protect her apartment seemed to be working. There was no "other" voice in her head, nothing but her own pure, consuming desire for the man in her arms.

Over the softly playing music, she heard the tortured gasps of their breath, the tearing of his shirt as she fumbled with the buttons and he took the quicker route and ripped it from his body. His bare chest against hers felt wonderful. His bare cock against her pussy would feel even better. She started tugging at his jeans.

Without breaking the kiss he helped, yanking them down and kicking them off his feet. She hadn't had this with him before, the snuggled intimacy of a dim room, the softness of a bed. Part of her had wondered if she could ever be as aroused as she'd been pressed against that rock, against the hard earth. Now she knew that had been a groundless fear. They could be locked in a closet, they could be in a dusty attic or they could be in a grand suite in a beachfront hotel. It didn't matter because there was nothing in the room but Ferrin.

She slid her hand down his muscular body to find his cock, rigid and swollen in its nest of soft dark hair. He gasped into her mouth when she touched it, closed her hand around it. Already his hips pumped forward and a drop of liquid told her just how ready he was.

Their energy swirled around them, glowing in the darkness, making the moment even more intimate. Their passion created its own veil to shield them, to protect them from whatever might happen. How could anything bad happen, when they felt this way, when their bodies fit together so perfectly? She spread her legs, settling him between them so the smooth skin of his cock pressed against her clit. Sparks flew through her body.

She lifted her hips, begging him to enter, but before he could something stopped him.

Something tall and blond, glowing white in the gloom.

Aleeza's lips fell open and she stared in wonder. There was no other response possible when Dorand looked the way he did just now. He stood naked at the side of the bed, every chiseled, perfect muscle in his chest and stomach standing out in sharp relief. He looked carved of pure moonlight, and her pussy spasmed at the sight.

"You can't do this without me," he said, and something in his voice told her he didn't just want them to be safe. He wanted to be a part of this, wanted them to want him there for himself and not his powers.

She'd never imagined herself as part of a triumvirate. It had never been possible for her or any Gunera that she knew of. But more than that, the idea had never made her entirely comfortable. She'd always thought a three-way meeting of magic was the sort of thing people planned carefully. Surely a hell of a lot more time needed to be spent talking and organizing something like this. They weren't average people—they were supers, and the interaction of their power could have consequences outside the bedroom.

And then there was the Carantha question. Aleeza knew now that she wasn't being haunted by her spirit, but that didn't mean her men weren't haunted by their lover's memory. Maybe all they were looking for was a way to fill the void left in their lives. Maybe Aleeza herself wasn't as special to them as she wanted to believe.

But right now, she knew she had no time for deliberation. Whether they wanted her or just another third to replace Carantha, she couldn't bring herself to care when her body hovered so close to pure bliss.

Ferrin watched her, his body poised just above hers. She could feel how badly he wanted to simply thrust into her, taking the decision away and sending Dorand back into the cold.

But he didn't, wouldn't. He would allow her to invite Dorand in. Maybe he even wanted it. She knew she did.

She held out her hand.

The colors around them changed when Dorand climbed onto the bed, his cock heavy and hard. Some of the green-gold faded, brightened, absorbed by Dorand's white. Her own bright blue aura even shone through for a few moments. She noted it but was too nervous to care.

She saw the two men exchange glances, then Ferrin slid down, tugging her with him to the edge of the bed while Dorand ran warm hands up her arms to pin her wrists against the sheets. She tensed. How did they know what to do? Had they planned this? Or were they simply in sync from years of bedding one woman together? Or maybe —

Ferrin spread her legs and pressed his tongue against her clit, and she stopped caring.

Her cries were just barely audible over the music, but they echoed in her head. Ferrin rested her heels on his shoulders, circling his arms around so he could grip the tops of her thighs while his tongue swirled and teased, dipping inside her, feathering over her soft, wet skin.

Another tongue found her right nipple, flicking gently over the hard peak. She rolled sideways slightly, pressing her breast farther into Dorand's mouth. He took it eagerly, his breath hot as he sucked her in, sending pleasure shooting down to her pussy.

She tried to reach for his cock, but he kept her wrists help tightly in his hands. "Let us do this," he said, a request as much as a command.

She was happy to obey, but they weren't going to be doing anything for much longer. Already there was enough pressure built in her pelvis to make her explode off the bed. Ferrin was wickedly talented with his tongue and seemed to know exactly where to touch lightly, where to press harder and where to avoid altogether for fear of triggering her release. She knew he was trying to prolong this for her but she didn't think it would do any good.

She'd expected this to be awkward, expected to feel like an exhibit, but she didn't. All she felt was the overwhelming pleasure they gave her, their caring and attention as Dorand took his mouth from her breasts and kissed her.

The kiss had the same passion she'd shared with Ferrin, just a different flavor. Ferrin's energy was a glass of red wine. Dorand's the high you got after a long run. Both were intoxicating, both sensations she knew she would crave for the rest of her life.

Dorand slipped his tongue past her lips, setting her alight with white fire, pure and clean and smelling of the forest. The connection between them flared, the light in the room changed, and as Dorand's tongue delved into her mouth, Aleeza came with a deep, shaking intensity that made her scream.

Still Ferrin did not stop. He increased his rhythm, hitting her where she was sore and overly sensitive. It was too much, more electricity than her nerves could handle. She tried to move but he and Dorand held her fast.

She squirmed beneath them while Dorand kissed her, caressed her, swallowed her moans into the heat of his mouth. Within moments, pain gave way to pleasure and she could feel the pressure within her building again, swelling to a magnitude she wouldn't have believed possible.

Ferrin chose that moment to thrust his finger into her, and she screamed. Her body arched off the bed so high she thought she might actually fly if the two men didn't keep her in place. She came so hard it hurt and healed at the same time. Her pussy clamped down on the fingers Ferrin worked inside her with a vengeance. The sensation was beyond amazing, but it still wasn't enough.

"Fuck me, please. Somebody fuck me." The words were barely out of Aleeza's mouth before Ferrin lifted her hips off the bed. Dorand grasped her behind the knees and helped her roll back, legs over her head until her knees hit the mattress. It was a move that would have made her karate master proud, though she doubted Sensei had ever intended the defensive back roll as a bedroom maneuver.

Aleeza immediately came onto all fours, flipping her hair out of her face to watch Ferrin at the end of the bed. He stood inches away from the mattress, his cock thick and swollen, leaking fluid that she couldn't wait to taste. As Dorand came to his knees behind her, she motioned for Ferrin to join them.

"Oh gods, yes." She cried out as Dorand slid into her with one long, swift stroke. Then she parted her lips and took Ferrin inside her mouth with the same eagerness.

He was too long for her to take him all, but she tilted her head back and took as much as she could, relaxing her throat and letting Dorand's thrusts push her forward, taking Ferrin deeper and deeper. Eventually he hit a place inside her that made her want to gag, but her profound desire to give him pleasure helped her fight the urge, working through the momentary discomfort.

Soon they were moving as one, three pieces of a puzzle that fit together perfectly. Ferrin's hands were on her shoulders, his cock in her mouth. Dorand's fingers dug into the flesh of her hips while he thrust into her slick heat, faster, deeper. Their rhythm built swiftly, each of them urged onward by the moans that filled the room, the slap of skin upon skin, the suckling sounds as cocks disappeared into hot, wet places and emerged glistening.

And as their passion rose, so did their power. Behind her closed lids, Aleeza could see fireworks of green and blue and gold, accents on a field of white that shone more brilliantly than anything she'd ever known.

"By the gods, please." Dorand cried out behind her and began to thrust even faster, harder, ramming into her body. Ferrin did the same, fucking her mouth until she could hardly breathe, until a metallic taste rose in her throat and she did gag.

Still she didn't stop. She wanted to stay here forever, caught between two elemental forces, fire and water, two great powers that might very well destroy her. But it would be a sweet destruction, of that she had no doubt.

"Come, Aleeza, please baby, come for us." Dorand's fingers moved to work her clit, but still release hovered out of her reach. Then he slid a thumb deep into her ass, and it was as if that was the thing all of them had been waiting for.

She came, groaning around Ferrin's cock, struggling not to bite down on the delicate flesh between her lips. Seconds later, Dorand spilled himself inside her pussy, and Ferrin jerked between her lips. The salty, musky taste of Ferrin's come hit the back of her throat and she swallowed greedily, wanting that piece of him inside her. Both men continued to thrust slowly, gently until finally they all grew still, the sound of their heavy breath once again the only sound in the room, save the music.

"Holy shit." Ferrin was the first to speak, the awe in his voice making Aleeza open her eyes and let his softened member slide from between her lips.

But he wasn't looking at her or Dorand. His eyes were fixed on something else.

"Careful, don't move too quickly. Just in case." Dorand sounded almost frightened, and Aleeza turned to look at him over her shoulder.

That's when she saw it…and almost screamed. But somehow, she knew that would be a bad thing, a very bad thing. The flame flared at the same time the anxiety within her flared. The damn thing was already four feet tall. If it grew much larger, it would scorch her ceiling.

"Goddess…what did we do?" She swallowed hard as Dorand pulled out and gently positioned himself between her and the massive flame her tiny little candle had become.

"What did you do is more like it," he said. "I tried to ground the power, but I couldn't. You were in control once our three magics joined together."

"But I didn't try to do that. I didn't think about fire…at least I don't think I did." God, what had she been thinking? There had been something…something about the two men being elemental forces.

"What's that sound?" Ferrin asked, moving toward the door to the bathroom. Even before his hand touched the knob, Aleeza knew what he would find there.

"No, wait! Ferrin, I—"

She was too late. Ferrin had already opened the door, letting out a rush of water that drenched him nearly to the waist and quickly spread out into the room. In seconds the entire bedroom was standing in three feet of water, the bed an island in the center of it.

"My landlord is going to kill me," Aleeza muttered, still in shock that a tiny thought about fire and water could have caused all this.

"At least we don't have to worry about the fire." Dorand kicked her nightstand over, and the giant flame fell down into the water below, quickly dying out.

"Shit! What am I going to do? This is bad, guys, very bad," Aleeza slid her feet to the floor and began wading through the water toward her dresser drawers, unplugging the stereo as she went—the electrical outlets were above the waterline at the moment, but no sense taking chances. She had to get some clothes on and go tell Mr. Fiorelli that she'd accidentally left her bathwater running or…something. She'd think of an excuse on the way.

"Where are you going?" Dorand asked as she pulled a black camisole out of her underwear drawer and threw it on.

"I have to go downstairs and let my landlord know what happened. I've been renting here forever, so maybe he'll cut me—"

"Wait, don't go yet." Ferrin waded through the water to the window and threw it open. A rush of cold air swept in the room and made her shiver. "Walter said my people can mimic other magic, right?"

"Right." Dorand looked suspicious, and Aleeza couldn't say she blamed him. Ferrin had a smile on his face that wasn't entirely nice. But then, when was Ferrin entirely nice? It was part of his charm.

"Then let me try something really quick. Aleeza get back on the bed with Dorand."

"Ferrin, I'm not sure about this, I mean—"

"Trust me, I'm not trying anything dangerous." Ferrin leaned down, put both hands in the water, and started to chant softly under his breath. Aleeza crossed quickly to the bed and climbed up, moving into Dorand's arms without a second thought. It felt good to touch him, to touch them both. More than good really, it felt…necessary somehow.

Ferrin's hands began to glow a pale, robin's egg blue and then pink and then blue again. Finally the light shone lavender and grew bright and strong. Ferrin continued to chant, moving his hands back and forth through the water. Slowly, white mist began to form above the water. It grew thicker and thicker as Ferrin continued to cast, and eventually began to leak out the window into the cold night.

The water level in the room sank until, finally, all that remained was a slight dampness on the hardwood floor. The planks still might buckle a bit, but that was infinitely preferable to the major water damage that had looked unavoidable.

"Sambucus magic?" Dorand asked, laughing as he hugged her more tightly to his side.

"Yeah." Ferrin smiled, but his astonishment was clear on his face. "I can't believe it worked, but I just thought of the color of their aura when they cast and spoke that mutation spell Cato uses."

"Which one?"

"The grape juice to wine one, but I substituted water to vapor."

"That's amazing. Do you think the same thing would work—"

"I'm sorry to interrupt this little chat on magic theory, but would you guys mind if we talked about what the hell happened here? You know, why we ended up with three feet of water on the floor and the huge fire in the first place?" Aleeza tried to pull out of the circle of Dorand's arms but he held her tight.

"I can think of a better idea. Why don't we help you practice grounding a little less destructively?" His hand moved down her back and then farther down, over the curve of her bare bottom and down between her legs, slipping fingers into where she was still swollen and wet.

"Practice?" Aleeza asked, though she already had a pretty good idea what Dorand had in mind if his rapidly recovering erection was any clue.

"Yes, I think some practice is definitely in order." Ferrin gave her a look that made her nipples tighten of their own accord and strode toward the bed. His cock wasn't recovering as quickly as Dorand's, but for some reason the sight of him, halfway between arousal and rest, was extremely erotic. She wanted to take him in her mouth again, just like that, and feel him grow thicker, longer, between her lips.

"Okay, let's practice." Aleeza pulled her tank top over her head and threw it to the floor. "Sleep is overrated anyway."

She giggled as both men tackled her at once and they rolled across the bed in a pile of arms and legs. Laughter soon gave way to moans and soft cries of pleasure, and Aleeza knew it was going to be a very long night.

Or maybe not nearly long enough.

Chapter Thirteen

ɞ

"Reglanus! I know you're there I can feel you on my skin. Show yourself!" Kali paced the floor in her three-inch heels, the sharp click of metal on wood accentuating each furious step.

He'd lied to her! Lied! She'd been prepared to risk her life, her beauty, her newfound power, all for him, for their cause, and he'd lied!

Did you expect anything else from a demon, my love?

"When that demon is mine in magic-fast, yes. I did, and I still do. I don't care if this man really is Daeisthai, I'll kill him. And then you'll have no choice but to honor our agreement." Kali glared at the thick mist floating above her couch. She'd seen Reglanus take more concrete form, even fucked him when his skeletal face and wickedly curved cock were in plain view. The fact that he was hiding himself now, made her even more worried. He knew she feared his demon form on some level, even though it excited her. By not revealing that form, he was getting as close as a demon got to sweet-talking her.

She didn't want to be sweet-talked. She wanted what she'd been promised.

I thought you'd be pleased, dear Kali. Now there's no need for you to risk yourself. You can stay female, stay as beautiful as you are now forever.

"And turn my chance as head of the new coven over to another? I don't think so, Reglanus. I won't let you free of our fast, and if I don't set you free, you won't be able to fast with the man and Aleeza—"

Who says we need Aleeza?

"What do you mean?" Kali walked slowly toward the mist, wishing she could see the creature's features more clearly. To her surprise, Reglanus suddenly appeared before her, more concrete than ever before.

See. Look how your power grows. You can force me from my formlessness with just a wish.

He smiled but Kali thought she heard the hint of caution in his tone. He didn't fear her, but he respected her power more now than he ever had before. Every murder she had helped commit was worth it, in exchange for that flash of respect in his black serpent's eyes.

"You want me to bear the child?"

Yes. What stronger coven could we dream of than if our third is the product of two Daeisthai parents?

"I can't conceive, Reglanus. You know that. It's why Monven turned me out, the entire reason I agreed to magic fast with you in the first place. I can't mother a child, but I might be able to father one."

You couldn't be a mother with Monven or with a witch of another coven, but with one of your own kind…

"What are you saying? Speak plainly, and no lies this time. It is breach of contract to lie to your magic-fast partner. You know that. I could condemn you back to hell and not suffer any of the consequences."

No, you could not, my love. I never lied to you. I didn't know your brother had survived until a few days past. Your mother swore she had killed the babe only months after his birth.

"My brother?" Kali felt the news hit her somewhere near where she'd once had a heart. A brother, family, what she'd longed for all those lonely years growing up in foster homes for abandoned witches, teased by her peers for being a freak without a coven, with magic that never found its true nature.

Even with Monven, after years of what she'd thought was a happy and productive magical union, that lack of family had come to haunt her again. He'd wanted a child, someone to carry on his legacy, to benefit from his accumulated power. When she couldn't give him that child, when her lack of clear magical lineage left the doctors powerless to help her conceive, he'd turned on her. His mistress had been pregnant with his son, and Kali had been granted a divorce without alimony. Monven needed the money for his son…and his power had been strong enough to force Kali to sign the agreement he'd had drawn up against her will.

"Why didn't you ever tell me? When you came to me and told me of my heritage, why didn't you tell me about my brother?" Her voice was louder than she would have liked, but she couldn't help herself. It was either scream or cry, and she would never cry in front of Reglanus or anyone else, ever again.

Your twin was dead, or so I assumed. I didn't want to cause you pain.

"Please, spare me. You're as tender hearted as I am."

Reglanus laughed. *You're right, my love. I didn't see the point in it. A dead man can father no sons or daughters for our coven. What use is he?*

"So you want me to sleep with my brother? And try to conceive our next generation?"

Does that…trouble you?

Kali thought for a moment. "No. Not if it will work."

It will work. I'm sure of it. And then we will use our magic circle in the woods for another purpose entirely.

"And that would be?"

It is a circle of transformation, calling forth into solid form. We will use it to grow the babe in your womb, nine months' worth in a single night, the night of Samhain.

"Then we won't have to wait for the rebirthing of the coven. We can perform the spell as soon as the baby is born," Kali said, a smile upon her lips.

As soon as we can prick its finger and gain a drop of second-generation blood.

Reglanus smiled too, and his hooked cock began to swell.

"You don't expect me to fuck you after you've been such a bad boy, do you? You kept secrets from me, secrets I had to find out from my spies not your own scaly lips." Kali loosened the ties at the top of her corset and tugged it down, letting her breasts spill out the top. Reglanus' forked tongue darted out to sweep across his bottom lip and her pussy gushed. She like that forked tongue more than she would ever admit to the demon now scuttling across the floor toward her.

I expect that you will fuck me as soon as I have served my penance, my love.

Then his impossibly large hands were on her hips, forcing her to the ground, ripping away her tiny satin panties and wrenching her legs apart. Kali moaned and brought her hands to her breasts, plucking at her nipples as Reglanus went to work on her pussy.

She still didn't trust the demon, but she craved him and was willing to give his plan a chance. If she couldn't conceive, they still had Aleeza, and Reglanus, for all his trickery, couldn't break their magic fast without her permission. Kali held the power, and very soon, might also hold a babe in her stomach.

The thought made her womb ache, ache and begin to spasm as Reglanus worked his tongue deep inside her, deeper than any mortal tongue could ever reach. She came, screaming, a victorious sound.

Now she just had to find her dear brother and bring him to her. His seduction would be easy enough. She'd never met a man who could resist her, and she was sure her twin would be no different.

* * * * *

Ferrin watched Aleeza grow progressively more disturbed the closer they came to her mother's home. She was practically gnawing her bottom lip in half by the time they mounted the aging steps to what had obviously once been quite a nice bungalow but now looked to be in need of several major repairs.

"You're going to be fine." Dorand put his arm around Aleeza's shoulders and hugged her close. She melted into him, but the anxiety clear on her face didn't fade a bit.

"I'm sure she doesn't bite. Even if she does, if she looks anything like her daughter, I'll take one for the team." Ferrin laughed at Aleeza's astonished look.

"You're gross—that's my mother." She moved away from Dorand to punch him on the shoulder.

"I don't discriminate. Women can be sexy at any age. I'm sure you're going to be totally smoking at fifty." He pulled her close before they reached the door and gave her a quick, but thorough kiss that left her grinning.

"Fifty?"

"At least forty."

"Thanks. I'm sure you'll look okay yourself," she said, her eyes shining up at him. God, was he just imagining it, or did he see more than a little affection in that look? Last night had been amazing, but none of them had made any grand declarations.

Looking at her right now, however…it was all he could do not to tell her how much he loved her. How he was certain he loved her enough and wanted her badly enough for it not to matter what her mother the reproductive guru had to say.

"We should go inside. I don't think we've been followed, but after yesterday it doesn't seem smart to stay out in the open too long." Dorand's face was unreadable, but Ferrin could see the tension in his body. They had shared Aleeza last night openly, willingly, but this morning things had still been tense between them.

Ferrin couldn't help thinking that Dorand was a little too eager for this meeting. He'd been more than understanding last night, even suggesting he and Aleeza talk alone, but Ferrin sensed that a part of his brother would be more than pleased if it turned out their suspicions were correct, that Ferrin and Aleeza could never be together again without him. Their magic had worked well together as a triumvirate last night, and Aleeza and Dorand had nothing to worry about where the mingling of their magic was concerned.

But Aleeza and Ferrin were another matter entirely. He wanted to howl at the unfairness of it, the fury that threatened to overtake him when he thought of it. That he would never be truly allowed into the depths of her body again. He would be forced to make do with her hands and mouth while watching his brother get what he himself so fervently desired. One day, he might even have to watch her belly grow with Dorand's child and not his, theirs, the dream children…only the strongest will he possessed kept him sane. Kept him from striking out, from letting his blackness take over.

Even now on her mother's porch, having just stepped over magical wards intended to keep out evil, he could still feel the whisper of that "other" voice the second Aleeza was in his arms. It shivered down the back of his neck, urging him to throw his woman over his shoulder and get the hell away from Mona and whatever magic she might work upon them this day.

Aleeza was his to claim, his to bed, his to —

"Dorand's right." Ferrin stepped away from her quickly and stuffed his hands in the pockets of his coat. "We should get inside. Better get this over with."

"You heard it again, didn't you?" Aleeza asked.

He nodded, tried to smile and failed.

She lifted her hand as if to touch his face, then thought better of it and crossed her arms over her chest. She suddenly looked so small, standing there in a white fleece sweatshirt and black track pants, more a teenager than a powerful witch determined to find a killer. He wanted to protect her from her mother, from this black magic, even from himself if that's what had to be done.

"I heard it too, but not as strongly as yesterday. Maybe —"

"Are you coming inside or are you going to stand out there making out with your boyfriends all day?" The shout from inside cut Aleeza off mid-sentence and brought the anxiety rushing back to her features with a vengeance.

"I'm coming, Mona, keep your panties on," she yelled back before she squared her shoulders and set her face in what Ferrin was coming to know what her "tough girl" expression. "Come on, guys. I guess it's time to meet the folks. Or the folk, I guess. My dad ran off when I was six. Remind me later to ask you if you've ever met the bastard."

She opened the door and motioned for them to follow.

If looks could kill, Ferrin had no doubt he and Dorand both would have fallen down dead as soon as they stepped inside the little house. The air reeked of cleanser and roasting chicken, and the surfaces had the intense shine of things long allowed to be dirty, suddenly scrubbed in the face of guests.

He offered his hand to Aleeza's mother, gave her his best, most heart-melting smile. "Mrs. Perkins, it's a pleasure to meet you."

She frowned and ignored his hand. "I'm sure it is."

Dorand and Ferrin exchanged looks. Maybe Aleeza had been right.

Mona turned away, heading toward the back of the little house. "You might as well come on. I've made some tea for you."

Ferrin followed, his gaze wandering into the rooms they passed. Aleeza had grown up here. As a child she'd played here, cried here…had she run to this forbidding, sour-faced woman in front of him when she suffered the hurts every child suffered?

He couldn't imagine it.

They sat at the scratched wood kitchen table while Mona poured them tea in faded china cups. She poured herself a whiskey.

"Sorry I'm not offering it around," she said. "Medicinal. I figure I'm going to need a drink while you all explain to me how my daughter managed to break a two-thousand-year-old curse—a curse for the benefit of her and everyone else—and why she is now allowing two men who should know better to use her body like a goddamn inflatable doll."

Automatically, Ferrin and Dorand both reached for Aleeza's hands. Her skin was cold as death. Her eyes glittered.

Sometimes Ferrin wondered what it would have been like to have known his birth mother. His adopted mother had been a kind woman though old enough to be his grandmother. She'd passed when he was twelve and left a void in his life that sometimes he'd wished could have been filled by a real parent. But other times, like now as he sat at that table and watched the woman he loved being treated so cruelly, he thought maybe he was better off without one. He'd never been big on compassion himself, but he knew damn well he would treat a child of his better than the family dog. Speaking of dogs, he suddenly wanted to leap across the table and attack.

Dorand, as always, was the one who knew what to do instead. "It wasn't her fault, Mrs. Perkins. Aleeza's been cursed."

"No, you idiot Amiantos. Aleeza *was* cursed. Now she's just—"

"No." Dorand cut her off before she could say what Ferrin suspected would be another insult. "There's demon magic going on here, ma'am. Aleeza was under a demon's influence. That's why she broke the celibacy spell. She didn't have a choice."

"There's always a choice."

"Forget it, guys." Aleeza's voice broke. "I figured we'd find her in a pissy mood."

"Don't I have a right to be angry?" Mona slammed her empty glass on the countertop. "I'm your mother—don't I have the right to an opinion? I know you don't give a shit what I think. I know you didn't even come to me for help after you broke the Gunera curse despite knowing that aside from being your lousy mother, I'm an expert at reproductive spells and curses. I had to dose you up with herbs myself. Good thing I did or who knows what you might have made while you were out fucking your little boyfriends."

"That's why I came here, Mother! To ask you for help. Could you quit screaming for a fucking second?"

"That's a nice way to ask for help."

"Fine, please. Will you please help me? Do I have to be on my hands and knees? I'm your daughter for fuck's—"

"Don't you dare pull the daughter card. You don't have any respect for me as your mother—you never have. How was I ever supposed to help you? From the time you were six, you would run and hide the second you got a skinned knee. You shut everyone out, even people who love you. How could I—"

"I'm not shutting you out now, am I?" Aleeza covered her face with her hands but not before Ferrin saw the tears start to roll down her cheeks. Mona did the same a second later, her shoulders shaking quietly. The room was completely silent except for the soft sobs that came from both women.

Ferrin exchanged glances with Dorand. The two men stood up in unison.

"I think we're going to wait outside for a while," Dorand said. "May we look at your garden, Mrs. Perkins?"

Mona nodded from behind her fingers.

* * * * *

Aleeza wiped her own tears away and watched her mother cry, barely feeling the kisses both men planted on her forehead before they let themselves out the back door. She'd made Mona cry again, for the second time in two days. It was a new world's record and one she didn't want to repeat again.

She was tired of hurting, tired of making her mom hurt. No matter who had initially been right or wrong, they were both going to be fucked as long as they kept resenting each other.

"Mona," she said. "I—"

"No." Her mother lifted her face from her hands. "No, Aleeza, you listen to me. I tried to tell you yesterday. I wanted to talk to you…but I've never been able to talk to you. And…that's probably my fault." She poured herself another drink then surprised Aleeza by pouring a second and setting it on the table before she sat down. She nodded. "Drink up."

Aleeza took a cautious sip. Mona nodded.

"You know, when you were born…I was so excited. I had my boys. Now I wanted a girl. And your father, he felt the same. The way he used to smile at you." She shook her head, a ghost of a smile crossing her face. "It doesn't matter. But he spoiled you, Aleeza, and I admit I was jealous. Not of you, of him. Because you loved him so much. When you fell down, you wanted Daddy. When you woke up in the morning, you wanted Daddy. I just couldn't compete. And when things fell apart between me and him…"

"He wanted me." The words felt strange in her mouth, wrong, but she knew she was right.

Mona nodded. "He didn't want me anymore, he didn't want your brothers but he wanted you. We fought for the better part of a year. Then your magic decided the issue for us when it turned Gunera. I told him he couldn't have you. You needed to be with your own people, to learn to use your magic." She wiped her nose on her hand. "It was true…but it wasn't right. I used you to get back at him, to punish him for leaving. Most of all I punished him because you loved him best. I didn't know why I wasn't good enough…"

Tears poured down her face, down Aleeza's face too. "Mona…Mom…"

Mona shook her head. "I'm so sorry, baby. I just wanted to know you, to be close to you. But you didn't want me. You never did. Once he was gone, you just…closed off. And you never let me help you, and you never talked to me if you didn't have to, and I couldn't do anything about it but let you go. Before you started hating me more than you did already."

"I never hated you," Aleeza managed.

"I just didn't know how to talk to you. I never knew how to talk to you. But I always loved you, baby." Mona started crying in earnest, and before Aleeza knew quite how it happened she was crying too, crying in her mother's thin arms. She cried for all of the lost years, for all of the nights she'd lain awake thinking of her father and wishing he'd come back, and hadn't even noticed her mother standing just outside the room wanting to come in.

Minutes passed that felt like hours before they finally released their hold on each other. Mona poured them each another drink and gave her a watery smile. "Okay, honey," she said. "We'll talk more later."

"Yeah, we will."

"Meanwhile, let's get those men back in here and see if we can figure out what's going on." She shot Aleeza a look. "I still don't approve, you know."

"I'm sorry." She looked her mother right in the eyes. Knowing what she knew changed things, changed her feelings, but not toward Ferrin and Dorand. "But they— they're very special men. And we're powerful together."

"Amiantos don't usually work in threes. Neither do Gunera."

"Ferrin isn't Amiantos."

Mona nodded. "He didn't feel like it. What is he? Onterantu? Bizanna? You need to be careful if he's not

Amiantos, you know. There's a good reason why we're not supposed to be with anyone but the undefiled."

Aleeza took a deep breath. "He's Daiesthai."

"What?"

"He's Daiesthai."

"That's not possible." Mona's face was paler than Aleeza had ever seen it. "No, he can't be. They're all gone. They're extinct."

Aleeza shrugged. "He survived."

"By the gods." Fresh tears started in Mona's eyes. "Aleeza, you can't be with him. You can't let him touch you, you can't—" She swallowed. "You can't make love with him. Not ever again. Never. Do you understand?"

"I think we should bring the men back in now. You can tell all of us about it. That's why we're here, Mon—Mom. To find out why. There's some serious shit going on, and we need information."

"I don't think I can have him in my house. He's Daiesthai. Don't you know what that means?"

"No. That's why we're here."

"Aleeza…baby…they're why the curse was cast to begin with." Mona's eyes were so large in her face Aleeza thought her mother might be having a stroke. "The celibacy curse. When Gunera and Daiesthai mate, they make demons. Sometimes actual demons, monsters who rip their way out of their mother's wombs. Some half-breeds, not quite demon, not quite human. Those children…so many had to be killed. Little babies, killed before they took their first breath, never given a chance to live…demon babies."

"Goddess." Aleeza felt a wave of bile rush into her throat. "How do you know this?"

"There were scrolls left behind, but I've had visions as well. Midwives from ages past. They've come to me in my sleep. The horrors they've described…I can't even repeat. Even the children who look human consort with demons. They're never fully mortal and have no soul, no empathy, no compassion. They're all monsters, no matter what form the child may take on the outside. I can't let that happen to you. You can't let that happen. You have to leave him. He can't ever touch you again."

Aleeza shivered, her chest tight. All these years she'd wondered why Gunera were cursed. There was no pleasure in discovering the truth, only a cold pit in her stomach. She could almost hear the screaming women, the crying men, parents whose minds and hearts were ravaged by the innocent act of creating a child. Or what would have been an innocent act, had demons not played their part. Her flesh crawled.

A noise at the door made her turn her head. Ferrin stood there, his face white. She didn't know how long he'd been listening but it was obviously long enough.

"Ferrin…"

"He needs to wait outside," Mona said. "I'm sorry, but I can't have a monster in my house."

Aleeza snapped her head around to glare at her mother. "Mona!" Dammit, just when they'd been gaining some ground with their relationship, she had to show her nasty side.

When she turned back, Ferrin was gone.

Chapter Fourteen

The little park had seen better days, but the stiff grass still felt cool and good under his heated skin as he sank to the ground. More than anything he wished he was home, back in the forest with his family.

Maybe they weren't his blood, but they were his family nonetheless. They would never have looked at him the way Aleeza's mother had.

Not that he blamed her. She didn't know him, and he was screwing her daughter. The unhappy accident of his birth was merely icing on the cake of dislike he knew had been baking from the second she laid eyes on him.

So to keep from getting angry, he'd left. They obviously needed information from Mona. Maybe if he wasn't there, Dorand and Aleeza could get it. That was the most important thing, to stop the demon from gaining power, from achieving whatever end it desired. What Ferrin wanted, what he could never have…it was secondary. He had to remember that. Lives were at stake, maybe even his own if he couldn't force this black power back into hibernation.

From where he lay, he could just see Mona's ramshackle front porch. This was as good a place to wait as any.

Time moved slowly. Birds chirped, children laughed, cars passed. A couple of men in ill-fitting black sweatshirts ran around the perimeter of the park, jogging, watching him—

Ferrin sat up, the muscles in his arms and back tensing. The "joggers" looked exactly like the guys who'd attacked Aleeza yesterday. They'd either picked an awfully convenient place for a daily constitutional or they'd been following them. Ferrin knew which he was betting on.

He pulled himself to a crouch and waited, resting on the balls of his feet. The men had disappeared behind some bushes. When they re-emerged, he'd be ready. There was no way he would let them reach the house if that's where they were headed.

Under his breath he muttered the first words of one of his favorite attack spells. It was designed to arrest, not harm, and even though the thought of harming those men brought a cruel smile to his lips, he needed them awake and able to talk.

Something moved, a black-hooded head appearing from the hedge. He focused his power and shouted "Recanto!", the last word of the spell.

The man went down. Where was the other one?

Quickly chanting a protection spell for himself, Ferrin got up and starting edging toward his fallen enemy. He could keep the man paralyzed and still get the information he wanted.

Footsteps thundered along the grass behind him. He turned, raised his hand, opened his mouth to speak but it was too late. There were five of them, and even as Ferrin's spell hit one, the others cast at him, breaking through his magical shields, knocking him flat into swirling, silent darkness.

* * * * *

"Ooh, you're more handsome than I thought you'd be. What a pleasant surprise."

Ferrin opened his eyes to find a woman smiling at him, familiar dark eyes shining in her beautiful face. He started to sit up, but stabbing pain in his head forced him back down. "Who the hell are you?"

The woman's smile widened. "Just a friend."

"My friends don't usually…" he stopped. Had she captured him or was she his rescuer?

Captor, he guessed, since he was naked on her couch. He resisted the urge to cover himself with his hands. Let her have a good look if that's what she wanted. "Were those guys your goons?"

She dipped her head. Her smile did not waver. Something about her made Ferrin ache. Not his muscles or his skin, although certainly he'd felt better. But something inside him, a yearning. The closest feeling he'd ever had to this was when he'd watched Aleeza and known he couldn't have her.

But no, that wasn't it either. This woman felt familiar, the way Aleeza did, but Aleeza didn't make the hair on the back of his neck stand on end. There was something wrong with this women, something…dark hidden beneath her beauty.

"My name is Kali," she said. The name whispered from her lips into the room, echoing in his head. "I want to help you."

"The only help I want is help getting out of here. No, wait. You know what? I don't want any help. I can get out of here myself." He tried to sit up again, ignoring the pain. Stars swam in front of his eyes. He clenched his teeth together to keep from groaning.

Kali laughed. The sound crawled up his spine. From a table by the couch on which Ferrin lay she picked up a small, steaming cup and held it out to him. "Drink this."

"No thanks."

"It's just tea," she said. She lifted the glass and took a sip, opened her mouth a little so he could see she was indeed drinking, and swallowed. "It will make you feel better. You're probably a little dehydrated. You've been asleep for hours."

"How many hours?" He took the glass from her but did not drink, afraid of her answer.

"Fifteen or so," she said.

Shit. Dorand and Aleeza…did they think he'd stormed away angry? That he was sulking now, hiding? Why had he left them to begin with? Had he wanted to punish them, to…no…he'd only wanted to give them some privacy, wanted some of that privacy for himself. Wasn't that right? By the gods, he could hardly remember. His head ached.

He wondered where they were now. Were they angry? Were they hurt?

Were they looking for him?

And most importantly, did they give a shit where he'd gone, or had they skipped off to bed together, their sanctioned pairing making it even easier to forget him?

He didn't want to believe it, but he couldn't help that a part of him did. His stomach clenched, and he forced down the tea in an attempt to still it.

"I need to go."

"Rushing back to that Gunera woman so quickly?"

"What?"

She stood up gracefully, her lithe body covered by a loose red silk wrap. Ripe breasts strained against the fabric, hard nipples creating sharp points in the softness. Ferrin didn't want to look, but he couldn't help it. His cock shifted. It knew what Kali was after and wanted it, even though the rest of him did not.

She noticed his beginning arousal and slipped the robe off her shoulders. "Ferrin. I've been watching you. I've been…wanting you." Her musky fragrance assailed him while the sight of her soft curves made his mouth water.

He didn't want her. He wanted Aleeza. He just wished his cock would get the message.

"There's nothing special about me."

"You know there is," she said. "Daiesthai man. Don't you know what you were made for? How good it could be?" She ran her right hand up her body from thigh to breast, stopping to rub a circle over her nipple on the way up. Her nails were long and red, filed into sharp points. As he watched she scraped one along the smooth skin of her breast and left a mark.

Ferrin swallowed. There was no hiding his erection, no matter how much he wished it wasn't there.

"You'll never be able to have what you want from the Gunera woman. Not with your third there. You'll never be able to take her, to make her bruise and bleed, to feel your own blood pouring over your skin…this is the Daiesthai way. I know what you need, Ferrin. I can give it to you if you let me."

"I'm not interested."

Her eyes narrowed. "Do you think they're waiting for you? Do you think they're not taking this opportunity to fuck each other's brains out?" She put her arms on either side of his face, leaning over him. He tried to slide back, away from her, but it only brought his face closer to hers. "Think of it, Ferrin. The two of them, their bodies twisting together, your brother's cock deep, deep inside the heat of her cunt…just the way they were when you saw them that first night."

"How did you know about that?" He tried to shut out the image she described, but he couldn't. His erection jerked. The sane part of him knew he should get out of here. He didn't want to touch this woman, didn't want to listen to this.

But he was trapped by her eyes like a fly in a spider web, unable to look away, unable to ignore the sense that he needed her.

Unable to ignore, too, the voice that now started roaring in his head. His blackness swirled and shifted. He saw Kali's face through a filter of darkness.

Take her! This is what we want! She'll give us what we want!

He squeezed his eyes shut and turned his face away. Bad move. Kali's pearly teeth nibbled at his neck, just over his racing pulse. He could not keep from gasping.

"I know enough about you to know I can give you everything you need," she whispered, her breath hot on his skin. "We could mean so very, very much to each other."

The warm, incense-heavy air in the room swirled against the hypersensitive skin of his cock. Kali pulled him up to a sit. His head still throbbed but not as badly now. He could sit up. He could look at her.

She picked up a riding crop from the floor at her feet—he noticed several other items down there as well, but couldn't make out what they were—and slid the tip between her breasts. "You could hit me with this if you want."

The beast inside him roared but he did not speak. He still had the strength for that, even as his mind clouded with black, seething need.

"Not ready yet? How about if I do it for you?" She lifted the crop, made it sing through the air to smack down on her breast. Her skin flamed where it landed. She closed her eyes, the tip of her tongue sliding out to lick her lips.

"No." He barely managed to choke out the word.

"Are you being disobedient, Ferrin? Do I need to punish you?"

He looked away, clenching his jaw so hard he thought his teeth might break.

The crop whispered again and landed on his upper thigh, a hairsbreadth away from his throbbing cock. His hips jerked. A groan escaped his lips.

Again she smacked him, on his other thigh this time. Sweat broke out on his forehead. He fisted the couch cushions, desperate to keep still, fighting himself not to grab the crop from her hand and hit her back, *hit her, throw her to the ground and climb on top of her, bite her, fuck her, it's what we want —*

"No!"

Kali grinned at him and adjusted her stance, spreading her legs and placing one foot on the edge of the couch by his side, taunting him with the flesh between them. She dragged the crop up the inside of one trim thigh, rubbed it over her pussy. The leather gleamed with her juices.

He could not drag his eyes away, and she knew it. She leaned backward, tilting her pelvis, and ran the slick tip of the crop up his swollen length. He groaned but did not move.

"Not enough? Let's see…what else do we have to play with?"

Ferrin closed his eyes, trying to rid himself of the sight of her pussy, of the crop on his cock. All he had to do was lean forward and he could taste her, bury his tongue in her. All he had to do was grab her and he could bring her onto the couch and impale her in one quick motion.

She slapped him across the face. His eyes snapped open and a growl more animal than human escaped him. The sound scared him. It also excited him. Something built within his body, something great and terrible, the thing that had always been hiding, forced to hide. Now he could let it out—he knew he could—with this woman who was a stranger and familiar all at the same time. He didn't want to, didn't want to touch her, but his body was almost out of his control.

Think of Aleeza, think of—

But it didn't help. Thinking of Aleeza and how he loved her only made the animal roar louder in his head because he could never have her, not the way he wanted, and here was this woman who practically begged him to fuck her like they were both about to die.

And maybe they would. And in his confused state, that didn't seem like such a bad idea.

She slapped him again, and before he could stop himself he hit her back.

Her cry of pain sent a shiver through his body as she fell to the floor, her hand clasping her cheek. Almost immediately she sat up. Her eyes glittered with triumph and tears, and her lips curved in a wicked smile. "I knew it," she said.

His breath came in hard gasps as she knelt before him and ran those sharp nails up his thighs. He was glued to the couch, unable to take his eyes off her. Thoughts of Dorand and

Aleeza were very, very far away as she grabbed his hips and pulled them forward so his ass just rested on the edge of the cushions.

He struggled, tried to pull away. She muttered something under her breath, words he didn't recognize, but suddenly he couldn't move. He was trapped, unable to do anything but watch as her tongue darted out to snake over the tip of his cock.

"No! Damn it, no!" Again he tried to move and found he couldn't. The captivity only fueled his rage, and his rage only fueled the black lust in his head. He wanted to scream, to cry. He was totally helpless as the beast within him roared and shook, ready to unleash itself in any way possible.

Kali's mouth sank over him, swallowing the length of his erection.

For a long moment he just watched, feeling the wet heat of her mouth envelop him, the gentle suction that already threatened to blow the top of his head off.

"No! NO!"

"Yes." She reached out and raked her nails down his chest. Droplets of blood beaded in lines across his skin. Her mouth descended upon his again.

His throat ached as he struggled against her invasion, his tongue preferring to crawl down into his stomach rather than mate with hers. But still his cock pulsed, thick and hard, almost as if it too were enchanted. But by what magic? He'd never met a spell he couldn't master. This couldn't be happening to him. This couldn't be real—he was too strong for—

He snapped his teeth together, trying to fight in the only way he could, but she was too fast for him, pulling back an instant before he would have bitten off her tongue. "Ferrin. Stop fighting me."

Again she rested her foot by his side, but this time she reached down and slid her fingers into her pussy, spreading her lips with one hand while the other rubbed in slow circles. "Together we can be everything you've ever wanted to be. We can do everything you've ever wanted to do."

He watched her hands, mesmerized by the sight of her long fingers disappearing into her body and coming back out gleaming wet. It was almost enough to make him forget the power pressing his body to the couch, the itch of another's magic between his thighs.

"You don't have to be scared anymore. You don't have to be alone. I'll be here, I'm everything you want, everything you need."

She reached over him, behind him, to grip the back of the couch and lift herself up. The movement brought her pussy right into his face, hovering only inches away from his lips. He could practically stick his tongue out to stroke it without moving his head.

Kali tilted her pelvis forward. Her fragrance filled his nostrils. He could not get away.

She kept talking. He didn't know the words, didn't understand them, but they sounded good, right. The darkness within him grew as she spoke, shifting and changing. He tried to fight it but could not. There wasn't enough strength in him anymore to fight.

Something foul and dark spilled over him, ripped through him. He tried to speak the words of the liberty spell but couldn't even remember them. He couldn't find language anywhere in his head as he shrank inside himself and the blackness took over.

They tumbled back on to the floor. Somewhere deep inside Ferrin something screamed, horrified, furious. He didn't want this, didn't want any of this, but her nipple was between his teeth. He yanked his head back and her scream of pain and delight was too much for him to refuse. Too much to deny.

He hit her again and she hit him, their hands moving almost in unison, a dance he'd never experienced but somehow knew intimately. More blood ran down his chest as she scratched him, tearing at his skin. The beast within him roared and shook.

Her mouth reached for his but he pulled away. There was enough of himself left, enough of the man who knew this was wrong, to refuse to give her that. He would not kiss her. He would not kiss her lips but he would let her bite him, scratch him. He felt tears run down his cheeks when she picked up something small and vibrating from the ground and shoved it into his ass, sending tingling, throbbing pain and pleasure rolling though him. He shoved his fingers into her pussy, into her ass, bent down to suck and bite her nipples. All of these things he would do, but he would not kiss her as a lover.

The crop sang through the air again, snapping on his back. "Fuck me!" Kali screamed. "Fuck me now!"

The thing that used to be Ferrin growled and shifted, positioning himself above the inferno of her pussy, ready to thrust into her. It would work—this time it would work. It was what he'd wanted for so long, all he had to do was obey, just obey her, and obey him, and the children would be—

Children?

Kali hit him again. Ferrin's cock danced just outside of her. Every muscle in his body shook. He wanted to shove into her so badly, wanted to thrust mindlessly, to bruise her with his cock and hands and mouth.

But children…

Those were Aleeza's children. It was Aleeza he wanted to be with, Aleeza he wanted to make love to. Not this woman. Who was this woman? By the gods, what had she done to him? What was he doing?

The voice hesitated. So did Kali. Their indecision colored the air. "Fuck me!" she screamed again. "Don't wait, do it!"

Ferrin pulled himself away. "By the gods, I call upon my soul, my freedom…" The liberty spell wasn't working. Usually something eased as he said the first words. Not this time.

He tried again, reciting the entire thing but to no avail. His power was too caught up with the woman, his soul too filled with blackness. It was as if he'd given away his right to freedom, or maybe there was too much darkness in him at the moment to get rid of.

If only Dorand was there. He could help—he could ground the energy and expel it.

Fuck Dorand. Stupid "undefiled", stupid bastard with his white magic and his—

No! Not "fuck" Dorand. *Be* Dorand. What would Dorand do? How would Dorand fight an evil like this, an evil that seemed to come from his very heart?

Where the words came from, he did not know. He could not recall hearing them before. All he knew was that he concentrated on Dorand, on the white light of Dorand's power, and suddenly it was as though that light filled his own body. Words fell from his lips, words of purity and strength, and as he spoke he stood up, disentangling himself from Kali's arms and legs, his erection subsiding as his blood pumped again and his head cleared.

He had won. He was Daiesthai, but he had mimicked the magic of the man he loved most in the world and that magic had saved him. Or maybe the love had saved him.

"Fuck you, brother! I'll take what I want, with or without your consent." Kali hissed the words from the floor, her face twisted in an expression that transformed her beauty into something feral, fearsome.

Ferrin had a split second to realize what she had said, to realize why those brown eyes looked so very familiar, before she whipped her legs sideways, knocking him off his feet. He hit the ground hard, barely recovering his breath before she was on top of him, pinning him to the floor with a few quickly spoken words, trapping him again just as she had on the couch. This time the horror wasn't just from being trapped.

"I'd hoped we could have a little fun, but you've obviously spent too many years among the undefiled to know what fun is anymore. Do it, Reglanus."

"No! No, wait, you don't know what you're doing. You'll make a monster, a—"

His words gave way to a scream of pain as the mist floating near Kali's head moved over his body. The aching in his balls grew even worse, a throbbing that made him writhe on the floor, seeking a way out of his own skin. He twisted and fought the thing above him, but it was no use. His cock hardened against his will, swelling until it was nearly purple. It pulsed with the furious need to spill seed, to release the horrible pressure.

"Thank you." Kali smiled and spread the lips of her pussy with her own fingers, guiding his length to her opening and dropping her hips. The second he was surrounded by her slick heat, Ferrin felt the aching grow even more intense. He was going to come any second, no matter what his right mind had to say about it.

"No, by the gods. Don't do this! If we are brother and sister, the baby could be deformed, sick—"

"We're twins, brother, and the baby will be fine. It will be able to spill blood for its coven—that's all we need." She began to rock back and forth, grinding her clit against him. In seconds she threw her head back, raven hair flying around her shoulders, and came. He joined her, the release a painful jerking forced from his cock by black magic that gave him no pleasure.

Instead, he felt violated. His skin was covered in a cold sweat and his stomach threatened to empty itself all over the woman on top of him. But maybe that wouldn't be such a bad thing. He couldn't free himself from whatever spell she had cast, but he could cover her in bile. A small repayment for rape, but it was a start.

"Damn you!" She screamed as his vomit coated her breasts, and pulled herself from his body. "Yes, I know, Reglanus. I don't require your guidance. Make yourself useful, and bring me a towel." She spoke to the mist, answering some voice only she could hear, then lay down on the wood a few feet away, and lifted her hips into the air.

"Wouldn't want to lose any of your precious sperm, brother." She retrieved a towel that floated through the air and began to clean herself, smiling at him, a mad smile that did not reach her eyes. "Now, tell me about yourself. What was it like to grow up with a coven, with people who gave a damn if you lived or died?"

"Fuck you." Ferrin spit at her, but this time she was too far away.

"Now, now. We've got so much lost time to make up for. We're brother and sister, the only two Daiesthai in the world, and now we'll soon be new parents as well. Seems it would be best if we could find a way to get along."

"You're a sick bitch, and I'm going to kill you at the first opportunity." He whispered the words, staring straight into her eyes. Sister or no, he knew he spoke the truth.

"We'll see about that, brother. If this doesn't work, maybe I'll kill you first." She paused for a moment then smiled again. "Or maybe we'll just have to fuck again. Tell me, Ferrin, would you like to be on top this time, or do you prefer the bottom?"

"I didn't fuck you, and I will never fuck you."

"Hmm…for some reason, I doubt you'll have the choice." Her eyes grew distant for a moment, as if she were listening to some far-off ocean, then cleared. "No, no choice at all."

The mist moved over him, and his cock immediately began to throb. He moaned and shuddered, squeezing his eyes shut against the sound of Kali's laughter.

Chapter Fifteen

ℰℐ

"There's no way you're staying on this investigation." Gavyn paced behind his desk, pausing now and then to glare at Aleeza and Dorand sitting opposite. "Hell, you are the investigation!"

"Exactly, Gavyn. I am the investigation, so who has more at stake than I do? Than Dorand? This is his clan brother who has gone missing, who is in danger, who might even be the next victim and—"

"Who is a member of a cursed coven capable of recreating one of the most evil groups of witches the world has ever known. There's a witch out there casting demon-fasting spells, and you're sitting in front of me, curse-free, ready to help her out. If you're right, if she's got the Daiesthai male, you're next."

"Maybe, maybe not. We don't think the woman knew that Ferrin existed when she started the spell in the Amiantos woods. She was going to make herself a man for goddess' sake. Don't you think she'd rather stay female, give birth to the baby herself if that's an option? She may not even need me anymore."

"Mona's report says that Daiesthai females are infertile."

"Mostly infertile, most, not all."

"Okay, so we can be *mostly* certain that the witch is still going to need you, Aleeza." Gavyn stopped pacing, snatched up the phone on his desk, dialed, and spoke brusquely to whoever was on the other end. "Send a unit up to my office, the best we've got. Aleeza is going into hiding until Samhain, and I want to make sure she stays hidden."

"You're going to lock me up?" Aleeza stood up fast, sending her chair scraping across the floor. Dorand stood beside her.

A part of her had feared this when she'd decided to tell Gavyn the truth, but she hadn't seen that she had a choice. She now knew exactly what this demon-fasted witch wanted, a second generation for a spell that would bring a kind of misery to the world it hadn't known since the dark ages. A trip back to Walter on Monday had revealed more specifics as to why the demon had contacted Aleeza in the first place and why she hadn't heard a whisper of evil in her ear since the day Ferrin disappeared.

The witch had to have him. She and the demon must have taken Ferrin, kidnapped him. Aleeza and Dorand were certain he'd been taken against his will. It had been two days since he'd disappeared from her mother's house, and no one had heard from him. He wouldn't have run off without calling, without telling anyone in the Amiantos coven where he'd gone. At least that's what they'd told themselves. The alternative was that he'd succumbed to the blackness within and gone off to find this demon-fasted witch of his own accord. No matter how tempting that voice, Aleeza couldn't think that Ferrin would give in.

Still, it bothered her more than she would admit that she hadn't felt any touch of the demon in her mind in two days. Did that mean that the witch had achieved her goal? Even now, was she pregnant with the next generation of Daiesthai witches?

"Gavyn, please. You can't send me into hiding. My mother has me dosed up on so many herbs, I probably won't be able to get pregnant for years. I'm not fertile, and I won't be for a long time. I'd be useless to—"

"For every spell, there is a counter spell, Aleeza. You know that. Anything your mother could work could be unworked. If this witch wants you pregnant badly enough, they would find a way to make sure you conceived. Not to mention that, if this Daeisthai female theory is wrong, there could be another Gunera out there who is free of the curse and fasted with a demon. If I don't send you into hiding, you could be in danger from one of our own people."

"The theory isn't wrong, Gavyn. I can feel it in my gut!"

"Fine, even if you're right, we've still got a leak, someone close enough to you to get the ingredients needed for a hex portal spell. Whoever he or she is, I have no idea, but considering how much time you spend at work, it's likely it's someone on my own goddamned staff!"

"If it is someone on your staff, how can you be sure Aleeza will be safe in the custody of whatever unit you choose?" Dorand spoke for the first time, but his question obviously gave Gavyn pause. Aleeza was learning fast that though Dorand was a man of few words, the one's he did speak were usually very well chosen.

"I'll pick two of my strongest coven members," Gavyn said, shooting Dorand a measured look.

"That's fine if the Daeisthai theory is correct. But what if it is a Gunera female who fasted with the demon? She'd need to be powerful to break the curse. Weak or strong, every Gunera is a suspect," Dorand said.

"Which is part of the reason we came to you for help, Gavyn," Aleeza said.

"Oh, my being your boss and head of this company wasn't enough to earn me the truth? Good to know, Aleeza. I'll keep that in mind the next time I'm handing out assignments." Gavyn scowled but held still, crossing his arms over his chest. He was at least listening, so she'd better make her request while she still had the chance.

"I want a detailed list of every assignment for the past six months. I want to know who worked what and when. I'm hoping I'll be able to narrow down my list of suspects, find out who might have had the motive and opportunity to get in with this Daeisthai witch or—"

"Or who might have been strong enough to form the demon fast herself," Gavyn finished with a nod. "That makes sense, but that's work you could do while you're in seclusion. If you don't get taken into custody, then our leak is going to know that we're on to them. Your mother, the Amiantos council and I all know that you're curse-free. It's only a matter of time before word gets out to the rest of our coven. It will look—"

"What?!" Aleeza fisted her hands at her sides, resisting the urge to punch something. How could he? How could he have shared her secret without letting her know?

"It will look suspicious if I don't take you into custody. You could, after all, be a suspect."

"How could you tell the Amiantos? Gavyn, I—"

"They're the client—they deserve to know what's going on with this case."

"But they could have a leak on their side! Those men who were following me, they knew I was on the case almost before I did, and—"

"You hadn't met an Amiantos in years before you were assigned. There was no way they could have gotten hair or the fluids they would need to form a hex portal," Gavyn countered.

"They could if they'd broken into her apartment," Dorand said. "I don't like to think one of my coven is responsible, but it's not outside the realm of possibility."

"Even more reason to protect Aleeza. She can't go back up to those woods without being a target for either a lingering demon spell or an Amiantos coven member with a demonic agenda."

"Gavyn, I can't sit on my ass in some safe house while someone I care about is in danger!" Aleeza regretted the words the second they were out of her mouth.

"You just put the nail in your coffin, honey. I'm sorry, but you're not going to think clearly if you're letting emotions cloud your judgment. You're going into hiding, end of story. I'll get my best people on the case and they'll get to the bottom of this, thanks to the good work you've done so far." The knock came at the door. Perfect timing for Gavyn. "Come in."

"Sir, you asked for a team?" Pater asked from the doorway, a lit cigarette in his hand. His brother Sean stood beside him, also smoking. Both of them were dressed in regulation Gunera Bounty uniforms. Everyone who worked in a collections unit was required to wear the navy blue jumpsuit. Only investigators were granted the privilege of street clothes.

"Aleeza's going to safe house five. Take the back way and make sure you don't have any tails. Keep the phone enabled but don't let her make any calls without running it past me first." Gavyn sat down at his desk and began to shuffle paper, clearly finished discussing the matter.

Aleeza shot Dorand a desperate look. She couldn't go with Sean and Pater, but she couldn't *not* go either. If she refused a direct order, she'd be up for coven-rejection or worse. If she went with them quietly, she could be condemning Ferrin to a horrible fate and helping usher in a reign of evil. No matter what Gavyn said, she knew that she was the best woman for this job. She and Ferrin and Dorand had an undeniable connection, one that she knew would prove valuable in helping track Ferrin down.

"Don't worry Aleeza, I'll keep looking." Dorand pulled her close for a hug, then bent his head and whispered in her ear. "You want to get out of here?"

"Okay," Aleeza answered. She'd made her decision. If Dorand had a plan to get her out of here, she was ready for it. She'd risk coven rejection or worse for either of the men she loved. She couldn't let Ferrin down, not when it had been her spell in the woods that had led the bad guys to him in the first place.

"Think fire," Dorand whispered, then he kissed her. Not just any kiss, but a soul-deep kiss. His tongue pushed past her lips, claiming her mouth, causing blue-white light to flare between them almost instantly. Within seconds, green-gold joined the white-blue, and Aleeza knew exactly what she had to do.

"What the—" Pater screamed as the cigarette in his hands burst into a roaring flame. He dropped the fireball to the floor and backed away, leaving the doorway clear except for the flame itself.

"Let's go." Dorand pulled her after him. They ran and jumped quickly through the fire. Aleeza felt the heat for only a second before they were on the other side. And then they were running, booking it down the hall before Sean could pull Pater to his feet.

"Get your ass back here, Aleeza!" She heard Gavyn screaming but she didn't turn back. She'd made her decision. Now all she could do was pray that she'd survive to face the consequences.

* * * * *

Ferrin woke slowly, fighting consciousness. He knew what awaited him in the waking world, and he wanted no part of it. Kali had been at him for what felt like weeks, but it could have been only a few days. He had no concept of time. The room she kept him in had no windows, and he'd been able to snatch only a few minutes of sleep at a time.

"Wake up, sleeping beauty." She laughed, her breath hot on his cheek. She'd moved him to a bed at some point, maybe yesterday. By that time he'd appreciated the softness, his spine aching from lying pinned to the hardwood floor. Too bad she hadn't given his cock a break as well.

She'd raped him again and again. As soon as her demon brought him to erection, she was on him. So far, they'd yet to conceive, but it was only a matter of time. Kali had a potion that put her body in a state of constant ovulation. She dropped an egg every day. It was just a matter of time until—

"I've got some good news, sweet brother."

Gods, please no. Let her kill me. Anything but good news.

"Open your eyes. I know that you're awake."

He turned his head away. Fighting did no good, but it made him feel better. He couldn't control his cock but his head still belonged to him.

Her fingers closed around his chin in an iron grip. She yanked his head to the side.

"Don't disobey me, brother. I may be pregnant, but that doesn't mean I can't still have my fun with you."

His heart sank. His prayers hadn't been enough. "You got what you wanted—now let me go."

"Oh, no. We still have work to do." She smiled like the Cheshire cat. "We're going to cheat nature."

* * * * *

"Turn right," Aleeza commanded. "And pull into one of those parking spots over there, out of sight from the road."

Dorand swung the car in, straddling two spaces, and braked. Good enough. They didn't have time to waste.

Even coming here was a risk, but they had to go somewhere. They needed to get on the Gunera Bounty website database to get the records Aleeza wanted. The only Gunera she knew who had a computer with an approved i.p. address and might be willing to give them access was Raven. Aleeza had never particularly liked her cousin, but at least Raven wasn't blinded by obedience to Gavyn or anyone else for that matter. Her cousin's blasé attitude when it came to work and coven was finally going to prove itself useful instead of a royal pain in the ass.

They sped up the rickety stairs to Raven's furnished efficiency on the third floor. Please let her be home, please let her be home. Aleeza had no doubt that Gavyn had people on their trail. It was only a matter of time before they gave Raven's apartment a drive by. If they were safe here now, it was only for a few minutes. She pounded on the door even harder until the bones in her hand began to protest.

"Hold on, hold on." Raven's voice came muffled through the door as chains and locks rattled. "Where the hell have you—Oh. Aleeza." Her gaze flitted to Dorand and back to her cousin. She tugged at her pigtails and bit her lip. "Hi. What are you doing here?"

"You were expecting someone?"

"Um, yeah. Just a—friend from school. Hey, come on in." Raven scanned the street as she ushered Dorand and Aleeza into her cramped apartment. "It's such a nice surprise, you know, to see you. And who is this?"

"This is Dorand." Aleeza watched the two shake hands, alarm bells buzzing in her head. When had her cousin started dressing like that? Her plaid skirt was way too short and her blue sweater tight enough to leave nothing to the imagination. She looked like some Catholic schoolgirl fantasy run amok. Not to mention that Raven was fidgeting nonstop. The girl was never nervous, at least not that Aleeza could remember. Now she looked ready to jump out of her skin.

"Nice to meet you," Dorand said.

"Sure, hi. Nice to meet you." The room was spotless, another surprise. Raven was a notorious pig, and it had always amazed Aleeza that she managed to look clean and tidy when Aleeza knew for a fact she picked most of her clothes out of wrinkled piles on the ground.

But right now, there wasn't a pile of semi-clean laundry to be seen. The place even smelled nice with candles burning on the tiny table, and soft music playing on the stereo. Aleeza had suspected she wasn't the only Gunera who tried to build a sexy, seductive atmosphere in her living space. If you couldn't live it, at least you could find some comfort in the trappings of romance.

"Raven, I need some help, I want to use your—" she began, then stopped.

Something clicked in her mind, and suddenly Aleeza knew exactly was wrong with this picture. She enjoyed a little luxury in her bedroom, yes. But she didn't light candles or dress for sexual role-playing when she was expecting company. What would be the point? Until a few nights ago she hadn't been capable of seducing anyone, and Raven shouldn't be either.

Shit. She'd come here looking for a way to track down the Gunera leak. Instead she'd found the traitor herself. Raven, with the shadow-walking skills of someone three times her age. Raven, who had been working as her apprentice during the months when the dreams were the worst. Her cousin had sold her out—there was little doubt in her mind. Now she just had to find out if she was merely a leak or the demon-fasted witch they were looking for.

"Sure." Raven's blue eyes widened above her eager smile. "Anything I can do to help, you know that."

Aleeza reached out and took Dorand's hand, giving it a quick squeeze. If her suspicions were correct—and the sinking feeling in the pit of her stomach told her they were—she needed to handle this very, very carefully. Dorand seemed to read that light touch because he moved back toward the door, blocking the only exit as Aleeza turned back to Raven.

"My apartment has been contaminated with black magic, and I'm afraid to go back there until I figure out how it happened. So I was wondering if I could use your computer to get on the Gunera Bounty site?" Aleeza moved into the room, quickly locating all the doors. There was what looked like a bathroom to her left, and the doors to two bedrooms on her right. The first bedroom was dark, but in the second, more candles burned.

"Oh my god, that's horrible." Raven moved casually to the bedroom door and closed it but not before Aleeza had a good look inside.

There was no one there, no Ferrin tied to her bed, which made Aleeza think Raven was merely an accomplice, not the demon-fasted witch. But why would she agree to such a thing?

Don't be dumb, 'Leez.

Of course. Not money, not power but the very thing Aleeza herself had been willing to risk her magic, her place in the coven, and her mental wellbeing to gain. Raven had wanted to get laid. Wanted it badly enough to help someone work black magic in Aleeza's apartment. But she hadn't had a hex portal under her bed to help persuade her—she'd just been selfish and horny.

The little, fucking bitch. Aleeza gritted her teeth and walked closer to the romantic table set for two.

"I know. I couldn't believe it. A hex portal, under my bed."

"That's…wow. That's really scary. Do you have any idea who might have done it?" Her voice was free of guile, and when Aleeza turned to face her, she saw that Raven's eyes were the same. She looked shocked, frightened and completely innocent.

"You know, you really are very good. If someone had told me it was you, I never would have bought it, even with your less-than-stellar record of service to the coven." Aleeza smiled and casually crossed her arms, eyes glued to Raven's face, searching for the slightest break in her act. "You're a fantastic actress. You should consider a change in careers."

"What do you mean?" Her look of sweet confusion was priceless. Time to up the ante with a little creative truth-telling.

"I mean, if I didn't know for a fact that you'd sold me out to get your fuck on, I would totally buy this innocent act." Aleeza held her breath as the girl met her eyes in confusion, wondering if Raven would keep up with the denial, and what she would do if her cousin refused to take the bait. Luckily she didn't have to wonder for long.

"If you try to hurt me, you are going to be very, very sorry," Raven whispered, still looking anything but repentant.

"You helped work black magic on your own cousin—your family, not just your coven—and that's all you have to say for yourself?" Aleeza struggled against the urge to cross the few feet that separated them and slap the younger woman—hard.

"Don't act like you're any better. You were powerful enough to break the spell with gray magic. If you hadn't been, don't tell me you wouldn't have dipped into black. It was only a—"

"Don't you dare. There is no way to excuse what you've done."

"I wasn't making excuses. Now get out of my house, and take your *friend* with you." Her bottom lip trembled, but she still managed to look haughty, imperious as she pointed to the door.

"Oh please, we're not going anywhere until you spill it—all of it. Who are you working for? How long have you been working for them? And why, if you've broken the curse, don't you want to be the vessel for the next generation? Come on, Raven, don't you want to give birth to a few demon babies?" Aleeza stalked toward her cousin, grateful that she'd worn her boots. She would be able to look the slightly taller woman in the eye, and hopefully Raven would read the price she would pay for withholding information loud and clear.

"I'm not telling you anything. It's too late, anyway."

"What do you mean it's too late? Where is my clan brother?" Dorand's voice was menacing enough to make the hairs at the back of Aleeza's neck stand at attention, but for some reason Raven didn't seem intimidated.

"Really, Aleeza, I don't understand you. You break the curse but you still choose to fuck an Amiantos. You could have done that anyway. You did know that ri—"

Raven's words became a strangled yelp as Aleeza leapt upon her, hands closing around her cousin's neck. The rage that surged through her was as powerful as any demon-inspired hatred. She wanted to punish her, beat her to within an inch of her life, make her pay for all the evil she had worked in the name of her own selfish desires.

They hit the floor with a thud, Aleeza on top, fingers tight on Raven's thin throat, but her cousin didn't even try to fight back. Instead, she lay there, tears sliding from her closed eyes, almost as if she wished for death at Aleeza's hands. Slowly, Aleeza loosened her hold enough for Raven to suck in a breath of air and start to sob in earnest.

"She's never coming back to me. It's been days, and...nothing. I did all of this—betrayed my family, my coven—for nothing." Raven continued to cry as Aleeza moved to stand over her cousin and Dorand crossed the room.

Of course. "Your lover is a woman."

"I gave her everything, did anything she asked, but I can only be with women. That's why I can't get pregnant. I can't have sex with men. Not even she was strong enough to completely break the curse. At least not then. She might be now, but she doesn't care what happens to me, doesn't care if I live or die."

"Who is it? Give us her name." Dorand's voice was softer now, as if he too sensed the real reason behind Raven's lack of penitence was simply that she'd lost her will to live. She was so addicted to this woman, so deeply mired in black magic, she might never work her way free.

It would have been enough to move Aleeza to pity if she didn't know that Raven was probably at least partially responsible for the murder of three people, one of whom was Dorand and Ferrin's third. No matter that they were learning to love again, they never would have lost that woman if it hadn't been for a power-hungry witch and Aleeza's own cousin.

Aleeza wondered for a second if that was the reason behind her being chosen as the Gunera who would bear the next generation of Daeisthai. Was it simply because Raven had easy access to Aleeza? And she happened to be powerful enough to suit the purpose? Her stomach roiled. With family like this, who needed enemies?

"I can't tell you, but I bet Aleeza can guess…if she takes time to ask the right questions."

"Listen, you little bitch—"

"Wait Dorand, I think she literally means she can't tell us," Aleeza said, her hunch confirmed when Raven nodded, sadly. "She's under some sort of safeguarding spell. A lot of the criminals we track use them, to keep accomplices, witnesses, whatever from talking."

"Can you break the spell? We don't have much time," Dorand said, moving to the window as a police car zoomed past, siren wailing. Thankfully it kept moving. They hadn't been found, not yet anyway.

"I can't break it, but I can ask her yes or no questions. She should be able to nod an answer. Even if she can't nod, that tells me something, usually that the answer is yes." Aleeza paced the ground in front of Raven, staring down at the girl's bowed head and trying to think of what woman, what witch would have been able to consume her so completely.

"Is the woman someone I've met?"

Raven shook her head "no" but met Aleeza's eyes, as if to urge her to get more specific. Her eyes flitted toward the bedroom doors and back again. Aleeza took a quick glance over her shoulder but both doors remained closed.

"Is the woman someone who I've heard of?"

Raven nodded "yes", and again took a pointed look toward the bedrooms.

"Oh…shit. The woman who moved in with you? Your roommate, the one who grew up in a supernatural orphanage?" Aleeza suddenly wished she'd taken Raven up on the offer to come to dinner last spring. She might have been able to sense something off about her cousin's new roomie, been able to intervene before it was too late.

"I'll search her room, see if I can find pictures, notes, anything that might lead us to where she's taken Ferrin." Dorand disappeared into the second bedroom.

"She has Ferrin?" Aleeza asked. She already knew the answer, but it never hurt to confirm the facts.

Raven nodded and fresh tears started running down her face.

"She's hurt him."

Another nod, and Aleeza felt her own throat grow tight. She was going to kill this woman. Kill her and then think about killing Raven.

"Is he still alive?" The words were barely a whisper, forced out through lips that felt strangely numb. He couldn't be dead, she'd felt his power moving through her less than an hour ago. If he was dead, the magical remnant wouldn't have survived, would it?

Raven didn't nod either way, just stared at her, eyes once again flat, lifeless. She didn't know, but that look made it clear—Raven wouldn't be surprised if Ferrin was dead, not surprised in the least.

"Go sit at the table, I'm going to bind you to the chair. I'll call Gavyn as soon as we leave. He and the coven elders can decide what to do with you."

"No, Aleeza, please. If you tell him, I'll be outcast. I'll have nowhere to—"

"It's either tell Gavyn or I'll take care of you myself. I don't think you want that, cousin."

Something in Aleeza's voice must have made Raven see the truth in that statement because she nodded. "I'll tell him. Just go before it's too late."

"Go where? Can you at least tell us her name, maybe what kind of—"

"Kali. Kali Meronyi." Dorand came back out into the room, carrying a thin sheaf of papers. He held them up. "An electricity bill, a water bill…all to an address downtown."

"You're kidding." After all this, their witch was going to be tracked so easily? It was hard to believe.

"I guess evil demon-fasted bitches like to take a hot shower now and then." Dorand smiled, but it wasn't a nice smile, not at all. Aleeza was glad. Now wasn't the time for nice, now was the time for payback.

Chapter Sixteen

ɛ℧

"Stand there." Ferrin's skin crawled when she touched him, but he let her stand him by the head of the low bed. His heart raced as his eyes scanned the room. There had to be a weapon, a way out, something…anything.

This couldn't be happening. He couldn't be standing beside his long lost psychotic sister, contemplating murdering both her and the child she carried. His child. After seeing what he and Aleeza could have had together, after realizing that—thanks to his heritage—he could never have children, even the thought of killing the product of an incestuous rape bothered him.

But there was no choice. This couldn't happen, and he would have to be the one who made sure it didn't.

Kali left him and went to stand in front of the low altar at the foot of the bed. Her back was to him—she'd become that certain he was no threat. For the hundredth time Ferrin wondered how long he'd been here, even as he kept searching for a weapon. She was summoning her demon now—he only had a minute before the thing came and his chance was gone. The cocky bastard he had been when he'd first met Kali would have sworn he'd never be bested by a demon, but now…he knew better.

As she started to speak, his eyes caught a flash of silver. Slowly, carefully, he pushed aside one of the pillows, revealing the ceremonial knife she'd left there. Whatever ritual she planned, it must involve blood. The knife's dark energy throbbed along his skin when he touched the handle, making him shudder. Still he held it tighter. This was the only weapon he'd been able to lay his hands on since his arrival. He couldn't waste the chance, no matter that something within him warned against giving this weapon blood.

Kali's voice grew louder. Her nude body shimmered in the candlelight as she raised her arms, smoke from the incense on the altar obscuring her features. Her head fell back, face tipped to the ceiling, eyes rolling back in her head.

Ferrin crept up behind her, the knife clenched in his fist. If he slit her throat she would die almost instantly. But, if he jammed the blade through the base of her neck, would that be faster? Maybe, but it wouldn't be as easy as it sounded. Her throat was delicate, thin, and it would be hell to hit the exact spot. He didn't want to slip and lose his chance.

He raised his arm, preparing to strike, when some unseen force grabbed his hand. The knife burned his skin with a cold fire, but still Ferrin clung to the weapon.

It is not necessary. Ferrin shivered. It was the voice of a demon, of something evil crawling through slime. And through his distaste and fear, he realized something about that voice was as familiar as home. He'd actually begun to miss it, to crave Reglanus' words in his mind during those times when it was obvious the demon was elsewhere. *You will have your revenge. Be ready.*

Ferrin gritted his teeth, fighting the urge to drop his knife as Kali's demon converged from the ether. Bit by bit, Reglanus coalesced, more solid than Ferrin had ever seen him. What the hell was the demon up to?

Why not simply tell Kali she was in danger, why tell him he would have revenge?

Trust me, my son.

Ferrin sucked in a breath and dropped the knife to the bed with a soft thud. Whether he trusted the demon or not, he no longer had the strength to fight it.

"You are certain we don't need the power of Samhain?" Kali asked the demon, the excitement clear in her voice.

I've consulted with my brothers. Neither the Fire Festival nor the spell in the woods are necessary. Your power has grown. Being reunited with your twin has given you great strength. Once he has fasted with us both, there will be none in the world stronger than our triad, than the son who will be born tonight.

Kali turned to Ferrin and smiled, seemingly unaware of how close she'd just come to death, and led him back to the bed. "Kneel there and be ready," she said, giving his hand a squeeze. "Our child will be born tonight!"

Ferrin swallowed. The demon caught his eye and shook his great horned head. His face looked like a cross between a bleached cow skull and a giant snake, his body a horror of scales and bones too close to the skin's surface, but his eyes were warm, welcoming. The mad part of Ferrin was sure that he could trust this man, this…thing, to help him.

Kali lay down and pulled Ferrin to his knees beside her on the bed, placing Ferrin's hands and her own on her flat stomach. "Reglanus will start the ritual," she said. "Just repeat what he says, and focus your energy."

The hell I will, Ferrin thought, but he nodded anyway. The demon made a face that looked almost like a grin.

"I'm ready." Kali settled herself more comfortably on the bed and looked at the demon. "Let's go."

* * * * *

"I don't like this. It's too quiet. Shouldn't she have guards or something?" Aleeza followed Dorand around the side of the abandoned warehouse, sticking close to the side of the building. Her voice was soft and firm, but he read the anxiety on her features loud and clear. "I know I'm used to tracking human criminals, but in my experience bad guys this bad always make sure they're protected."

They hadn't seen a soul since they pulled the car into an alley several blocks back, but they had both begun to sense Ferrin. The closer they got to the address on Kali's bills, the stronger his energy became. He was alive, he was close, and they were on their way to find him. Dorand knew he should have been thrilled, but something in him was screaming that this was a trap, that they should wait for reinforcements.

Too bad they didn't have any reinforcements to wait for.

"I would think so. There were at least those two men who were following you." Dorand stopped, listened and then crept closer to the parking entrance to the building with a tight sigh. Trap or not, he didn't see any choice. They had to keep going. They had to find Ferrin before it was too late.

"You think this is a trap too."

"It feels wrong. I know that's Ferrin's energy, but there's something—"

"Off about it, almost like it's being—"

"Channeled through another person or thing. Yeah." Dorand jumped down off the sidewalk onto the ramp that led down into the bowels of the building, and turned to help Aleeza clear the five-foot drop. He lifted his hands to her waist but froze when he saw the look on her face.

Love. By the gods, it had snuck up on them so quickly it still took his breath away.

"You realize we just completed each other's sentences." She smiled, and he felt the warmth of it wash over his skin.

"Like an old married couple already." He returned her smile, but a part of him felt a sharp stab of regret. He loved her—there was no doubt in his mind—and he knew she felt the same, but would they ever have a chance at a relationship without Ferrin? No matter what they knew about his heritage, the past two days had taught Dorand that he didn't want a life without his clan brother. Love him, hate him, envy him, Ferrin was a part of him, a part he never wanted to live without.

"Let's go get him, Dorand. We can do this. I know we can." She leapt off the ledge into his arms and kissed him like the world was coming to an end. In that second, he knew she wasn't just talking about Ferrin's rescue. She was taking about them, all three of them, and the life they could have together.

"I love you. Thank you," Dorand said, the words hot and wet against her lips.

"I love you too. Thank you for what?" She pressed closer to him and her breath quickened. Even now, the slightest touch and they ached for each other. Dorand wondered if it would always be this way years from now when their older children were learning the ways of the coven and he, Ferrin, and Aleeza were arguing over who would check their spell work and who give the younger kids a bath.

She smiled and ran a cool hand down the side of his face. "Never mind. I know."

"Are you a mind reader now?"

"No I—" The smile dropped from her face, replaced by a stricken look.

"What's wrong? Aleeza, are you all right?" She moaned, one hand flying to her head, and Dorand scooped her into his arms as her knees buckled. "Talk to me, tell me what's—"

"He's back, oh god Dorand, he's back. Stronger than ever." She cried out and writhed in his arms, but Dorand held her tighter, closer. "Let me go, you have to let me go. I have to go to him, have to stop—"

"Never. Listen to me, Aleeza. Concentrate on my voice. You can fight this. You're strong enough to—"

"No, I can't. I won't." She screamed, but Dorand could tell she was speaking to the voice in her head and kept urging her to fight.

"You choose your destiny. You choose what to do with your magic."

"No, please, Dorand. Let me go!"

"You heard the lady, let her go." The voice came from the darkness just inside the garage and Dorand swung around in time to see fifteen men dressed in black sweatshirts moving out of the shadows.

Scratch that, not men, witches. Their power wasn't strong, but it was there, yellow and sick, throbbing nastily through their auras. Dorand let Aleeza's feet drop back to the ground but held her close to his side with one arm. He would need two hands if he planned to take this to the combat level, but magic he could work better with Aleeza's aura melding with his own.

"Lend me your power, Aleeza."

She moaned but didn't answer yes or no. Dorand decided to take that as a yes, dropping the shield between them as the men began to advance. The second he felt their magic collide, he knew he'd made a big mistake.

He screamed as he felt the demon's power burn along his skin, seeking entrance to his mind but blocked by Amiantos magic. That didn't keep it from hurting like a son of a bitch. He dropped to his knees, and Aleeza fell from his grasp, rolling onto the ground. Their attackers chuckled and drew even closer.

Dorand rallied the last of his strength, the last of his magic, and prepared to do battle. So a demon attack had weakened him, so what? Now maybe this might actually be a fair fight.

* * * * *

At first Ferrin didn't understand what he was feeling, he was so focused on holding back the power that raged and twisted inside him. He sensed the beginnings of some sort of struggle, yes, but was the struggle outside or within himself?

His power bucked and raged and fought to break free. Before him on the bed Kali's body gleamed gold, her lips curved in a beatific smile as she waited for her stomach to grow. The demon's words filled the air around them, a rising wind that stirred the curtains and made Ferrin's hair dance.

Everything he was, everything in his soul, wanted to let his power go, to ride with the demon through the blackness surrounding them. It would be so easy to just release it, to release himself. For the first time in his life he would know what he truly was, how it felt to be what he should have been. What it was his birthright to be.

But he would not, could not. This situation gave new meaning to the word "wrong". An abomination rested in his sister's belly, and a demon called his power. Ferrin gritted his teeth and thought of Dorand. Of Aleeza. Where were they? Did they know what had happened to him? Were they coming for him?

Something shot through him, a spark of pure energy that felt like Dorand. Ferrin lifted his head. It was probably only his own power imitating the Amiantos light Ferrin knew so well. Still, he focused on that spark. The reminder of what goodness felt like was heartening, especially with the seductive blackness around him so thick it was hard to breathe.

Then another light joined the white, an electric blue light and a breath of the fresh, sweet air that was Aleeza, and Ferrin knew she was here. They were here, both of them. A sob of relief escaped his lips before he could think to hold it in.

Kali heard and opened her eyes. Whatever she saw on his face made her smile. "Yes, brother," she said. "You see now, how strong we will be. How our child will give us more power than we ever dreamed."

Ferrin nodded. "I see now." He looked away, afraid she would see the hope in his eyes. Around him the smell of pine strengthened. Dorand. Aleeza. He could wrap them around him and keep himself safe inside.

They had to be close, maybe even fighting Kali's followers. He had to stay focused on the ritual, keep Kali and Reglanus focused as well until Dorand and Aleeza could find him. As if called, the green-gold energy he and Aleeza created together swirled through the air, a gleaming banner. Kali frowned.

"What is that?"

Nothing, my love said the demon. Ferrin glanced over at him, pricklings of misgiving sneaking up his spine. Surely the demon knew something was wrong, sensed the magic of other witches nearby?

The green-gold strengthened, glowed. It wrapped around Ferrin. Aleeza. She was here, she was coming, she was sending her power to him to keep him strong…

But this wasn't her power. This was something else, something that looked like her and smelled like her but somehow, indefinably, was not her, and Ferrin struggled to get away as the energy wrapped around him and squeezed.

"No, by the gods!" He screamed as the energy shot through him, rotten and twisted, soured by something that was not of this world.

Not of this world yet, but I will be…one way or the other.

"Let her go! Damn you," Ferrin raged at the demon, struggling to lift his hands from Kali's bare stomach and lash out at the creature who hovered at the opposite side of the bed. Reglanus had to have Aleeza in his power. There was no other way he could be stealing her magic.

There's only one way to help your love.

"Reglanus? What's happening? Is something wrong?" Kali asked. She didn't seem to hear the words her demon was speaking in Ferrin's mind.

Send the energy into your sister. Get rid of it and you will be at peace.

"What about Aleeza, what have you done with her?"

She and your brother walked right into my trap. A succubus spell. I'm taking her magic, just as I'll take yours if you don't agree to help me.

"I'll never help you," Ferrin screamed.

"You will help him. You will do as he says, you will aid this spell, or you will die!" Kali screamed, taking his chin in her hand and twisting his face to hers.

Send the magic into your twin. Disable her before she kills you.

"No. No!" Ferrin gritted his teeth and struggled to pull away from his sister. He succeeded in lifting Kali off the bed, but they stayed melded together. There was no way to free his hands, and without his hands, no way to channel this power anywhere else. He hated this woman, despised her for everything she had done to him but he didn't want her dead.

"What are you doing? Hold still! If you do anything to damage our child or interfere with this magic, I will kill you, brother. Do not doubt that." Kali hissed the words, her eyes glimmering with menace.

"Why do you want this now? I could have killed her before!" Ferrin ignored Kali as she began to spew more threats. This was between him and the demon now. Something had happened, something to change the distribution of power, though what that had been he couldn't say.

We're not going to kill her, dear Ferrin. We're just going to get her out of the way.

"He wants to get you out of the way." Ferrin repeated the words to Kali, the truth suddenly becoming clear. "You're not pregnant. He lied to you to get us here, in this ritual with nowhere to run."

"You're a liar! I can feel the baby kick already! The tests were positive, all three of them," Kali argued, but he could see the faint glimmer of doubt in her eyes.

"I'm not lying. The demon's tricked you. Help me. We've got to get my hands—"

"Never!"

"Help me or I won't have a choice. I'll do as he asks. I might even kill you." A cold sweat covered his skin, and Ferrin trembled with the force of holding the power within him. He didn't have much time. This was her last chance, a chance he wasn't at all surprised to see her pass up without a thought.

"You're a liar! Do what Reglanus says—do it now!"

With a roar of frustration, Ferrin pushed the sick, green-gold magic into his sister. He didn't know if he could trust the demon, but the power was too much to fight. He couldn't contain it or control it. If he didn't channel it somewhere, he was going to burn himself alive. If he killed Kali, well, it just might be her day to die.

Kali screamed as the energy powered into her body, her golden glow throbbing with streaks of dark green. She rolled from the bed to the floor, Ferrin's hands falling from her easily now that the ritual was complete. There, she curled into a ball on her side, gripping her stomach in pain.

"Damn you! You've broken our covenant. I'll send you back to hell so fast your—" Kali broke off with a sob, her hands flying to cover her eyes. She was suddenly crying, bawling like a small child, wild, abandoned wails that made Ferrin physically ill. The pain that radiated from her petite frame was epic, more pain than even a traitorous demon could possibly cause. Whatever it was that had broken this woman, turned her to the demon-fast in the first place, it was far worse than anything Ferrin had ever known.

For the first time since he laid eyes on his sister, he actually felt sympathy for her. While he had been growing up in the warm loving light of the Amiantos woods, where had Kali been? Who had loved her? Shown her that life could be more than pain and power? Had there ever been anyone who had helped her learn to listen to the voice of goodness within her, the voice that Ferrin finally realized had always been within him as well, as strong as that black seed that he had always feared?

"Yes. You win, yes. I'll free you, if you vow to stop this." Kali's whispered the words through her tears. The malignant glow that covered her skin faded, leaving her pale and limp on the floor, her large eyes nearly black with despair.

"Are you all right?" Ferrin asked, picking up the knife from the bed and positioning himself between Kali and the demon. Reglanus was fading, no longer as solid as he had been moment before.

"As if you care." The words were quiet, hopeless, and her eyes didn't focus on him when he crouched down beside her.

"I won't lie, I don't have any love for you, but you're my sister. I wish we could have met before…before you came to this." Ferrin felt something hard in his heart shatter. She'd raped him, hurt him, threatened to kill him, but looking into her face right now, all he could see was that little girl she'd once been. A little girl who had obviously been scared, hurt and ashamed by what she was, a little girl who had never had anyone on her side.

As he gently pushed the hair from her face, it was almost as if he could see that life, flashes of Kali alone in some sort of halfway house. Kali beaten by a group of other witches in a locker room, Kali smiling up into the face of a much older man on her wedding day, full of hope for the first time in her life. Hope that had later turned to despair when that man betrayed her.

"You were right. There was no child," she said, tears in her eyes once more. "I'm sorry, Ferrin. I'm so sorry."

Ferrin didn't know what to say. His throat was suddenly tight, tears at the back of his eyes. How could he forgive her, but how could he not? She'd broken him in a way nothing ever had, but amidst those pieces he'd found his true self, a self that was far better than he had ever known.

"Kali, I—"

"You have to run, try to get out of here. It was a wasting spell. It would have killed me if I didn't free him from the magic fast. Now he's at liberty to join with you and Aleeza. That's what he's wanted all along," she whispered, swallowing with obvious effort, fear clear in her eyes as she stared at the misty form of Reglanus now growing solid once more. "I took some of his power by breaking the fast, but it won't take him long to recover. Get out of here, find Aleeza and free her from his spell if you can."

"Come with me. I'll carry you out of—"

"No, there's no time. Run Ferrin, and no matter what you do, don't go into the Amiantos woods!" She pulled herself into a seated position and took the knife from his hand. On unsteady feet she stood, making her way toward the demon. "Let's see if a demon can bleed, Reglanus. I've been curious about that for some time now."

Ferrin turned and ran for the door, trying not to think about what would happen to Kali now that she'd decided to battle the demon. If Reglanus had wanted her dead, surely he would have killed her already. There were only two Daiesthai left in the world. He couldn't afford to kill Kali until he was certain that Ferrin was bought and paid for. She might suffer, but she'd bought him some time and provided a much-needed distraction.

Ferrin flung open the door and ran down the steep metal steps, his bare feet freezing. The temperature had dropped significantly since the last time he'd been out of a climate-controlled room and he wished for some clothes as he raced around the first landing and hit another flight of stairs.

He could feel Aleeza and Dorand, could almost hear the sounds of a struggle somewhere below him. He would find them, free them and then they would all get the hell out of here. No matter how strong he felt when linked with their power, he didn't want to take another shot at Reglanus until he'd had time to heal.

And to eat a fucking sandwich. Gods, he was hungry, so hungry that even the fear and anxiety rocketing through him couldn't keep his stomach from growling. Running down the stairs was making him dizzy. Kali had given him water but no food.

He was so dizzy, in fact, that at first he assumed the sight at the bottom of the stairs was just a hunger-induced delusion.

"Ferrin, I'm so glad I've found you." Aleeza stood over Dorand's body, blood on her hands. Dorand lay frighteningly still at her feet, his face slack as if in sleep…or something worse. "Now we can become what we were destined to be."

"Aleeza, step back away from him." Ferrin moved closer, close enough to see that Aleeza's skin was marked with scrapes and bruises, and her eyes clouded and unfocused. "Aleeza, can you hear me? Aleeza!"

She blinked once, and then shook her head. "Ferrin…run, it's—"

Her words ended with a moan as she sank to the concrete beside Dorand. Kali's men attacked Ferrin from behind, and it wasn't long before he knew exactly how Aleeza had come by her bruises.

Chapter Seventeen

෨

He woke with a cry, his muscles and limbs jerking in a vain attempt to fight the men who surrounded Aleeza. It was too late—he knew it was as soon as he saw her body twist and that strange light in her eyes—

He was alone. Gingerly, Dorand sat up, one hand instinctively going to his bleeding forehead as if to hold the blood back. The signs of the earlier fight were everywhere, from the broken two-by-fours the men had used to beat them to the blood spattering the garage floor, but he didn't need the silence to tell him everyone was gone.

Everyone, including Ferrin and Aleeza.

Groaning, Dorand dragged himself to his feet. There was no time, no time to waste waiting to feel better. He had to go, to find them. Before it was too late if it wasn't already. The dim light coming through the entrance to the parking area told him not much time had passed, but if they had taken Aleeza's car they could get back to the Amiantos woods pretty quickly.

They had to be taking them to the woods. He even knew about where they would be, thanks to their predictable four-corners pattern from the earlier murders. East, south, west. Somewhere north of the center of the forest, they would be setting up the gruesome finale.

Every nerve ending screamed at him to hurry, but he tried to use his head. Thirst racked his body, and after losing blood he couldn't afford to ignore it. He made his way along the dusty floor to a spigot on the wall. After waiting for the brown water to turn a more neutral color, he held his mouth under the cold stream until his throat stopped burning and his vision lost the fuzziness associated with dehydration.

How to get back home was the question. They'd come in Aleeza's car, which might or might not still be outside. Downtown Savior City was rife with bums and coven rejects so even if the thugs hadn't taken it, the thieves might have. Hitchhiking wasn't an option. People with vehicles rarely dared enter this area. Not that it really mattered. Even if there had been motorists thick on the streets, no one was going to pick up a hitchhiker half covered in blood, and if he tried to walk, it could be hours before he reached a phone where he could make a call to his Chieftan. And that was assuming he made it through the streets alive. In his condition, he was easy prey for people who would kill him for the clothes he wore or for organs to sell on the black market.

No. He had to find some mode of transportation. He made his way to a small booth near the entrance of the garage and rifled through the drawers, looking for keys. There were a few rusted heaps in the back of the garage. Surely one of them still had to be in working order.

"I'll take you to find them. I know where they've gone."

Dorand spun around, instinctively bringing his hands into fists in front of him. It was a female voice, but he was never one to underestimate the "weaker" sex. The woman who stood a few feet away was naked, her golden skin torn, covered in blood and dirt. She waved a weary hand. "I'm not going to hurt you. I don't think I could even if I tried."

"Who are you?" As if he had to ask. Even beaten and bruised, the woman throbbed with dark magic. This had to be Kali, the woman they'd come here to find and destroy. This was the witch who had fasted with the demon, who had killed Carantha, kidnapped Ferrin and delivered Aleeza into the hands of evil. Dorand's throat tightened and he fought the urge to run at the woman, fists flying.

"I'm Kali, the one you came here to kill. I don't blame you, but I think it would be in your best interests to let me live, at least until we find them. My car is on the next level down. I can drive—"

"You can't think I would trust you to take me to the bathroom, much less drive me somewhere in a car."

"So you drive." She stumbled and grabbed the wall of the garage to keep herself upright. "I don't care, and I don't care if you trust me or not. But you have to believe me. I don't want to hurt Ferrin or Aleeza, I just want my revenge. That demon bastard betrayed me, and I'll see him sent back to hell or die trying."

Dorand hesitated. The truth of her words hovered around her, but at the thought of being closed up in a car with the woman responsible for Carantha's death—his fists clenched.

Kali's eyes narrowed. "If you want to keep Ferrin and Aleeza from finishing what the demon started, you'll drive me to the woods. I know exactly where they're going, and if we hurry, we can still stop it."

* * * * *

Ferrin struggled against the ropes binding him. The rough bark of the tree scraped his already aching back, but he didn't care. Had the knot holding his left wrist slipped a little bit? Maybe this was working. He concentrated on that side, twisting his wrist, ignoring the pain as the prickly hemp cut into his skin.

Pain was good, anything to keep his focus from what lay before him.

The torch-lit clearing looked like a place from another world. Technically it *was* from another world—Reglanus had already cast the circle, so the clearing was set apart, a place between worlds and within all worlds. A place where the kind of ritual the demon had planned could work.

Raw power crawled over Ferrin's skin, something else to ignore. He could not give in, especially not now, when Dorand might be dead and no one in the world was on their way to help the woman he loved. But gods, it would be so easy. Aleeza's naked body gleamed in the firelight as she slept, tied to the low stone table with her arms above her head and her legs spread just enough for him to see the treasure hiding between.

The scent of her assaulted him, almost physically caressing his skin. He wanted her so badly. She was made for him, born for him. All he had to do as reach out and take her, and together they and their children could have everything he'd ever wanted, power, love, safety —

No! He couldn't let his mind think those thoughts. No matter how badly he wanted it, no matter how hard and heavy his cock, he could not. To do so would be to destroy the balance of good and evil, force everyone else he loved to live in a world consumed by violence and pain. And he would be a fool to believe that pain wouldn't touch him, Aleeza or their children. If they were fasted with demons, they would never be truly free, never safe. Reglanus had betrayed Kali, maybe even killed her. Surely he had learned his lesson, that the power Reglanus offered was nothing but a pretty lie.

He had learned that. Hadn't he?

Aleeza stirred, her head turning toward him. Her back arched a little off the stone, as if she was trying to get comfortable. The movement made her breasts rise, made the light dance off her hard nipples. His cock jerked.

"Look at her, you can hardly control yourself," said that girl—Raven, he thought her name was—Aleeza's cousin if her word was to be believed. It made sense. If anyone could get close enough to gather the ingredients for a hex portal, it would be a trusted family member.

She smirked as she took a good, long look up and down his body. He wanted to look away but refused to do so. He had nothing to be ashamed of. She was the one who had sold her soul for the chance to get laid. She'd been Kali's lover, and now she served Reglanus for the chance to claim a place as a bride of the Daeisthai coven. He'd tried to convince her that the demon's promises weren't worth a shit, but she hadn't listened. But then, what else was new?

"You're going to fuck her—you won't be able to help yourself. You know you want her."

"More than anyone will ever want you," he said. Raven's hand shot out. She slapped him across the face—hard.

Damn. Baiting her was a very bad idea. The pain caused by a Gunera woman, no matter how vile, only served to increase his desire. Must remember to avoid angering her in future, at least until he could finally put an end to all of this.

"Liar." Her angry face twisted into a smile. "*You* want me. I can tell."

How should he respond? If he denied it she might hit him again. If he agreed she'd think she had power over him. That might serve his purpose eventually, but it was too soon to tell. So he said nothing, only stared at the fire flickering over her head.

"It's a shame," she continued. "If I'd been a little more powerful I could have broken the curse, and it would be me about to create a new world, a new magic. But no, it had to be Aleeza. Why she gets everything, I don't know. Everyone acts like she's some sort of hero or a fucking angel of mercy. She's not. She lied and cheated and worked gray magic, and she's not even in trouble for it. My coven leader was going to give her a full pardon."

By the Gods, this girl was worse than Kali. "Don't you think being chained to a rock as a demon sacrifice is punishment?"

Raven snorted. "She won't be a sacrifice. She'll be mother of the new race. The Daeisthai will worship her as a goddess for centuries, the dark Mother Mary. Hardly seems like a punishment."

"Raven." The cold, smooth voice of Reglanus echoed through the clearing. "Time to leave our guest to gather his energy. If we want the spell to work without the full moon of Samhain, we need to put the wheels in motion. Another hour and the moon leaves Saturn."

Raven ran one finger down Ferrin's chest and stomach, sliding it all the way to the tip of his cock. He gritted his teeth but could not help his body's instinctive reaction. Raven smiled a melancholy grin. "Such a shame. Aleeza's a lucky woman."

Ferrin renewed his attempts to free his left wrist as she sauntered away to consult with the demon. How she'd gotten here he didn't know, but then he wasn't sure how any of them had gotten here. His last clear memory was of Aleeza's beautiful, confused face as she stood over Dorand's still body.

Dorand. Was he really dead? Ferrin didn't think so but he couldn't be sure. He dared not try to call his brother's energy here. To do so would warn Reglanus that Ferrin hadn't given in to him. The only way to get through this was to make the demon think he wanted to submit and follow his Daiesthai instincts, lull him into a false sense of security so that he could grab Aleeza and make a run for it.

The breeze rustled through the trees outside the clearing but did not touch Ferrin's skin. Reglanus' circle was strong enough to keep out the very forces of nature. That did not bode well for rescue or escape.

Reglanus walked the circle again, his voice low, slithering through the sacred space. Ferrin's skin crawled. How the demon's power called him, how he yearned to respond, to let his father-brother-mother-demon-ruler set him free, to impregnate the girl who waited for him. She was his, his birthright. Why couldn't he?

The sparks of purity and hope in his heart ignited, struggling valiantly against the demon's words, but Ferrin could feel himself sinking into darkness just the same. His chest expanded. His breathing deepened. Something in the air smelled like home, like sulphur and smoke. The blackness within him turned to flame, flames rising through his body and into his mind.

Reglanus looked like smoke himself, silvery and indistinct in the gathering darkness. The torches still burned, but their flames were smaller, somehow, suffocating as the gateway opened and the unnatural poured into the circle.

Aleeza stirred, a tiny moan escaping her lips. She looked so beautiful tears came to his eyes. His dark queen waiting for him. Tonight their love would bring something long-gone back to life. Aleeza would give birth to a new world today, a new era.

Her eyes opened. For a second he saw panic there, but whatever Reglanus' spell, it seemed to be working because the fear disappeared. Her lips curved into a sexy smile. "Ferrin," she said, and her voice was honey poured over his skin. "Why are you all the way over there?"

He cleared his throat. "Because…" Why? Why was he all the way over here? Think! "Because we shouldn't do this, Aleeza. We can't—you know that. You know it."

"Why not?"

"I don't know." But he did, didn't he? There was a reason. It just didn't make much sense now.

Cool hands unfastened the knots binding him to the tree. "Why don't you go touch her, my son?" Reglanus said. "Just go see how you feel."

Ferrin rubbed life back into his hands and took a few steps toward Aleeza, Reglanus' chants receding, a buzz in the background. He'd unchain her and they would escape. That was what he would do. They needed to escape.

Her eyes met his as he stood over her. She bit her lip. The sight of that plump bit of flesh disappearing between her perfect teeth made his insides twist.

He reached for her arms, intending only to slide his hands up to unlock her, but his palms found her breasts instead, lifting them, squeezing them together. She gasped and arched her back further. The movement made her legs fall open. Ferrin groaned.

"I love it when you touch me," she said, and for a second there she wasn't bespelled Aleeza. She was just Aleeza, and the rest of the world fell away. Reglanus and Raven no longer watched them. The clearing was not a space of magic but just a clearing. And the woman he loved lay naked before him and begged him with her eyes to make love to her.

He bent his head to her, rolling each nipple in turn between his teeth. Heat caressed him from her skin, and when he slid his left hand down the soft curve of her belly to dip between her legs he found even more heat waiting for him there.

Her hips lifted as he brushed his fingertips over her clit. A growl escaped his throat, coming from somewhere low in his belly, somewhere so deep he didn't know it existed within him.

Aleeza's eyes glowed as she looked at him, and he saw on her skin the reflected glow of his own eyes. It was complete. Somehow he'd finished the spell, accepted the demon's suggestion. Maybe when he touched her, when he dipped his fingers into her slick heat or when he took that delicious nipple into the cavern of his mouth…it didn't matter. They were walking on the path now, the path that led only to one place, and as Ferrin climbed onto the stone slab to bury his face between her legs, he knew there was no way to turn back around.

* * * * *

Kali's breath rasped so loudly Dorand was sure they would be heard long before they reached the location. She was weak from her battle with the demon, barely managing to keep pace with him as they raced through the dark woods. A few miles back he'd offered to carry the bitch, just to make sure they didn't alert the demon or his followers of their arrival, but she'd refused.

Once Dorand saw the tableau before them, however, he realized they could have been beating gongs and still gone unnoticed. The clearing was tightly enclosed in a magic circle, nothing coming in, nothing going out until the spell was complete.

In the center of the clearing, illuminated only by flickering torchlight, lay Aleeza and Ferrin on a slab of granite. Or rather, Ferrin was lying down while Aleeza hovered above him, his cock buried in her throat as her legs straddled his head. From his position Dorand could see her gleaming pussy, could see the tip of Ferrin's tongue teasing her. As he watched, his throat grew dry as bone and his cock hard as iron. She came, throwing her head back and grinding herself down onto Ferrin's face.

"The spell has started," Kali said softly beside him. "We're too late."

"No, we can't be." Dorand watched Aleeza sit and turn around, sliding down Ferrin's chest to take his cock in her mouth again. The green-gold glow of their desire hung glittering in the air around them. The looked like a painting, the most erotic painting he'd ever seen.

"We might have been able to break the circle before they were both on the altar, but now…" Kali trailed off, then sucked in a deep breath as if she was fighting tears. "I'm sorry. Truly I am. I know you won't believe me, but I wish I could go back and give that demon bastard a different answer."

"Wish in one hand and shit in the other. Let's see which one gets filled first." Dorand suppressed a roar of rage, digging his hands through his hair and pulling until his scalp ached. There had to be a way into that circle. Frantically he mentally thumbed through his knowledge of demon lore. For every spell there was a counter-spell. If only he'd given in and bought a cell phone when Ferrin had pushed him to get with the times, he might be able to call Walter right now and find out.

"I know which would get filled. My entire life was one big fistful of shit, topped off by my husband leaving me for his mistress. Reglanus promised the one thing my heart desired. I let that desire and my anger overwhelm me. But—"

"What your heart desired? Do murderers have hearts?"

"I didn't murder anyone. I just collected people for Reglanus."

"You *collected* Carantha and good as signed her death warrant. Keep reminding me of that, and you won't live to see that demon sent back to hell." Dorand shut his mouth so tightly his teeth ground together and his jaw ached. He had to maintain control. He couldn't let his temper get the better of him, not when he needed the use of reason so badly.

"A baby. I wanted a baby. Everything else came later, the power, the promise to rule the Daeisthai. When I first fasted with Reglanus, it was simply because I wanted to have a child, wanted to feel that kind of love. The demon took advantage after—"

"The devil made you do it? Sorry, I'm not buying." Dorand knelt on the ground, clutching a fistful of earth. He had to think, think of where natural magic would lead him, let the magic of creation fight this spell of death. It was a death spell, no matter that the use of intercourse mimicked a creation spell. He, Ferrin and Carantha had used sex to speak with the dead. Now Reglanus would have Ferrin and Aleeza use sex to bind their eternal souls to the demon realm and be soul dead for the rest of their very long lives.

Damn! There was something there. Sex and death, polar opposites that were so very intimately related in magic. Their triad had used sex to transcend the physical realm, to reach beyond and bring the spirit of the dead a voice it could never have without that magic. Reglanus attempted to use that same power to transcend the boundaries of Ferrin and Aleeza's flesh, of their human souls, to fast to them in a way that would make room for the demon to fit between them like the piece of a puzzle. A piece that would never be removed.

But how to stop him?

Dorand watched Ferrin's hands twist in Aleeza's dark hair as she bent her head over him, swallowing him. From the pulsing of his hips and the way he forced himself deeper into her mouth, Dorand guessed he would climax soon. What would happen then? Did they need to actually have intercourse to complete the spell?

"If he comes now, is it done?"

"Not if he comes in her mouth—that's not how babies are—"

"Don't you dare." Dorand turned to the woman and took her by the upper arms, shaking her like a doll. "You will answer my questions and help me stop this, or I *will* kill you."

"I'm sorry." She winced in pain but didn't close her large, brown eyes, eyes that looked so fucking familiar it gave Dorand the creeps.

"Talk."

"They'll keep going if he comes in her mouth," Kali said. "No matter how many times they each come, they'll keep going until she's pregnant. Reglanus is using all of his power to make sure of that, see? You can just barely make out—" she gasped, her hand flying to her throat.

Dorand saw her at the same time as Kali. Raven, standing nude not far from the stone table.

"She betrayed me, that little fucking bitch. That's why my coven followers attacked you. She must have had them in her control. Reglanus can't cast a spell into the physical world without a human conduit. That succubus spell in the garage. I thought maybe one of the men…but I should have known," Kali whispered. She shook her head. "I can't believe she had it in her."

"When we found her, she was all dolled up waiting for you and said you hadn't called in days. Why shouldn't she betray you? The better question is how the hell she got out of the binding spell Aleeza cast."

And why Aleeza's coven head, Gavyn, hadn't detained her. She must have escaped before Gavyn arrived, which gave Dorand hope. Maybe Gavyn had called the Amiantos council.

Maybe his brothers and sisters were out looking for them right now. Not that it would do much good if he couldn't stop what was happening in that clearing. If the demon finished the spell, there was nothing any of them would be able to do to save Ferrin or Aleeza or themselves.

"She was always very powerful, but she's more powerful now that she's made a deal with Reglanus. I had her under a safeguarding spell. She shouldn't have even been able to tell you where to find me."

"She didn't. We found electric and water bills in your room." Dorand began picking his way around the circle, positioning himself behind the demon. Once he decided what in the hell he was going to do, that seemed the best place to be.

"There were no bills, not in my name. They were all in my coven followers' names and most of them aliases." She laughed, a weak, bitter sound that turned to a wheeze as she hurried after him. "Raven must have printed those up for you to find. Clever. If I'd only known, I would have found her so much more attractive."

"Shut up, let me think." Dorand hissed the words over his shoulder.

Riding in the car with the woman, watching her struggle into a black sweatshirt three times too big and wade through the knee-deep leaves barefoot, listening to her talk—all of it made her far too real. He'd vowed to kill Carantha's murderer, but Kali was still very much alive. The longer she stayed that way, the less likely he would be able to follow through with his intent. He still hated her for what she'd done, but she was no longer a faceless thing he could destroy.

Hell, he probably never could have done it. The desire to shun black magic, murder and anything so blatantly dark had been imbedded in his very genes.

By the gods, that was it!

"What are you doing?" Kali asked.

"I have to get in that circle," Dorand said, peeling off the sweatshirt and stiff jeans he had found in Kali's car. It would be best to be naked, nothing to impede him when he tried to make contact with Ferrin and Aleeza.

"Are you mad? You'll never penetrate a sacred circle, at least not and live to tell about it."

"It's not a sacred circle. It was walked by a demon, not a witch. I'm Amiantos. I can't conduct any of his spells." Dorand turned to the clearing but was stopped by a surprisingly strong hand on his arm.

"No, but he can use Ferrin and Aleeza to kill you as soon as you get close enough. Not to mention Raven and there could be some of my men nearby. Reglanus didn't want them here before but if he's feeling cautious, he could have lookouts hidden or—"

"There are no men. We would have seen them by now, and Ferrin and Aleeza won't hurt me. Even under the demon's power, Aleeza never tried to harm me, only to stop the blood when one of your goons slipped a knife in my ribs."

"Fine, but you do realize what you've just said, don't you? You've been beaten and knifed. You're hardly in prime form to go combat a demon and three possessed witches." Kali held his arm more tightly, her features drawn and worried, as if she actually cared that he might be walking to his death.

"Your concern is touching, but I'm going in that circle. If you want to help, find a way to distract Raven. Tell her you've come to have make-up sex. She acted as if she loved you, might as well use that to our advantage." Dorand wrenched his arm free and stalked toward the stone table, where Ferrin was now on top, seconds away from sliding his cock inside Aleeza.

"Wait! Here, take this." Kali pulled a knife from the front pocket of her sweatshirt and held it out to him. "Reglanus has one just like it that he'll use to cut the baby out of Aleeza."

"I don't have time for—"

"Please! Listen. As soon as they conceive, Reglanus has a spell to make the child grow nine months' worth in a few hours."

"I won't—"

"I know you're going to try to stop that from happening, and this knife can help. It's a blood keeper. If you can get Aleeza and Ferrin to willingly spill blood on the knife, and then cut your own hand, you'll be their keeper until you choose to set them free. Reglanus won't be able to touch them."

"That's black magic, Kali, and you know it."

"Aren't the people you love worth a little taint on your soul?" Her eyes looked black with the moonlight shining behind her, their soulless depths sending a shiver down his spine. Dorand looked to the clearing, then back to the knife in Kali's hand. Ferrin was inside Aleeza now, his buttocks clenching as he fucked her, harder, faster. It wouldn't be long now.

"If I fail, the blood keeper is coming looking for you." Dorand took the knife and ran. There was no more time to think, only to act—and pray.

Chapter Eighteen

ഇ

"Yes, Ferrin. Yes!" Aleeza screamed, her pussy contracting around the cock Ferrin thrust ruthlessly between her legs. She'd lost track of how many times she'd come, as well as how many times she'd opened her mouth to protest only to find her lips unable to form the words.

Stop him! You have to stop this! Remember what will happen if you conceive, remember —

"Aleeza." He called her name, raking his teeth against the delicate skin at her throat, and the weak, quiet voice of sanity fled.

There was nothing in the world but him, his body hot above her, inside her, his skin pressed so tightly to hers it felt like they would merge into one being. The torchlight and their green-gold magic filled the air, blocking out the world, blocking out everything except the bliss of making love to this man.

"Reglanus! Look out!"

But it didn't block out that voice. Aleeza's head snapped to the side and she saw her, Raven, standing nude only a few feet away. How the hell had her cousin gotten here? And why the fuck wasn't Aleeza lunging from the table to get her hands around the bitch's throat?

"Ferrin, stop, stop!" She screamed the words as loudly as she could, before the black cloud of drunken lust could descend on her mind or numb her lips. They'd been tricked, she and Dorand led into a trap set by her cousin. She was sure of it. Now she and Ferrin were on their way to selling themselves to the monster who stalked around the circle, and Dorand was probably dead and —

"Fight it, Ferrin. Fight it, Aleeza. I'm—" Dorand's words broke into a roar of pure rage, and Aleeza turned in time to see him struggling toward the stone table though the demon clawed and tore at his skin. Dorand swung his arm up and around, hitting the monster upside the head with the hilt of the knife he held in his hand. The thing howled and floated away, once again becoming mist.

"Fuck, Aleeza. You have to get out of here, out of this circle." Ferrin pulled his cock from her body, gulping for air as if emerging from too long underwater. "You have to get out before it has time to refocus its power."

"But what about you?" Aleeza sat up and swung her legs over the side of the table, her vision dancing with gray spots. The abrupt release from the demon's influence was dizzying. She wasn't sure she could walk a straight line right now, let alone fight her way free of a circle of power.

"I've got to help Dorand. He's been wounded already and—"

"Dorand isn't affected by the demon spells—you are. If you go over to help him, you might end up helping kill him. We've both got to get out of here—preferably in different directions. Once we're gone, Dorand can—"

"Aleeza!" Ferrin caught her around the waist as her knees buckled. She was so fucking weak, and feeling every bruise Kali's thugs had inflicted now that she wasn't high on sex magic.

"I'm fine, but I think I did something to my ankle when Dorand and I were fighting those witches in the garage." Aleeza said. "I'm not going very far on my own."

"Neither of you are going anywhere. Get back on the table." Raven appeared inches away from Ferrin, and Aleeza felt him stiffen against her.

"She's got a gun, Aleeza."

Dorand reached her side, then stilled. Just his presence there was enough to give Aleeza strength. Too bad that wasn't enough. The strongest magic they all possessed was no match for a speeding bullet.

"You think he won't break his word to you, Raven?" Kali's voice, contemptuous and full of pain, entered the circle, even if her body could not. "You think he'll deliver his promises? He won't. He lied to me."

"He didn't want to lie to you, Kali," Raven said. "I convinced him Aleeza was the better option. That having a healthy child to start the new race was better than the inbred mutant you would have conceived. And he'll keep his promise to me. I'm a Gunera woman, after all. I'm one of the only witches powerful enough to raise this child."

"My child?" Aleeza knew there could be no child, but she couldn't help the pain that shot through her at Raven's words, or the anger.

"No, *my* child. You don't think you'll survive the birth, do you?"

Ferrin and Dorand reached for Aleeza's hands at the same moment, holding her back. Bullet or no bullet, she was ready to rip Raven's cold blue eyes right out of her head.

Their touch calmed her, centered her and sent a spike of lust straight to her pussy. There was something here, something about the connection of the three of them that made them powerful. Without knowing how or why, she knew that what she and Ferrin had not been able to achieve on their own, they could achieve with Dorand's purity added to their power. Together she and Ferrin were nearly hopeless in the face of their bodies' demands. When Dorand was added to the mix, she wanted him just as badly as she did Ferrin. The distraction was enough to clear her head.

And beneath her own desire throbbed Ferrin and Dorand's. They both wanted her, needed her…but they wanted and needed each other as well. Once they'd been part of a powerful triad. She knew without either of them telling her that they both hoped to be again. Knew too that she was more powerful than Carantha had been.

"Let's test that one out," she said below her breath, as Raven and Kali continued to bicker and taunt each other from opposing sides of the circle wall.

"You never cared," Raven shouted, voice thick with unshed tears. "You used me from the beginning, so you can't blame me for getting some of my own back."

Do not lose focus, Raven, my love. Reglanus was still misty. Aleeza guessed holding the circle and the blow he'd suffered from Dorand had sapped more of his strength than he would like to admit. *Why are you wasting time? Get rid of the Amiantos.* If he noticed his former fast-partner, he gave no indication.

"Aleeza, I need your blood," Dorand whispered. He slid the blade against her arm. She tried not to flinch.

Blood magic was dark magic, the strongest and darkest there was. Blood hadn't even been a requirement in the anti-celibacy spell, which had been the darkest magic she'd ever dared to work.

Would an Amiantos even be able to cast dark magic? Even an Amiantos who could communicate with the dead?

She shook her head. Why was she even thinking twice about this? If Dorand wanted her blood, he could have it. "Go ahead," she whispered, steeling herself against the pain.

But it didn't hurt. Instead a rush of heat bloomed in her muscle, heat and a curious draining sensation. She turned to look at him, but he wasn't looking at her. Instead his hooded eyes were focused on the demon, and his lips moved in a chant she'd never heard before.

The draining stopped, and something rushed into her now, something blinding white tinged with black. It roared through her body. It was all she could do not to scream. She bit her lip hard enough to taste blood, her fingers squeezing Ferrin's.

The whole thing seemed to take hours, but it couldn't have been more than a few seconds. Reglanus hadn't even finished his sentence, Kali was still yelling, and chaos still ruled in the still air of the circle as Ferrin turned to her, his eyes dark with worry.

"Aleeza," he said. "What's—"

He looked down and saw the blood running down her arm, saw the blade in Dorand's hand. Something passed between the two men that Aleeza did not understand. Her ears roared and buzzed, the buzzing slowly settling and becoming something else, a steady rhythm. She knew somehow what it was. It was Dorand's heartbeat, and it pulsed through her own veins. He'd connected her to him, and in a flash she saw him reach out his knife to slice Ferrin's arm and knew what he was doing.

So did Reglanus. With a roar he surged into his solid form and lunged for Dorand. The two fell sideways, leaving Aleeza and Ferrin alone to watch, horrified and helpless, as Reglanus' ghostly fingers closed around Dorand's throat. The fingers didn't look completely formed, but it was clear from the mottled hue Dorand's skin quickly took on that they were solid enough to kill.

Aleeza's own breath came in gasps. The connection between them meant she experienced Dorand's desperation for air. If he died, would she die too?

Beside her Ferrin shouted, his words lost in the echoing rasps of her breath in her ears. Her vision fuzzed around the edges. She was going to pass out, was going to die…

"Dammit, Aleeza! Breathe!" Ferrin's words finally came through to her. Raven, who'd been staring transfixed as Reglanus choked the life out of Dorand, leapt at her just as Aleeza realized what was happening.

Through their connection, Dorand was taking her breath. She was keeping him alive somehow, but her panic was making her gasp, which was providing less oxygen when they needed more to share.

Clenching her fists, she focused on breathing deep and slow, on feeling the air fill her lungs. Almost instantly the wheezing in her chest eased and images in the clearing came back into focus.

She had a glimpse of the trees and flames around her before Raven slammed into her, knocking her to the ground with a painful thud. Raven's fingers clawed at her face, her eyes, her cousin's lips twisted in an ugly grimace of fury.

Still trying to breathe as deeply as possible, Aleeza brought her knee up, wishing it was a man who held her down instead of a woman. Still, no matter what sex you are, being slammed in the groin isn't comfortable. The second of surprise and pain halted Raven's movements long enough for Aleeza to pull back her fist and punch her cousin in the face.

Raven screamed and lifted her own fist, but by then Ferrin had joined the fray. The firelight gleamed off his naked body as he yanked Raven backward by the hair and dragged her away.

Aleeza rolled to her side, to where Dorand and Reglanus still struggled. The demon realized his choking wasn't helping at the same time Aleeza grabbed for one of the torches. He lifted his terrible face to her, but his power over her had ceased. She was Dorand's now, protected by his Amiantos purity, and the movements of Reglanus' lips as he tried to bring her back under his spell did not affect her.

Dorand reached for her, but he was not offering his hand. It was the knife, the one he'd used to bind her to him, and as his eyes caught hers she understood.

She grabbed the knife from him. Reglanus lunged for her but missed.

Unfortunately, Ferrin didn't. She'd thought Reglanus' spell had been aimed at her, but it had not. The man staring at her now through Ferrin's eyes was not Ferrin.

The demon turned into a whisper of smoke and disappeared, leaving them alone with the thing that used to be her lover.

On the ground Raven lay still and silent, but her aura told Aleeza her cousin still lived. She wasn't sure she cared. But she knew she cared about Ferrin and had to find a way to take his blood. Maybe if she could make him angry enough to rush at her—

"It has to be willingly," Dorand croaked, standing up beside her. "He has to give it—we can't take it."

The thing behind Ferrin's eyes glared at them as they approached. A thick growl escaped his throat.

"Is that Reglanus in there?"

"I think so." Dorand took her hand. The warmth of his skin and the leap of his energy were comforting. She belonged with him, was bound to him. Together they could be happy for the rest of their lives...except they were bound to the man in front of them, in a way no less profound. They could not kill him, could not leave him.

"Ferrin," she started. It was a mistake. Her voice seemed to remind the demon why they were there to begin with.

"Aleeza," it said. The voice came from Ferrin's throat, but it was not Ferrin's. She curled her toes in the dirt beneath her feet to try and keep from collapsing. Cold chills ran down her spine. "Come to me."

"Can it—"

"I don't know," Dorand said. "I think he might still be able to impregnate you in this form, even with my protection. I don't know enough about this kind of thing."

"He can." Kali's voice from outside the circle drifted through the trees, weak and raspy. "But he'd need to kill you first to free Aleeza from the touch of Amiantos magic."

As if waiting for this, the Ferrin-Reglanus thing lunged for Dorand.

Aleeza screamed and shoved him as he passed, but Ferrin was too strong.

He fell on Dorand, knocking the bigger man to the ground. Instinctively Aleeza sucked in a huge breath, but this time it wasn't needed. Ferrin wasn't trying to choke Dorand. Reglanus had learned that lesson. Instead he appeared to be trying to rip Dorand's head off.

"No!" she screamed. Tears sprang to her eyes as she forced herself to kick Ferrin in the face. It hardly fazed him. She leapt forward, grabbing his arms, digging her nails in as she tried to tug and pull him away, but nothing worked.

"Ferrin...I love you," Dorand gasped. Ferrin hesitated.

He did not pause for long, but it was long enough for Aleeza to see what Dorand was up to, and how it might work. Trying to still her trembling, she ran her hand up Ferrin's arm to the spot behind his ear where he liked to be kissed, and tickled him. "I love you too, Ferrin."

Again, the beast hesitated. Dorand seized the opportunity to raise his head, snaking his hand around Ferrin's neck and pulling him close.

Aleeza's insides contracted as she watched her two lovers kiss, a kiss of pure love and trust, a kiss of rising passion. She felt it inside her own body, felt Dorand grow aroused as the two men's tongues entwined. Felt too her own arousal at the sight, her desire to join the pile and share their bodies.

Ferrin pulled his head away and screamed, a howl of agony. Aleeza jumped, frightened, but when Ferrin turned to her it was his eyes she saw. "Quick," he gasped. "Take it before he—aaarrgh!"

His eyes shifted, Reglanus coming back, but then as Aleeza held the knife aloft Ferrin showed through again. She didn't wait for Reglanus to return, cleanly slicing his shoulder with the blade.

This time she was ready, but the force screaming into her doubled. She stumbled, falling, while Ferrin's heartbeat changed into time with theirs. Both of their power rushed in her heart, in her brain. Both of their energies lifted her, bathed her.

She had only a glimpse of white light flashing into the clearing. Ferrin glowed with it, like a photo negative against her closed eyelids. He was screaming, and Dorand was screaming, so it did not surprise her that she was too. It surprised her even less that another voice screamed below theirs, the voice of the thwarted demon as he was sent back to hell. There was no place for him now, no way to regain his power. He could not impregnate Kali or Raven, and Aleeza was no longer available. She was bound, Amiantos by blood, and so was Ferrin.

How long the light blazed and the sounds of tearing agony went on, she did not know. She knew only that when they finally stopped, her entire body buzzed with the energy the three of them generated, with love and desire and sheer, simple gratitude that they were all alive.

She opened her eyes. The clearing still glowed white mixed with blue mixed with green-gold, but something else hovered there, something pale pink and vaguely human-shaped.

Beside her Dorand gasped and sat up. Ferrin followed. She felt the two men clasp hands, felt their sorrow and awe, and knew she was looking at the spirit of Carantha.

"More powerful than we were," she said, her voice a whisper through the trees.

"Carantha," Ferrin said. Once again his voice sounded different, but this time it was the tears choking his throat. "Carantha, we miss you so much."

Carantha nodded. She stood closer to them now but still hovered outside the circle. Aleeza could not make out her features. "I miss you too. Every day. But I'm moving on now and you should too."

"We…it's so hard." Dorand's voice was innocent and wounded as a little boy's.

"Not as hard as it seemed, is it? You have a new woman now, a powerful woman. Strong and brave. I've watched her, watched all of you. It's time to let me go now." Still Carantha glided outside the circle, and Aleeza had a sudden, horrible realization that she knew what Carantha was doing here, where she was going. Her gaze shot to Kali at the same moment the other woman realized it too. She leapt sideways, only to freeze in mid-air, caught in an otherworldly power.

Carantha's ghostly hand was extended, her fingers curled. "You're not going anywhere." Her features, delicately beautiful a moment ago, changed, became a parody of delicate beauty. Her rage was terrible to behold.

"Have mercy on her, Cara," Dorand said. "She helped save us in the end."

"Perhaps that will gain her a few moments of peace," said Carantha. "But you see, I am only here to collect her. Her fate is not up to me."

Two other shapes appeared at the edge of the circle. Rimer Lorcan and Lymera Brown. The other Fire Festival victims.

"I think we should get out of here," Ferrin whispered. His unease blew across her skin like a cool breeze. In it she felt his sorrow. Kali was his sister—she read the knowledge in his thoughts. She'd done horrible things to him, things Aleeza could not see because he was resolutely trying not to think of them, but she was still his sister.

"Please show her some mercy," he said.

"We will show her the mercy she showed us," Rimer said. Aleeza could not make out his features, but his image flickered and twisted with rage. She shivered.

Ferrin and Dorand did the same, and the three stood up as one. "Carantha, we're going," Dorand said. A tear ran down his cheek. "We love you, we will always love you but we cannot watch this."

"I will always love you," Carantha said. "But my world is different now. You will understand when we meet again." She glanced at Aleeza. "All of us. I look forward to getting to know you, Gunera woman. A long time from now. Until then, take care of them. I place them in your hands."

Responding somehow to the unearthly formality of the dead, Aleeza bobbed in a quick curtsy. It was the right thing to do. Carantha nodded.

"Now go, my loves," she said. Already she was gliding toward Kali with the other two close behind. "Let the dead handle the dead."

Kali's screams followed them as they ran from the clearing.

Chapter Nineteen
Ten Months Later, August 1ˢᵗ, Lammas

ℰℴ

Dorand lay back on the picnic blanket, closed his eyes and tilted his face toward the late summer sun. The sounds of the Eagles' song *Witchy Woman* floated to him from the bandstand, making him smile. The tribute band sounded almost exactly like the real thing, and he was enjoying himself tremendously.

"I still think they should have hired the Rolling Stones tribute band." Ferrin shifted slightly on the blanket beside him, his first sign of life in nearly an hour. His dark glasses hid his eyes completely, and Dorand had assumed he was asleep.

"I like this song. It reminds me of Aleeza," Dorand said, watching the small beads of sweat on his lover's chest roll down to pool in his navel.

They'd spent a good portion of the summer half-naked in the outdoors and Ferrin was looking more like a pirate than ever. He and Aleeza both had amazing tan lines. Just thinking about running his tongue over where dark turned to light, where what was public and what shown only in private collided, was enough to make Dorand thicker.

"This song's okay. The rest of the concert has sucked ass," Ferrin said.

"You suck ass." Aleeza spoke from Dorand's other side, a smile on her deep red lips. She'd gotten a bit of a burn and Dorand couldn't wait to smear aloe vera ChapStick over her lips—and then kiss it right off.

"I do not suck ass—that's Dorand."

"I was licking ass, not sucking. I think you're just jealous because it wasn't your ass." Dorand smiled when Ferrin punched him in the shoulder hard enough to hurt.

"Goddess, don't even start talking about that." Aleeza propped up on her elbows and took a long swig of the iced tea near her hip.

"Why, does it make you hot?" Dorand leaned over and whispered the words in her ear, inhaling the light saltiness of her sweat and that deep, exotic fragrance that was pure Aleeza. She laughed.

"You know it does, you jerk. Now stop with the seduction. I'm a sure thing when we get home, but right now we're on duty." Aleeza pressed a swift kiss to his lips, then pushed him away with a smile.

"On display is more like it." Ferrin's tone was dark, but the hand he snaked over Dorand's lap to pinch Aleeza's thigh decidedly playful.

"Quit bitching and keep looking like a wonderfully functional and deliriously happy triad." When Aleeza reached across his lap to return Ferrin's pinch, Dorand couldn't resist lifting his hips, and letting them both know where his mind was headed. "Dorand!"

"What? We've already raised a nearly thousand-year-old spirit and healed half a dozen witches once thought beyond the help of coven medicine. What more do they want?" Dorand asked. Since their magic-fasting, they had become the strongest magical force either of their covens had ever seen. Dorand's and Ferrin's death-speaking skills had grown threefold and Aleeza's healing power was greater than ever before. There hadn't been a hint of demonic activity in Savior City or the surrounding areas in nearly a year, and the three of them were happier than Dorand Triad ever imagined he could be. Other than the fact that his coven had basically exiled both him and Ferrin from the woods they had called home for over thirty years, everything was coming up roses.

"They need to see if our covens can play nicely before they offer any invitations to come back to the woods for the bonfire tonight," Aleeza said with a sigh that expressed just how much she was enjoying the first annual Gunera-Amiantos Lammas picnic.

You could cut the tension in the air with a knife. The Gunera stuck close to the stage and the beer tent while the Amiantos sat as close to the surrounding woods as possible. Ferrin, Dorand and Aleeza had spread their blanket between the stage and the woods, across the street from the beach in an effort to seem neutral.

Instead it made both covens unsure of which side they were really on. As a result only two or three people had made their way over to say hello in the three hours they'd been there. No matter how many times the triad had claimed to be both Gunera and Amiantos in power, owing no allegiance to one over the other, no one seemed to believe them. Dorand supposed old habits died hard.

"I don't really give a fuck if I ever go back to the fucking woods," Ferrin said, rolling over on his side and reaching across Dorand's lap again to steal a drink of Aleeza's tea. If Dorand didn't know better, he'd think the other man was deliberately trying to drive him to a state of arousal that would be difficult to hide.

"I don't know. The woods do have a certain power, and it was where we met," Aleeza said.

It had been over a year since Carantha's death and nearly a year since they'd bid her spirit goodbye. It was hard to believe he'd been away that long from what the Amiantos believed to be the source of their power with no ill effects. Or that he hadn't really missed the woods as much as he had expected when the verdict came down from the Chieftan that Dorand was no longer welcome there if he continued in a triad with Ferrin and Aleeza. Just being married to Aleeza might have been acceptable to the undefiled, as long as he didn't bring her up into the woods when he came to visit, but not a demon coven abomination.

The Chieftan was a bastard and his entire coven bigger bigots than he'd ever understood. He'd loved Ferrin before he'd known he was Daiesthai, and nothing that had happened changed that. He loved both of his partners and wouldn't stand for either of them being treated like second-class citizens.

"We have enough power and we could always make up a story about meeting at the horse races. Let's tell everyone we were all betting on the same horse, won the jack-pot, and decided to hold a three-day orgy at our new home to celebrate." Ferrin grinned and pulled his glasses off as he said the word "orgy", making it clear how he'd rather be spending the afternoon.

"We could say the horse's name was She Likes It Rough." Dorand said the words with a completely straight face, earning a giggle from Aleeza.

"But Dorand, I thought you wanted to go back," Ferrin said.

"I'd like to have the chance to visit from time to time, but I'd never want to live there again. The woods are tainted for me now." Dorand regretted the words as soon as they were out of his mouth. Both Aleeza and Ferrin fell silent, Aleeza plucking her lips with her fingers and Ferrin scowling fiercely toward the stage. Dorand knew how much it upset them, thinking of that night, of Kali, whose body had never been found, and of Raven, whose remains had been identified by dental records.

The demon Reglanus had apparently cast one last spell on his way to hell, a wasting spell that had destroyed Aleeza's cousin. She and Ferrin had both lost family that night. Betraying murderers or not, Dorand knew the memory of the loss still haunted them both.

"I think we've sunbathed enough. I'm ready for a dip." Dorand rose to his feet and stretched, pulling his long-sleeved white t-shirt over his head. He burned far more easily than his husband or wife and had to be careful in the sun.

"I'm game, anything to get away from *Hotel California*." Ferrin jumped to his feet with a grin as the band broke into the acoustic guitar version of the Eagles classic.

"I think you're both insane. The ocean is freezing cold. Not even the seals are swimming," Aleeza said, nonetheless grabbing her straw hat and coming to her feet beside them.

"Wimp," Ferrin teased, pulling her into his arms and stealing a kiss. His hands roamed down to take liberties with her luscious ass, which was barely covered by a pair of short shorts.

Thank the gods for short shorts, Dorand thought as his thickening cock swelled into a raging erection. He loved watching them touch, kiss. The jealousy that had been present at the beginning of their relationship was long gone. Once they were bound by the magic-fast of the blood keeper knife, and later by the vows of their people, they had fallen into a passionate but peaceful, way of relating. Their love was strong, fierce and equal. No one was ever left out in the cold, emotionally or physically.

"I'm a wimp? You were the one bitching about one little bite on the nipple last night."

"The little bite when you almost amputated my left pectoral?"

"I could have healed you after." Aleeza stuck her tongue out and pulled away from Ferrin to give Dorand a hug. Her face was even with his nipple, and her sharp little teeth clamped down hard enough to make Dorand grunt. "See, Dorand can take it."

She was right—he could take a little pain and dish it out far more easily than he could have dreamt of before. He'd been worried that his position as "keeper of the blood" in their relationship would taint their union, but his fears were unfounded. He had absorbed as much of Aleeza and Ferrin's power as they had his, each of them influencing the others equally, no one "in command" of the other. The only thing his position as keeper afforded them was that, within the eyes of the supernatural community, they were all Amiantos now. No demon or any demon magic could touch Ferrin or Aleeza. They were free to love and fuck as they would, with no danger of creating a new race of demon-witches, and for that they were all obscenely grateful.

"No, Dorand can not take it. I want your pussy today, little witch. And maybe he can enlighten me about that whole ass thing." Ferrin smiled, coming up behind Aleeza and leaning over her head to press a kiss to Dorand's lips.

Dorand moaned and opened his mouth to Ferrin's tongue, his cock throbbing. They'd become so much more free with each other sexually, far more so than they ever had with Carantha. Part of it was that their love had deepened in every way, and part because—

"Goddess, you two, can you wait for that until we're out of sight? I'm going to start glowing in public, and my mother is right over there on the blanket with Gavyn." Aleeza pressed closer to Dorand, her breath fast and hot against his chest. She loved watching them together as much as they loved watching her with each other. Seeing her get excited by his and Ferrin's contact was nearly as exciting as the kiss itself.

Life was good and likely to keep getting better if he had his way this afternoon.

"Come on, let's go. I have a surprise for you two."

"What kind of surprise?" Aleeza asked, her eyes already shining as she tilted her head back to look at his face.

"You'll just have to wait and see. I'll race you two down the beach." As soon as the words were out of his mouth, Dorand was off, using all his speed to pull ahead of the laughing man and woman behind him. He quickly crossed the quiet street and flew past the public swimming beach. He was going to make sure he reached the cove first, in time to turn around and see the looks on his lovers' faces.

* * * * *

Aleeza was out of breath but she forced herself to run faster. Dorand beat her every time the three of them ran, but occasionally she could hold her own with Ferrin. Whether it was because her dark lover really wasn't the best runner or because he let her win, she didn't know, but she enjoyed their competition all the same.

"You're going down, woman," Ferrin panted, arms pumping as he pulled ahead.

"Not on your life." Aleeza poured on the speed and managed to draw even with Ferrin in time to see Dorand disappear around a curve.

Aleeza couldn't wait to see his surprise. Knowing Dorand, it would be something wonderful and romantic. He played the tough guy, but his was the softest heart in their triad. It was a fact she was grateful for every time she came home from a hard day at work and found that Dorand had cooked an amazing meal for the three of them to eat out on their deck. Their new beachhouse actually wasn't too terribly far from here... Maybe once they'd seen Dorand's surprise, they could hoof it back home for a quickie.

She was dying to feel them, both of them. She wanted Ferrin's hot, sun-kissed skin at her back and Dorand's cool, hard muscle at her front. She wanted to feel one claiming her pussy and one pushing into her ass. They'd only fucked that way a few times, but every time felt better and better. It was quickly becoming her favorite position, the one that afforded them all the feeling of penetration, of merging into one body while their magic throbbed all around them.

Ferrin rounded the curve just seconds before she did and came to a stop so fast that Aleeza ran into him, knocking them both to the ground. She hit the sand with a giggle, smiling up into Ferrin's brown eyes above her until she saw the fear and uncertainty etched across his face.

A blanket made a spot of pale blue in the middle of a circle etched in the sand. Pink and blue candles surrounded it, and the scent of rosemary already lay heavy in the air. Dorand had set up a fertility spell.

"But—" she started, only to be cut off.

"But we've talked about it for months," Dorand said. His gaze traveled from her to Ferrin and back. "We all want it."

"But we don't know," Ferrin said. "We can't be sure the baby will be…I mean, in theory we're safe, but really if it's mine we don't…" he trailed off and looked away. Aleeza reached for his hand, grasping it firmly in hers. They had talked about this for months, about how badly they wanted a child. Conversations that went on for hours, going in circles, each of them alternately convinced it was a good idea or a terrible one.

She hadn't expected Dorand to take charge like this.

"We do," Dorand said. He took Ferrin's other hand, took her hand, so the three of them made a circle next to the circle in the sand. "I talked to the fertility expert."

"You talked to my mother?"

"I cornered her at Sunday supper last week while you and Ferrin were out back in the garden with your brothers."

"I should have known you weren't just volunteering to do the dishes."

He smiled. "She was fine with it, Aleeza. Excited even. I don't think she's holding out much hope for grandchildren from Simon or Blake."

"Who can blame them? I wouldn't want to marry an Amiantos woman. Frigid bunch of—"

"Ferrin!" Aleeza admonished. He and Dorand both had Amiantos women who were dear to them, and Carantha had been Amiantos. But she wasn't in the mood to rehash the frigid Amiantos women argument yet again. "So, what did she say exactly?"

"She said with us all under magic-fast there's no chance of a demon baby. The baby will be genetically like the father, but his or her magic will be a mix of all of us, and that includes me. Undefiled."

She didn't need to look at Ferrin to know how badly he wanted to believe it. He who'd grown up without a real family, an outsider…sometimes at night they talked about it, in the dark of their bedroom. Seeing the babies they could have had back when they met had affected him more than he realized, and more than anything she wanted to give him that family.

Seeing them weaken, Dorand started to smile. "Any baby is a risk. There aren't any guarantees. But we've taken a lot of risks to be together, guys. Isn't one more risk worth it? When you think of what we could have?"

"Yeah, it is." Ferrin's voice shook a little as he spoke, but his resolve came clearly through as well. "It's worth it to me. If it's what Aleeza wants."

She blinked back tears. Of all of them, he had the most to lose, had been the most damaged by the discovery of his true bloodline. But in some ways he was the bravest of them all as well. He was willing to reach for the brass ring, and her heart swelled with love for him. For both of them.

"Let's do it." She took the hands still held tightly in hers and stepped into the circle Dorand had drawn.

Dorand squeezed her hand, then turned to light the candles, letting the circle flow out from him. The air in the center grew still, quiet, the sun still shining down on their bodies as if the gods themselves were giving their approval.

Ferrin took her in his arms, his eyes staring into hers. "Are you sure?"

"As sure as I've ever been," she whispered back.

His kiss filled her with love, with pure, clean emotion which quickly turned to something a little wicked when his hands moved from her waist farther down. His fingers dipped between her legs. She smiled against his lips and tightened arms around his shoulders.

Dorand's warm body pressed against them from the side, and she stepped back to let her men kiss, to watch as their tongues entwined. Already her pussy was swelling in her shorts. Already she was desperate to feel them both. Their hands wandered over each other's strong, broad chests, down over flat stomachs. Her breath came faster. Her tiny bikini top felt too small as her breasts swelled and her nipples hardened. Quickly she reached up and untied it, letting it fall onto the ground.

The men's kiss intensified. Aleeza slipped behind Ferrin and reached around to unfasten his shorts and tug them off. His cock sprang free against her hand, and when she slipped around behind Dorand and removed his shorts both men gasped as their cocks rubbed together.

This was her favorite part. Well...one of them. Watching as her lovers stroked each other as their passion increased. She reached up to caress her breasts, to pinch her nipples softly. Their two strong bodies, one darker, the other pale, looked so perfect together.

Dorand's hands slipped down to Ferrin's ass, pulling the other man closer to him. Aleeza stepped forward to press her breasts against Dorand's back, to slide her hand between them and caress their swollen erections.

They turned to her, Dorand kissing her and spinning her in his arms so she stood firmly between them. Their energy glowed around them and combined. The white of Amiantos, the bright blue of Gunera. Bits of green-gold sparkled and twinkled around them, turning the energy into a different color, a new, powerful color that made her heart sing.

She leaned back against Ferrin's chest as Dorand kissed her throat, her collarbones. He leaned down farther, taking first one puckered nipple then the other into his mouth, nibbling, sucking with increasing pressure. She moaned. Ferrin's strong hands stroked her stomach, her thighs, teasing her by grazing over her shorts but not dipping to the place she needed him most.

She retaliated by rolling her hips in slow circles, grinding against his hard-on. His low groan made her smile, but the smile was lost as Dorand opened her shorts and knelt before her to pull them down all the way.

She needed the strength of Ferrin behind her as Dorand nudged her legs apart. His teeth scraped her thighs, her hipbones. Ferrin snaked a hand down her belly and gave her clit a gentle rub, just enough to make her hips buck forward before he took his fingers away. She groaned in frustration, grabbing his hand and putting it back.

He didn't stroke her. Instead he used his fingers to spread her open, to force her clit into prominence so Dorand could lave his tongue over it.

Heat raged through her. The sun beating own on them, the hot body behind her, the way her blood scorched through her veins and pooled in her pussy. Ferrin's hands stroked her, his teeth sank into her shoulder hard enough to make her cry out. Still Dorand licked and kissed, his movements so gentle she wanted to cry and so delicious she wanted to scream.

Her legs shook. Ferrin dipped down and slid his cock between them, rubbing against her opening, sliding between her slick, swollen lips. He thrust forward, and she looked down to see Dorand's tongue slide over the tip of Ferrin's cock. He slid back and Dorand turned his attention back to her.

"Please," she gasped. "Ferrin, please."

Dorand's hands on her thighs helped support her as Ferrin thrust into her from behind, tilting her hips so he could still play with her with his tongue. Ferrin's cock stimulated her opening with his shallow, fast thrusts, and Dorand sucked her clit into his mouth... It was too much. She came, her head falling back onto Ferrin's shoulder, her toes clenching into the blanket. Only their hands on her helped her stay upright as pleasure raged through her body.

Somehow she was on her knees on the blanket, with Ferrin still inside her, ramming all the way into her. She tilted her hips eagerly back, wanting more, while tugging Dorand toward her to kiss him, to take his cock into her mouth and give him back some of the pleasure he gave her.

The taste of him, salty and musky, filled her mouth. She relaxed her throat, leaning forward to take all of him into her while his hands played with her hair and he leaned his chest back to watch. She wished for a moment they were back in their house, in their king-size bed. They had mirrored closet doors and they all enjoyed watching each other, watching themselves as they took their pleasure. Here Dorand could not see Ferrin's cock plunge into her body, and neither could she.

With Ferrin's cock buried in her pussy and Dorand's deep in her throat, energy ran through them like a circuit. Power swirled around them, creating a breeze in the stillness of the circle, making the candles flicker and dance. Their moans bounced off the rocks protecting the little cove, sending their pleasure echoing back to them.

Ferrin's movements sped up, his fingers tightening on her hips. His indecision transferred itself to her and she pushed back against him, encouraging him to let go. To not be afraid anymore.

"It's okay," Dorand gasped, and she knew he felt it too. Slowly he eased his cock from her mouth, to concentrate on their third. "It's okay, Ferrin."

He hovered behind her for a long moment. His confusion, his need, his hope, coursed through her as they hovered together on the edge. She tensed and squeezed her muscles around him, waiting, wanting so badly for him to come inside her, give in.

It felt like forever that they paused there, but it couldn't have been more than a minute before he moved, thrusting into her, faster and faster, and without warning she clenched and splintered apart as he swelled inside her. His cries of pleasure were music in her ears. This time she did not blink back the tears.

"I love you," she whispered at the same time as Dorand said the same thing. He dipped his face to hers to kiss her, and as she straightened up they both kissed Ferrin in turn, feeling the bonds of love around them strengthen even further. Every minute, every day she loved them more. Every minute of every day she felt luckier and luckier.

She reached out to stroke Dorand, knowing he must be ready to explode. His heavy eyes told her she was right, and he pulled her closer, rolling onto his back so she could straddle him.

She lifted up enough to guide Dorand into her, sliding slowly down until her clit rubbed against his pelvic bone. He was thicker than Ferrin, and she had to stretch to accommodate him. His groan told her he enjoyed the process as much as she did.

She rocked forward, slowly at first, riding him as if they had all day. Which she supposed they did. Nobody at the picnic would care they were missing, and the circle around them was cast in such a way as to keep them hidden from prying eyes. No one but the gods would know what they were doing as Ferrin leaned forward again to kiss Dorand, to turn his head and catch one of her nipples in his mouth and suck on it.

She wrapped her fingers around his head, holding him close. Dorand shifted beneath her raising up on one arm, and Ferrin gasped. She looked down to see his hard-again cock, still wet with her juices, disappear into Dorand's mouth. Her pelvis tightened.

Ferrin wrapped his fingers in her hair, steadying himself while together they watched Dorand make love to Ferrin with his mouth. Aleeza moved faster, harder, reaching out to stroke Ferrin's chest, to stroke Dorand's chest.

With a cry Ferrin pulled away, his hand hard on her shoulder as he leaned her forward. She kissed Dorand, sliding her tongue into his mouth while Ferrin dipped his saliva-wet fingers between her legs then rubbed that moisture onto her puckered back door. She gasped, already tingling in delicious anticipation.

Dorand's hands stroked her breasts, her ribs, her thighs. The head of Ferrin's cock butted against her, then slipped inside. She groaned in pleasure. Having them both fill her…nothing made her happier.

They quickly found a rhythm, the two men thrusting into her like pistons while she threw her head back, waves of need washing over her. Dorand's face was a mask of bliss, his handsome features relaxed, his eyes glittering as he watched her ride him.

Quickly she reached the point of no return again, and she knew they were with her. Dorand's muscles tightened—his hips lifted. She let him drive deeper, butting against the entrance to her womb while she quivered with anticipation.

The men's fingers entwined on her hips as they clenched each other. She moved between them, filled with them, feeling their love rising like mist from their bodies. Never had she been so secure. Never had she been so loved.

She had everything she needed, everything she wanted, and as Dorand's back arched, as she felt them both quake and swell inside her, she knew she would soon have something else too. A child for them all to share, to raise together in the way they felt was right, not what either of their covens told them was the status quo.

No matter which of them actually fathered the baby, it would be theirs, and it would be unbelievably loved.

The air around them suddenly surged bright blue, then rose, then faded again, but Aleeza's aura remained a mix of the two colors for a moment as Ferrin and Dorand pulled from her body. She smiled to herself and snuggled close to her lovers on the blanket. She'd double check with Mona later, but even a relative novice in reproductive magic knew the implications of a double aura after conception.

"By the gods, do you think?" Dorand asked, echoing her thoughts.

"Twins," Ferrin said, but his voice wasn't sad. He was thinking of the future now, not the past.

"We'll have to wait and see, but yeah. I think so." Aleeza smiled as the men kissed her from each side then leaned over to kiss each other.

"See there, thank the gods you've got two husbands," Ferrin said with a smug grin. "You'd never be able to handle twins without us."

"Oh, I don't know. I can handle quite a lot." Aleeza took a cock in each hand and squeezed gently, a wicked laugh bursting from her lips as they both swelled to immediate, furious attention. "You boys, sometimes it's too easy."

"I'll show you easy." Dorand growled the words as he rolled her onto her side, biting down on her neck.

"Hey, I'm easy too." Ferrin grinned and kissed her and she giggled, happier than any witch in the world.

She'd gone looking for love and had found it twice over, first with her men and now with the babies that would be born. For a woman from a cursed coven, she was amazingly blessed. She sent a prayer of gratitude out to the sun, the moon and the stars as warm, strong hands roamed over her body, quickly bringing her back to the brink with their love and their dangerously wonderful magic.

Also by Anna J. Evans

છ

As the Lady Wishes

Bad Apple

Beauty Sleep

Decking the Hollisters

Deep Cover

Ellora's Cavemen: Dreams of the Oasis II (*anthology*)

Ellora's Cavemen: Jewels of the Nile II (*anthology*)

Ellora's Cavemen: Seasons of Seduction IV (*anthology*)

Enchanted

Love Fool

Main Attraction

Off the Deep End

Perfectly Wicked: Bad Apple

Perfectly Wicked: Main Attraction

Perfectly Wicked: Sinfully Sweet

Risking It All

Seducing the Enemy

Sinfully Sweet

Sultry Summer Fun

Taming the Madam

Wicked Delicious

Wicked Winter

Wicked Witch of the West Village

Also by December Quinn

∾

Accustomed to His Fangs

As the Lady Wishes

Blood Will Tell

Day of the Dead

Eighth Wand

About the Authors

ဢ

Anna J. Evans came back to her true love of writing fiction after working Off-off-off-Broadway and in a few Hollywood C-movies. She quit the biz to become a stay at home Mom-Writer and she's loving every minute of it!

Anna lives in Arkansas with her Air Force husband, her real-life romantic hero, their three kids and all the stories still making their way from her imagination to the page.

December Quinn is a multi-published author of romance and erotic romance. She lives in England with her husband and their two little girls.

December is a fan of high heeled shoes, corsets, cocktails, French fries, and rain. She is not a fan of airplanes, Brussel sprouts, or algebra. She still believes in dragons and the divine right of Kings.

Anna and December welcome comments from readers. You can find their websites and email addresses on their author bio pages at www.ellorascave.com.

Tell Us What You Think

We appreciate hearing reader opinions about our books. You can email us at Comments@EllorasCave.com.

Why an electronic book?

We live in the Information Age—an exciting time in the history of human civilization, in which technology rules supreme and continues to progress in leaps and bounds every minute of every day. For a multitude of reasons, more and more avid literary fans are opting to purchase e-books instead of paper books. The question from those not yet initiated into the world of electronic reading is simply: *Why?*

1. ***Price.*** An electronic title at Ellora's Cave Publishing and Cerridwen Press runs anywhere from 40% to 75% less than the cover price of the exact same title in paperback format. Why? Basic mathematics and cost. It is less expensive to publish an e-book (no paper and printing, no warehousing and shipping) than it is to publish a paperback, so the savings are passed along to the consumer.

2. ***Space.*** Running out of room in your house for your books? That is one worry you will never have with electronic books. For a low one-time cost, you can purchase a handheld device specifically designed for e-reading. Many e-readers have large, convenient screens for viewing. Better yet, hundreds of titles can be stored within your new library—on a single microchip. There are a variety of e-readers from different manufacturers. You can also read e-books on your PC or laptop computer. (Please note that Ellora's Cave does not endorse any specific brands.

You can check our websites at www.ellorascave.com or www.cerridwenpress.com for information we make available to new consumers.)

3. *Mobility.* Because your new e-library consists of only a microchip within a small, easily transportable e-reader, your entire cache of books can be taken with you wherever you go.

4. ***Personal Viewing Preferences.*** Are the words you are currently reading too small? Too large? Too... ANNOYING? Paperback books cannot be modified according to personal preferences, but e-books can.

5. ***Instant Gratification.*** Is it the middle of the night and all the bookstores near you are closed? Are you tired of waiting days, sometimes weeks, for bookstores to ship the novels you bought? Ellora's Cave Publishing sells instantaneous downloads twenty-four hours a day, seven days a week, every day of the year. Our webstore is never closed. Our e-book delivery system is 100% automated, meaning your order is filled as soon as you pay for it.

Those are a few of the top reasons why electronic books are replacing paperbacks for many avid readers.

As always, Ellora's Cave and Cerridwen Press welcome your questions and comments. We invite you to email us at Comments@ellorascave.com or write to us directly at Ellora's Cave Publishing Inc., 1056 Home Avenue, Akron, OH 44310-3502.

Discover for yourself why readers can't get enough
of the multiple award-winning publisher
Ellora's Cave.

Whether you prefer e-books or paperbacks,
be sure to visit EC on the web at
www.ellorascave.com

for an erotic reading experience that will leave you
breathless.